Only Human in Strangeville

Companions of the Convergence

By
Dakota Brown

Only Human in Strangeville

A Companions of the Convergence Shared World Novel

Inkwolf Press
P.O. Box 473
Ault, Colorado
80610

ISBN: 979-8-9864144-4-7

www.inkwolfpress.com

PRODUCED IN THE UNITED STATES OF AMERICA

10 9 8 7 6 5 4 3 2 1

Dedication

To Erica.
Thank you for being awesome and for your friendship.
Especially, thank you for asking me if I was ready for a
Yakutian Laika and for trusting me with one of your
wonderful puppies. I will always be eternally grateful to
have this amazing dog in my life.

Author's Note

Note the first: This was originally published through Vella.
It's been edited again since then.

Note the second: This is part of the Companions of the
Convergence world. I started writing this story and came
up with the cloud dog idea. Nimbus is based fairly directly
off my Yakutian Laika, Yuri. He's even on the cover. My
BFF Aeryn also has a Yakutian Laika who is Yuri's sister
so I decided she had to have a cloud dog in her world, too.
She agreed and we developed the mythology together from
that point. If you like the cloud dogs, look for more of
them in her Seven Sins series coming out fall/winter of
2024. THEN! Look for a cowrite from us that will tie our
two stories together.

Acknowledgements

So many people have helped me with this project and I'm so grateful to all of you. Thank you to my proofers, Andrea, Kirsten, R. Knight, and Aeryn Havens. Thank you for all the encouragement Alpha Team: Angie, Becky, Chelsi, Janet, Kelly, Michael, Sarah, and Stacy.

And of course, thank you so much for your extra support on Patreon. You're all amazing: Tina, Museholly, Nina, Latisha, Kelly, Ruby, Julie, Arkay, Tabitha, Wendy, Allison, Michael, Teri, Shay, Jacqui, Melynda, and Yashi.

Thank you so much to my editor Lynn, my PA Becky Hodges and a special thank you to Lou Berger for your encouragement to start writing this.

A huge super duper extra special thank you to Aeryn Havens for helping me develop the cloud dog mythos. Look for her own cloud dog in her Seven Sins trilogy.

And a super special thank you to all the Babes for always being there for me and each other.

Chapter 1

I took a deep breath when I stepped off the bus. The backpack hanging from my shoulders and the suitcase at my feet were all that was left of my past. Did I miss it? Yes, and no. Could I go back? Not if I valued my life. Which I did.

I pushed my glasses up the bridge of my nose and stretched while I looked around the small town of Beechworth. A normal enough sounding name for a town with a mysterious reputation. *Things* happened here. Stories of wishes granted, or nightmares encountered, littered internet chat groups, but nothing had ever been confirmed. I was intrigued. If I was upending my life, I wanted something enchanting out of it.

The sweet scent from the blooms on the tree next to me overpowered even the diesel exhaust as the Greyhound pulled away. I stepped deeper into the shade and studied my new home. Well, the bus stop at my new home, anyway. My first impression was of green. There was vegetation everywhere. Grass, trees, bushes, flowers, I felt like I was in a park, not at a bus stop.

Moisture glistened on the blades of grass, lingering dew from the night before. The rising sun glared just over the horizon. I'd slept in fits and starts on the overnight leg of the journey and I stifled a yawn.

The realtor who had helped me secure my apartment had assured me it was within walking distance of the stop. I had the address in my phone, but I didn't see anything nearby that looked like an apartment building.

There was an old three-story brick school not far from here, an actual park with a few early morning joggers, and a few other shops, one that appeared to be a coffee shop. My caffeine addiction was finely honed, and I could pick out a mecca of caffeine from a mile away.

I pulled out my phone and punched in the address. Sure enough, the old school was my destination. The pictures had looked promising, but it still made me nervous renting a place without having seen it. I'd had no choice. Surely, it couldn't be that bad? The outside was old, but charming enough, with vines climbing parts of the walls, fire escapes for the top windows, and a well-kept yard.

Mentally crossing my fingers, I grabbed the handle of my suitcase and dragged it across the street. The squeaky wheel was loud in the quiet morning, and I winced, hoping it wasn't bothering anyone. Maybe the birdsong would cover the sound.

I didn't encounter anyone on the quick trip across the street and down the sidewalk to the front door of the apartment complex. I opened the outer door and went inside. The mailboxes were to the right and someone already penciled my last name onto a slip of paper in a neat hand. My new last name. Miller. So common. So unremarkable.

The government had aided me with a new identity and resume, erasing who I had been with a few keystrokes. I'd chosen to relocate myself without their help beyond enough cash to keep me comfortable for about a year while I got my feet under me again. They were grateful for the things I'd found. I still wasn't sure I was glad I'd uncovered the trafficking ring. Well, yes, I was glad I'd found it and the government had shut it down. But personally, I'd liked my life, and now I had to leave it behind me and start fresh.

I'd already been given the code to the main door, and I hoped the landlord, or his agent was actually expecting me this early so I could get my key. After a long day on the bus, I needed a shower. I'd be getting a vehicle soon, but when I'd left everything behind, I'd left *everything*.

I missed that sporty little car I'd used to drive. I'd been warned to avoid getting the same car, doing the same things, having the same habits. I would do my best. They'd also given me money for a vehicle once I got settled. I could have had more, but despite everything getting turned upside down by my discoveries, I didn't feel right profiting from other people's suffering. I'd taken what I thought I needed to start over and felt that was fair compensation for giving up my entire life, but the extra money they'd tried to get me to take, I'd declined.

The code for the main door worked, and I pushed it open when it clicked. The office appeared to be off to my left. I parked my suitcase right outside the door and knocked quietly.

"Come in," someone said. His voice was smooth, rich, and calming, like a mortician's might be. His voice said he was glad I was here, but he was aware I'd lost something, and felt sorry for me.

Likely, I was projecting. No one here knew me. No one could connect me with anything that had happened in my old life.

I pushed open the door and had to make a forceful effort to keep my jaw from dropping.

"You don't need to knock if the door is unlocked," the man was saying while I stared.

3

Tall, dark, handsome, and movie star perfect, even in a t-shirt and probably jeans. His light blue-gray eyes contrasted with his dark hair and jawline beard.

"Hi," I stammered.

He appeared completely unaware of the effect he had on me, and likely others. Simply gave me a polite smile and waited for me to continue. When I didn't, his smile widened a little into amusement. Maybe he knew?

"Ms. Miller?"

My new identity sounded strange on his lips. I wasn't used to it yet. Maybe never would be?

"Yeah," I finally blurted. "Sorry. Long night." I yanked my glasses off my face and rubbed the lenses on my shirt, as if that could help my weird brain freeze. At least it gave me a quick break from the exquisite man sitting in front of me.

"I imagine so. I'm Oliver Cofield." He slid some paperwork toward me, and I shoved my glasses back on. "Here are all the things you should know, and here is your key. We'll need you to sign these once you've had a chance to go over them, but that isn't urgent. You should get some rest before you sign your life away."

My eyebrows rose, and he laughed.

"A joke. My apologies. I only require a deposit, which you've already made. Let's show you to your apartment."

He stood, and I followed mutely, trying to get my brain to start working again. It was not cooperating. Mr. Cofield was a fair bit taller than my five-foot five frame and he smelled like cinnamon when he walked past. That was weird as heck, but not unpleasant. Maybe I imagined that?

Mr. Cofield got the door for me and took my suitcase, waving away my weak protest.

"There is an elevator, but unless you require it, the stairs are faster."

"Stairs, fine," I continued to stammer, and my cheeks heated.

For his part, he simply carried my bag up a flight of creaky wooden steps and rolled it down the hallway to the last door on the right. He must know exactly where to walk because the ancient boards groaned under my steps, but the building didn't react to him at all.

Mr. Cofield put my key in the door and opened it for me. "The things you ordered arrived yesterday. I put the boxes in here, but otherwise the place has been empty since the last tenant left and we updated the room. I believe you will like it, especially the balcony. The view from this side of the building is the best. Here's your key and paperwork." He set them on a table, bowed slightly, and headed for the door.

"Please let me know if you need anything at all." He smiled, then left, the lingering scent of cinnamon hanging in the air.

I stared at the shut door for a solid minute before I shook my head, trying to jerk myself out of whatever weird brain space my landlord had put me in. Yeah, he was hot, but he wasn't that hot. Was he?

Someone had piled a bunch of boxes neatly along one wall. A few nights ago, in a cheap hotel near the bus station, I'd realized I was moving into an apartment and didn't even have a coffeemaker. I'd ordered a bunch of stuff and sent it to myself, then panicked the next morning when the tracking said most of it would beat me.

Fortunately, Mr. Cofield had assured me it was no issue to put the things in my room. The apartment had come with basic furnishings, a couch, desk, dresser, and a bed, but the rest I'd had to buy.

Rebuilding a life was a lot of work. But maybe it wouldn't be so bad here. Especially if my landlord had, like, an available brother or something.

I laughed at the thought and set about exploring my new home.

Chapter 2

Some unpacking and a solid amount of sleep on a perfect bed had me in a much better state of mind several hours later. I almost hoped I would run into my landlord again so I could act like a normal person instead of a brainless twit. My paperwork was read and signed. I pocketed my key, and grabbed my notebook with a list of things I needed to buy and questions to ask if I found someone to talk to, not to mention in case I needed to write down ideas.

Unfortunately, the office door was locked when I tried it, so I slid the paperwork through the mail slot and headed outside. Clouds had rolled in while I'd slept, and I shivered at the slight chill to the spring air. Despite the length of my shopping list, my desire for real coffee and the familiarity of a coffee shop were stronger than my need to buy groceries.

The short walk between my apartment and the coffee shop was possibly a dangerous combination, but so be it. It was a risk I was willing to take.

The earthy, rich scent of coffee mingled with a buttery smell that had me nearly drooling by the time I made it to the counter. Whoever ran this place clearly appreciated baked goods. Really high-quality ones. I wanted to plaster my face against the glass like a kid in a candy shop.

"What can I get for you?"

I hadn't even noticed the woman behind the counter, though she was nearly as remarkable as the baked goods. Her skin was flawless porcelain, and her eyes held an ageless depth I couldn't begin to describe properly. She wore hot pink lipstick and matching eye shadow. For the life of me, I couldn't figure out how old she was.

"Hi. I'm Hannah. I just moved to town. I think I'll be here a lot." I couldn't help my cheery grin.

"Jaz," she said and pointed at herself. "I'm here a lot, too." Her expression had turned interested, but she remained a little reserved.

Fair enough.

I ordered a latte and a pastry, barely refraining from ordering one of everything out of the case.

"Take a seat. I'll bring them out in a minute."

While she worked on my order, I found a seat near the front window, so I could see out. There was some sort of weird coating on the glass that blocked much of the light. Some sort of UV thing? Seemed odd, but they had plenty of lamps inside to make up for it and it didn't block the view.

One section of the place had comfortable-looking armchairs, a couch, and some low tables. Bookshelves lined the wall. I would explore those later. Reading was one of my favorite activities.

This area had more of a table and chair set up.

Jaz brought my drink and pastry.

"Is it always this quiet during the day?"

"Yes. Our main clientele are a bit more… nocturnal."

"Oh, you're open late?"

"Twenty-four, seven."

"Wow. That's amazing, especially in such a small town."

Jaz smiled at me. "Beechworth is a bit different from your standard small-town USA."

8

I almost blurted out that was part of why I'd chosen to move here, the rumors. But I didn't want to be 'that person.' So I clamped my lips shut on the admission.

"I'm looking forward to learning more about the town."

Jaz studied me, her gaze piercing me to my soul. "You would do well to keep your curiosity in check a bit until you get to know the folks here. They can be wary of strangers."

"Oh! Okay. I hope I won't be a stranger for long."

Her expression softened. "We'll see."

"Hey, anyone hiring around here?"

She tilted her head, thinking. "No. Don't think so. You could try over in Mayday Hills. Not sure what you're looking for, obviously, but I'm pretty sure Shady's Readery needs help. Quirky bookstore. A few of the bars are always looking, but I'd avoid those unless you're really into that scene. Um…" She tapped her teeth with a long, unpainted nail. "Couple of clothing places might need help. Not sure. Anyway, you'll find something. If you're looking for a more specific job, you might try the employment office. Also over in Mayday Hills."

"Thanks."

"You're welcome." Jaz moved off, and I settled in to enjoy my delicious latte.

***

The rest of my caffeine-fueled afternoon went quickly, though I noted that Mr. Cofield and Jaz didn't have the corner on the attractive-people market in Beechworth. The men and women at the grocery store were all extremely fit and extremely good looking. I would have thought them all related if they looked more alike. The little town had a lot to offer as far as fun shops, and I would slowly make my way through all of them. For now, though, I really needed to spend some time writing.

I pulled out my tablet and settled down on the balcony. A little music in my earbuds and I tuned out the rest of the world. The words flowed from my fingertips until I stopped and reread what I'd written. This was an adventure story and there was no need to describe the hero in such exacting detail. Not to mention he was starting to look an awful lot like my landlord. Grumbling at my treacherous fingers, I deleted the extraneous words and tried to settle back into the story. The main characters got well into their adventure for this writing session, but when things started to get a little spicy between them, I went with the extra descriptions again. Not only was the hero starting to really sound like my landlord, but the heroine took on a bit of Jaz's personality, only she had ebony skin instead of the porcelain of the barista's.

"This is not a romance," I muttered to myself. Instead of deleting everything, I left a few notes at the beginning of my chapter, reminding me to edit stuff out later. Then, annoyed, I shut my tablet and got up from the table.

A draft of cold air chilled the space behind me as I walked through it and back into the apartment. I rubbed my arms and thought about getting a sweater.

Instead, I headed for the shower, dropping my clothing on the bedroom floor as I went. I'd had a long day, and I deserved some relaxation. Someone had thoughtfully installed a showerhead with a separately handled sprayer, and it had excellent pressure.

Maybe it was the weird track my thoughts had taken while writing, or maybe it had just been a while, but I was feeling needy. The single life had been fine while I was buried in my work, but now I had more time on my hands, and likely would for the foreseeable future. Usually, a quick moment with the magic vibrator before bed to help me sleep was all I needed to stay satisfied. Hopefully, that would hold up. I wasn't looking for a relationship. I needed to make sure I was safe before I got involved with anyone else. No matter how hot they were.

Still, I couldn't help but think about a pair of blue-gray eyes and a perplexing but pleasant cinnamon scent as I aimed the jet of warm water from the hand sprayer at myself and played my fingers down my stomach. I really didn't want to think about my landlord in any way other than a business mindset, but I was so unable to focus on anything other than his gentle manner and his fantastic good looks, that I forced myself to imagine he had a brother.

This brother was every bit as handsome as Mr. Cofield—Oliver, but not my landlord and available. No, he was more handsome. Impossibly good to look at... like an elf in a fantasy novel. My brain went on a tangent, distracting me from the task at hand. I grumbled and jerked my mind back under control. I usually enjoyed the fantastical twists and turns my mind took, but the last one had proven to be all too correct and landed me in a world of danger. Now, I was free from that. The threat behind bars and my life completely upended. Even so, right now, I needed an uncomplicated fantasy.

So, just humanly good looking. There.

I managed to get latched onto that idea, imagining this person's hands on my body, caressing me, holding me, loving me, keeping me safe. Being safe is a big turn-on. I let my eyes flutter shut as my body responded to my hand and the warm jet of water, pressure building inside me as I worked myself toward release.

He would care about me, and my pleasure, and he had the skills to back that up. I was caught up enough in my fantasy that my legs went a little weak. I leaned against the back of the shower, propping up my foot and really getting

11

into it. He'd be appropriately sized to fill me and stretch me, but not so much that I had to worry about it being too much.

My breathing came faster, and I moaned softly as my pleasure crested and rippled through me, my inner walls fluttering around my fingers as I stroked myself. I gave myself a few minutes to enjoy the floaty feeling my orgasm, and the fantasy, had given me before bringing myself back to my current reality and finishing my shower.

I was well and truly ready for bed after that, and I curled up under my soft sheets. Tomorrow, I had another full day ahead of me. I needed a car and a job. Jaz's suggestion about the quirky book shop stuck with me as I drifted off. I wondered what exactly she meant by quirky. Did they sell esoteric books? Or maybe it had an adult section. Oh, I needed to get a few more toys if I was going to be surrounded by so many hot people all the time. Maybe I could squeeze that in tomorrow, too.

Those thoughts chased me into a deep sleep. My imagination was so good, I even imagined weight and warmth spooned around me, as if my fantasy man had come to life and was holding me while I slept.

Chapter 3

Of course, the next morning I ran across my landlord. Cheeks red and back to being tongue-tied, I stammered a greeting.

"Hello, Ms. Miller. How do you find your apartment?" Mr. Tall, Dark and Sexy was just coming out of his office.

"Uh, it's great. Thank you. I love the shower." If I hadn't been blushing before, my cheeks were certainly on fire now.

"I'm glad to hear that."

Change the topic! Change it now! I yelled at myself. "Uh, is there a bus system, or a ride share? I need to get to the dealership to get a car."

"Ahh, not really." Mr. Cofield's brows furrowed while he thought. "What type of vehicle are you looking for?"

"Small SUV. Something that will handle the winters." So different from what I'd once driven, but then I hadn't had to deal with winter, either.

He nodded. "Davin Longmire is the man you want to talk to. He has a number of new and lightly used vehicles and you'll get a better rate than if you go to the dealership in Mayday Hills. If you want to see his selection, I can call him. I believe he has time to come and retrieve you."

"Oh. Uh, really?"

Mr. Cofield nodded.

"Thank you."

My landlord went back into his office and picked up a desk phone. He dialed a number, apparently from memory, and, in moments, someone answered on the other line. I marveled at the old-fashioned phone and his ability to remember phone numbers. Automatically, I patted my pocket, making sure my cell phone was in its normal spot. I'd once dressed only in the cutest, trendiest outfits, but now I was a jeans and t-shirt girl. No matter how odd it felt. *Don't get noticed*, that was the new plan.

"He'll be right over. You can wait in here, or out front."

"Thank you, Mr. Cofield."

"Oliver is fine, if you prefer." His smile melted my panties.

He wasn't flirting with me. I was *nearly* certain. Still.

I needed to find a boyfriend or a fuck buddy fast. I did not need to be lusting after my landlord.

"Thanks, Oliver. You are welcome to call me Hannah. Ms. Miller sounds like you're talking to my mom." That was a blatant lie, but the sentiment was the same as if I'd been using my old last name.

He nodded. "Hannah then. Oh, look, Davin is already here."

I glanced out, expecting a fancy car. My eyes widened at the old pickup that rolled up to the curb.

My expression must have let my inner thoughts out.

"Ahh, he loves that truck. No need to worry, Hannah, the vehicles he sells are top-notch."

"Okay, thank you, Oliver." His name felt oddly intimate on my tongue, and the way he said mine sent shivers through me. "I'd better just, uh, go then."

"Have a nice day, Hannah."

I bolted before I could say anything inappropriate.

The day promised to be warm and humid. Birdsong filled the air, and the trees appeared to be at peak blossom.

I hurried down the sidewalk, slowing when I caught sight of the man who had climbed out of the big pickup.

"Fuck me, is anyone in this town not gorgeous?" I muttered to myself.

There was no way the man leaning against the truck could have heard me from here, but I swore an amused smile curled across his lips.

Davin had sandy blond hair, cut short. A neatly trimmed beard slightly darker than his hair, and broad shoulders stretched the material of his casual polo shirt. He wore slacks and dressy boots, but none of that concealed the muscles that filled out his clothing.

I really hoped my landlord knew what he was doing. I was screwed if Davin decided to be unfriendly.

His smile disarmed me a little.

"Hello, Ms. Miller," he said, voice smooth, comforting, but powerful.

"Hi. Hannah, please."

"Hannah. I'm Davin. It's nice to meet you. Oliver says you need a car?"

"I do. Thanks." Yeah, I definitely needed a fuck buddy. My ovaries had perked up and decided to cry a little at how his smooth voice went right through me. Trying to get myself under control, I thanked him when he opened the door for me.

His truck was old enough to have a bench seat, but not so old that it didn't have seatbelts.

"What brings you to Beechworth?" he asked casually as he climbed back into the cab and started the truck. It roared to life.

I sensed more than basic curiosity from the man. Maybe he was going to flirt with me? Just because he wasn't wearing a ring didn't mean he was available. So sue me, I'd looked. For that matter, Oliver didn't wear a ring, either.

"I needed a fresh start, and this place seemed quiet enough to get away from big city life." I'd come up with a fake back story. It was very similar to my real life, but different enough to mask the real details. I'd lived in Miami, according to my backstory. I'd certainly been there enough to know the area.

"City girl?"

"Beach babe," I added with a grin. That much was true. I'd miss the water, but I could visit again someday.

We drove through the small downtown I'd walked to yesterday. General store, grocery store, a few restaurants, and a bar. All the basics. There were other shops too. Antiques, crafts, things like that. I'd heard there was a farmer's market every Saturday. Not much beyond that. The mail came from a post office on the edge of Mayday Hills—I'd asked.

Davin gave me a quick once-over before returning his attention to the road. "Beechworth is a quiet town. It takes us a while to get used to new folks. I hope you give us a chance to adjust to a newcomer."

"Oh, of course. Everyone has been very nice, so far. I don't expect the entire town to throw open their doors to me."

He smiled and pulled into a small car lot on the far side of town. I could have walked the four miles, but it would have taken me an hour or more.

"Thank you so much for the ride."

"Not a problem. Take a look at what I've got and see if anything suits you. Keys are in the ignitions. Feel free to take them for a test drive."

"Wait, you don't want to go with me?"

"I will, if you prefer, but I don't need to."

"Oh. Okay."

"If you have questions once you've looked around, I'll be in the office. I feel people prefer not to have me staring over their shoulder."

"That's great. Thank you." I had no idea what to say. I'd never encountered a dealership like this. Keys in the ignition? What if I ran off with the car?

Davin slipped out of the truck and before I could put my hand on the handle, he opened the door for me and offered me a hand down.

I didn't need it, but I automatically accepted, his hand warm in mine.

"Prices are on the windshields."

Feeling in something of a daze, I headed over to the section of vehicles that had the small SUVs.

***

A few hours later, I was the proud owner of a new compact SUV that should withstand the snowy conditions we'd experience a few months in my future. It was the least stressful experience I'd ever had buying a car. Paying cash had sped things up a bit, but Davin hadn't batted an eye. I'd even gotten his number. Well, I had his business card and directions to call him should I have any problems with the vehicle. He promised to make sure I was happy. We'd see what actually happened if I had troubles, but I felt good about the purchase.

Wanting to get a better feel for my new home, I decided to head to the diner. I could use lunch, and local color always showed up at places like that.

Now that I had wheels, the trip took mere minutes. I parked on the street and headed inside. The building had a fifties façade, making it feel even more like an old-time, small-town diner. Inside, the tables had chrome edges and the barstools were black vinyl.

The woman behind the bar had a white-frilled apron, and another woman worked the grill, visible in the back through the service window.

The tables were about half-full, and I recognized a few people I'd seen working at the grocery store yesterday. Their tables were piled high, and they shoveled food in their faces with enthusiasm.

I took a seat at the bar.

"Hi, hun." Her nametag said May. She looked to be a bit older than me, with a friendly smile and a relaxed air about her.

"Hi. What's the special?"

She gave me a rundown of the menu, and I ordered. While I waited, a man slid onto the stool next to me.

"They're werewolves."

"Say what?" I turned and studied the man next to me. He looked fit, well-muscled, and, like everyone else in this town, he was attractive. His reddish-brown hair was a little longer with a curl to it, and he had green eyes. If I had to guess, standing, he'd be about six foot tall, maybe just a hair over.

He pointed at the folks I recognized from the grocery store. "Werewolves. Most of the people you see during the day are werewolves. The vampires come out at night, of course. Except the few that got stuck with the day shift at the coffee shop. You been there?"

"Uh, yeah." I thought back to Jaz. Vampire did kind of fit her, but seriously? I knew the town had a reputation for strange, but vampires and werewolves were a little out there.

"Bridger Sullivan, do not spread your conspiracy theories at my counter." May came back with my food and a frown for my companion.

"It's not a conspiracy and you know it, May." He turned to me. "She's the only normal one in Beechworth."

18

May snorted. "Don't listen to his nonsense."

I took a drink of my water and nodded. "Sure."

When May turned away to get Bridger a coffee, he returned his attention to me. "Haven't figured out what they all are of course, and they're careful, so I can't prove it yet, but if you find anything out, be sure to tell me. Don't go out after dark." He slid me a card, downed his coffee in a gulp, though it had to be steaming hot still, and left.

I glanced at the card. "Bridger Sullivan, Vampire Hunter," it said. And in smaller letters was a phone number and words about being willing to tackle werewolf problems and other supernatural creatures.

Just in case I needed to do novel research, I slipped it into my pocket before May returned.

"Now, hun, don't listen to Bridger. He's got a few screws loose. Just let me know if you have any problems with him."

"Thanks, May. I'm Hannah, by the way. I just moved here."

"Ahh, Oliver mentioned you. Welcome. Always nice to see a new face around here."

I wasn't sure, but I detected a hint of caution behind her cheerful words. Was Bridger on to something? Or was it just more of the wariness of newcomers that everyone had warned me of?

I could see why he thought the other occupants of the diner might be werewolves. I watched as they paid and filed out, their plates nearly licked clean from what I could see from the bar. Maybe I'd hit the coffeeshop tonight and check things out. Just to see. There was no such thing as vampires and werewolves, but the rumors about this town had to come from somewhere.

If nothing else, I now had two men's phone numbers. Not that I was attracted to either of them. No. Not at all.

Dakota Brown

Chapter 4

That night, back in my apartment and ready to visit the coffee shop, I hesitated with my hand on the knob, remembering what Bridger, the so-called hunter, had said about not going out after dark. To be honest, I was far more afraid of the human variety of predator than anything supernatural. Even wolves in the forest scared me less than humans did. At worst, the wolves would just kill me. Humans… I shied away from the things I'd learned toward the end of my old life.

The government had declared Beechworth safe, as far as they could tell. That didn't mean it was, or that there weren't run-of-the-mill bad guys around, but I couldn't let fear rule my life completely. A draft of cool air swirled around me. It had happened once or twice before, but I had no idea where the draft was coming from. I might mention it to Oliver when I saw him next.

Resolved, I opened the door and headed out into the hallway, my computer bag looped over one shoulder. I used a tablet when I was out and about for portability, but I only had one bag right now. Eventually, I'd buy more things, but not yet. Not until I'd settled into my new home for good. If I had to move quickly, I didn't want to lug a lot of things around.

I hurried down the stairs and almost plowed into Oliver at the bottom. He caught my arm as I did awkward gymnastics to avoid knocking him over, and I almost fell on my ass.

"I'm so sorry," I blurted out. "I was just heading out and I didn't see you."

He made sure I was steady before releasing me. Pleasant heat burned through my skin where he'd touched me and settled deep inside my stomach, warming me and reminding me of my daydream in the shower. There was no stopping the heat in my cheeks.

"No trouble. I really should improve the lighting in these stairwells. It always slips my mind." He glanced up at the light fixture before looking back at me.

Something else struck me then. "Oliver, I haven't seen any of the other tenants. Is that normal?"

"Yes."

I pushed my glasses back up my nose and considered how to ask for more information without being rude.

"Are you going out?" It was almost as if he were changing the subject.

It wasn't any of his business, but he'd been so nice, and it was possible he'd have more suggestions, like the car dealership, so I answered instead of pressing for more details. "Just over to the coffee shop."

Oliver studied me for a moment, tilting his head, before nodding slightly. "Take care."

There was far more caution in his voice than a simple trip a block over should warrant. He was gone before I could question him, muttering softly about increasing the brightness in the stairwells.

I caught myself staring as he climbed the stairs and jerked my gaze away from the fine view. "Damn it. Very clearly, I need to get laid." I also didn't want to jump the first attractive male I came across, so I'd probably be continuing my dry spell for a while. It was going to take some work to find an appropriate relationship. That thought did not comfort my needy self, and my good mood soured slightly as I headed out into the cool, humid night.

Insects sang and a light floral perfume floated on the air. The moon was not yet above the horizon, but the sun had only recently set, so it wasn't terribly dark and streetlights cast sulfur pools on the ground.

Something small moved in one of the pools of light. Weird.

Compelled to investigate, but carefully in case it was a raccoon or something wild, I increased my pace.

I stopped just outside the ring of light and stared, shocked. A small black and white dog lay huddled against the light post, its hair matted and dirty, laying with its muzzle between its paws. A small golden cord tied it to the post.

"What the heck?" I hurried into the pool of light.

The little thing whined at me and wagged its tail.

"Oh, baby." I dropped to my knees and reached slowly forward. The dog scooted toward me and whined, pushing its nose under my hand. That was enough for me. I scratched behind his ears. Though he was matted and wet, I could feel soft fur under all that.

"Well, we can't just leave you here." I put my hand on the cord that tied it to the post.

"Don't untie that creature," a deep, unfamiliar voice commanded.

I spun around, still crouched, and put myself between the speaker and the dog.

"Who are you?" I demanded. I couldn't see well outside the light, but already I would die for this dog. Something about this puppy compelled me to protect it.

"Those are nothing but trouble. Why don't you let me take the creature and be on your way?" The voice turned seductive.

I stood and planted myself in front of the dog. "Somehow, I don't think you have this dog's best interests in mind. How about I handle it and you fuck off?"

"That is no dog," the man said, coming to the edge of the light. His features were mostly obscured, but I got the impression of a hawk nose, sharp cheekbones, light colored skin, and a disapproving downward curve to his lips. He was taller than me.

I quickly reviewed what I knew of self-defense, hoped I wasn't completely screwed, and prepared to defend the dog, still whining quietly behind me. He had scooted to the far end of the lead that secured him to the post. I was probably screwed, but what else could I do? Wait... phone... I pulled it out of my pocket, swiped it open and dialed 911.

The man's frown deepened, and he waved his hand. The busy tone sounded, and he advanced into the light. "Move along."

I almost took a step away, but no, this man was going to hurt the dog. There was no way I was moving along. I'd faced down men with guns pointed at me. I wasn't completely defenseless against an unarmed man. I hoped. The dead line was weird, but I didn't have time to mess around with it. I'd throw the phone at the guy's face as my first move.

"Hey, there you are! Sandy, are you okay?"

I recognized the voice. The hunter, Bridger, also stepped into the light, his hand in his jacket pocket. Did he forget my name already? Or was that on purpose?

"No," I said through gritted teeth.

Bridger turned to the other man. "Maybe you should leave."

"Maybe you should mind your own business."

This time I felt the power in his seductive voice. For whatever reason, it hadn't affected me. Bridger pulled something out of his pocket. A squirt gun?

"Don't make me do it, demon," he snarled.

The man facing us sighed. "I sense that creature's interference. Hunter, you would be wise not to spread false accusations. It could prove unfortunate for you."

Bridger slowly tightened his finger. The man frowned and stepped back out of the pool of light, seeming to melt into the shadows.

"What was that?" The slight quaver in my voice now that the immediate threat was gone pissed me off, but it was better than a total freak out.

"Vampire, probably. Not sure. Anyway, didn't I tell you not to go out after dark?"

"Pretty sure you don't get to tell me what to do."

The so-called hunter stared at me for a moment before shaking his head and returning the squirt gun to his pocket. "Holy water, if you were wondering. Works every time."

"Have you ever actually seen anyone react negatively to holy water?"

"No. They always leave before I get a chance to hit them with it." He sounded disappointed.

The dog whined, and I returned to my initial purpose, untying the cord and holding on to it in case the dog bolted. Instead, it crawled into my lap.

"Well, that's adorable," Bridger said.

"Yeah, we need to get him to a vet. Know of any?"

"Yes, there's a twenty-four-hour clinic not far from here. Want a ride?"

"Are you sure? You've already gone out of your way for me."

"Want to make sure you get there okay. It's no trouble." He smiled at me, not looking at all bothered.

25

I lifted the dog and got to my feet, grateful for a little help at the moment.

"Looks like a puppy," he observed, giving the little guy a scratch. "Is that what all the fuss was about?"

"Yeah." I related the past few minutes while I followed Bridger to his car. It was a newer sedan, and he opened the door for me to get in.

The puppy seemed content in my arms and tucked its head under my chin.

"Poor guy. I wonder how it got there." Bridger started his car and pulled away from the curb.

"Yeah, really weird." I cuddled it closer. My hand touched something warm and wet, and I pulled my hand away and looked at a streak of red. The little dog whined.

"Hey, Bridger? Drive faster."

Chapter 5

The trip to the vet clinic didn't take long and they were able to see us right away. While a normal checkup would have been done during business hours, they were happy to take the puppy immediately because of the circumstances and the potential wound. They took him back, cleaned him up, and found his wound was minor. He only required a bandage.

It turned out he was a boy, not microchipped, not showing up on any of the missing alerts they had access to, and overall seemed healthy, though they gave him some fluids just to be on the safe side. The vet thought he was old enough that they could risk giving him his shots even if he'd gotten his vaccines recently, and they even helped me give him a bath. Under the dirt, he was an adorably fluffy black and white dog of unknown breed and fantastic personality.

He was also very hungry, and they sent me on my way with a couple of days' worth of puppy food, some antibiotics, dewormer, and a checkup scheduled for later in the week. This gave me time to figure out what to do with the little guy. They offered to let me surrender him and they'd figure out the rest, but I just couldn't do it. Something about the way he looked at me tugged at my heart. I'd never had a pet as an adult, and maybe it was time. I paid the bill gratefully, glad they were there to take care of the little guy.

Bridger patiently waited through the whole thing, though he did mutter something about werewolves when a woman brought a dog that might have been a wolf hybrid in to be treated for a minor laceration.

Another worry surfaced. I didn't know if my apartment was pet friendly or not. I felt that Oliver would probably overlook a day or two based on the circumstances. I'd have to talk to him first thing in the morning.

"What were you doing out, Hannah?" Bridger asked as I carried the soft little puppy back to his car. He had used a fake name for me earlier on purpose. Interesting choice, but I appreciated it all the same. Especially with my past.

"I was heading to the coffee shop."

"We could probably still go there. I don't imagine they'll mind the puppy, and it probably won't hurt him any. They let werewolves in all the time."

"Seriously?"

He nodded solemnly.

I'd already had too much weirdness for the night, so I just let it go. Sure, of course they did. And I really needed some comfort food. Now that the immediate danger to the puppy had passed, my heart was racing again. I'd just stood up to some random guy in the middle of the night. Yes, I'd done it before, but that didn't mean I wanted to do it again. Not to mention the bizarre circumstances. Why hadn't my phone worked? Where had the puppy come from anyway? And what was up with that guy? Not having any answers, I sighed and tried to focus on the coffee I was about to consume.

The puppy made an adorable grumbling noise and snuggled deeper into my lap.

"He's awfully adorable," Bridger allowed.

"He is the cutest, softest, most adorably fluffy thing ever." My voice dropped into the baby talk range and I wasn't even ashamed.

The little guy perked up at my tone and gave me a soft nose kiss before settling back into my lap.

"What are you going to call him?"

"No idea."

Something would come to me.

***

The coffee shop was actually crowded when we went inside. All conversation stopped and everyone stared, not at me, but at Bridger.

He waved casually and headed to the counter to ask about the puppy. The incredulous stares followed the hunter and only darted back to me after the young man behind the counter nodded, and Bridger gestured for me to enter. I tried not to stare in turn, but most of the people in the coffee shop had the same flawless skin as Jaz. From what I could tell, though, the range of skin tones was a nice surprise. I hadn't expected to see such a variety of nationalities represented in the coffee shop, but I was glad for it. I'd expected to miss the rich diversity of the neighborhood I'd lived in in my last life, and to see it represented here in this mecca of caffeine calmed me.

"What will you have?" the young man asked.

I ordered a decaf latte and a pastry. Bridger paid before I could shuffle the puppy around and get to my wallet.

"You can buy next time," he offered at my half-hearted objection.

"Sure, deal," I replied before realizing that obligated me to at least one more extended period in Bridger's presence. Of course, after stepping up to my side tonight and then carting me and the puppy around, I was willing to hang out with him some more. He'd never acted impatient.

We grabbed a seat on the couch by the fake fire in the corner, and I stretched my legs out, leaned my head back, and sighed. "What a night."

The puppy snuggled into my lap and made an adorable little happy grumbling sound before going back to sleep.

"Forgive me for eavesdropping," a smooth, cultured voice said. "But I'm curious, what happened? This town is typically very quiet. And how did you acquire that small piece of cloud sitting in your lap?"

I snapped my eyes open and stared. This man certainly had his own corner in the jaw droppingly attractive market of this town. Longish black hair, tied back, framed perfect dusky skin, piercing brown eyes, and a friendly smile. He sat down in a hastily vacated chair across from us and folded elegant hands across his knees. He wasn't wearing anything out of the ordinary, jeans and a plain green t-shirt, but he made it look like the most expensive outfit I couldn't have afforded, even on my formerly six-figure salary.

Grace. Every motion the man made was almost inhumanly graceful. Maybe he was a dancer?

Small piece of cloud was one way to describe the adorable floof curled up in my lap. It was surprisingly accurate, if overly poetic.

"I found him tied to a light pole." I suddenly didn't want to tell him, in case he knew the dog's owner. But, at the same time, if someone was looking for this puppy, they had to be heartbroken. I'd keep him safe, and the vet clinic had promised to look around for the owner. "This guy came up after I found the puppy and threatened me. Bridger showed up in time to help me get rid of the guy, and then we took the puppy to the vet."

The golden cord that had tied the puppy had vanished at some point at the vet clinic, probably misplaced. As pretty as it had been, I was much happier with the slip lead the clinic had given me, and I'd hit the pet store tomorrow for supplies.

"Ahh. Interesting. Forgive me, my manners are occasionally terrible."

I doubted that.

"My name is Katsuro."

"Hannah. I feel like you all know Bridger."

"Yes," Katsuro replied, obviously amused. "We all know Bridger."

"I'm new to the area. Probably obvious." I found myself a little tongue-tied under Katsuro's scrutiny.

He nodded. "Do you intend to keep the cloud puppy?"

"If the owner doesn't show up, yes."

"Very well. I'm the owner of this establishment. He is welcome in the coffee shop. I look forward to seeing you again." His smile lit up his eyes and drew me in, and I about melted in my seat. What was it with the men in this town?

Katsuro rose from his chair and left the coffee shop after a quick scan of the occupants that seemed to mean something to the rest of them.

I got a few more curious looks before the other patrons returned to their own business.

I finally managed to take a full breath.

"He was totally flirting with you," Bridger said, a hint of jealousy in his voice. "Also, I'm pretty sure he's a vampire. He owns this place and they're all vampires. Maybe don't flirt back?"

I raised my eyebrows, glanced around the coffee shop, then back at Bridger. Maybe the other occupants were more studiously ignoring us than they had been before, maybe it was just my imagination after a long night, but right now I didn't care.

"Sure, whatever, Bridger." I let my head fall back on the couch and dug my fingers into the little dog's fluff. I supposed I could move into the coffee shop if Oliver said I couldn't keep the dog, but I'd cross that bridge when I got to it. Either later tonight when I returned home, or tomorrow as soon as I could track my landlord down.

My heart sped a little, and not necessarily in anticipation. I really liked the feel of my new home, and my landlord, to be honest. I didn't want to move again so soon. The little puppy stood, stretched with an adorable rumbling growl, and settled back into my lap.

Yeah, somehow, I had to talk Oliver into letting him stay. Or talk him into breaking my lease so I could find a new place to live. I'd choose the puppy over being able to see Oliver, but the thought of not seeing him again was weirdly uncomfortable. I'd never experience the scent of cinnamon the same way again, especially if I had to move.

Beechworth was starting to win my heart—Bridger's insistence about vampires and werewolves aside—but this tiny, floofy creature had already claimed my soul.

Chapter 6

I startled awake, surprised to find a pair of soft brown eyes staring into mine. The little puppy poked me again, gently on the nose with his own snoot, then, seeing me awake, gave me a soft kiss before toddling toward the edge of the bed and whining.

Groaning, I grabbed my glasses and stared at the puppy, wondering what he wanted. He whined again, and my bladder reminded me that it was full. Oh!

"Hang on a second, little guy." I scrambled out of bed, threw on some clothes and gathered the squirming ball of fluff into my arms.

I didn't run into anyone on my way out, fortunately, and I put the puppy in grass still glistening with morning dew. He quickly squatted to pee, and I could practically feel his relief. I walked him a bit longer, cleaned up after him, and we headed back to the building.

Maybe I'd get lucky and get a chance to actually brush my hair and put on fresh clothing before I ran into Oliver. I still hadn't met any of the other tenants. He said it was normal. I thought it was weird as hell. Maybe I should start knocking on doors and bringing over tasty cookies or something.

The puppy stopped, yelped, and darted backward, just as a large creature slunk into my path. I scrambled back, reaching down and scooping up the puppy. The creature looked vaguely doglike, but it clearly wasn't actually a dog. It looked like a shadow had detached itself from the wall and taken the shape of a large, lean dog, except it had six legs. It stalked toward me in the early morning gloom. A faint scent of baked goods wafted over from the coffee shop, strong enough for me to notice, despite my fear. They must have been making cinnamon rolls. The cheerful scent contrasted sharply with my fear.

"Oh god," I whispered, backing farther.

The puppy trembled in my arms but didn't try to get away.

The creature blurred into shadow, swirled around me, and solidified on the other side. I was trapped between the creature and the building.

My heart raced and my hands trembled. There was no way this thing was real, except the puppy was reacting, too. I moved until my back hit the door. Mentally apologizing for any discomfort I might cause the little dog in my arms, I shifted him to a one handed grip and reached behind me.

The knob turned, and I almost fell into the entryway, but I slammed the door behind me.

"Oh my god," I breathed and quickly punched my code to get the rest of the way into the building.

"Good morning, Hannah."

I screamed and spun around.

I had no idea how Oliver had snuck up on me, but he stood in the hallway, studying me and the puppy in my arms. The scent of cinnamon that always seemed to accompany him strengthened. I had an insane urge to run my fingers along his jawline beard while I stared deeply into his blue-gray eyes. Then the current situation came crashing back and my stomach tightened in worry instead of misplaced desire.

My puppy squirmed, and I set him down next to me. He went to his belly and crawled toward Oliver, tail wagging.

"I didn't know you had a little nimbus." My landlord stared at the puppy for a moment with an unreadable expression before kneeling and holding out his hand.

"Uh, so, I didn't. I found him last night tied to a light pole. There was this creepy guy threatening me, and Bridger came by and helped drive him off. Then we took him to the vet, and, uh, well, he came home with me. I don't know what the pet policy is here." I ran my hand through my hair and realized I hadn't brushed it yet. Great. I looked a mess, and I was babbling like an idiot.

Oliver's hand hovered over the puppy for a moment before he touched the fluffy thing. His expression softened and a hint of a smile curled his lips.

"We don't openly allow pets," he said.

My heart sank. *Damn it.*

"But this little nimbus is promising to behave as well as he can. He is quite charming." Oliver gave him one last pat then stood.

"You can stay." It was as if he were talking to the puppy. Oliver turned his attention to me. "I will inform the other residents that they are not to take exception to his presence."

"Ahh, thanks. So, am I ever going to meet them?"

"Perhaps." One shoulder rose in an elegant shrug.

"Do you want me to pay extra? Pet rent, or something? Or is there anything else I can do to make up for having a pet when I'm not supposed to?" *Oh god, I hope that didn't come across wrong.*

Oliver's smile finally reached his eyes. "No, it's all right."

Relief settled the turmoil in my gut, though I had a lot to learn about taking care of puppies.

Nimbus. That was a good name. Though why both Oliver and Katsuro had referred to him as a cloud of some sort or another was beyond me.

My stomach got a little fluttery thinking about Katsuro, and Oliver, if I were being honest, now that I wasn't worried about getting kicked out of my apartment.

"Thank you," I said, again.

Oliver nodded. "Have a nice day." He went back down the hallway, and I went up the stairs. Today, I was heading over to Mayday Hills to see if I could find a job. First stop, Shady's Readery.

***

I fingered the thick paper and stared at my name on the outside in the fancy calligraphy. I'd pulled it out of my mailbox when I'd checked it out of habit. No stamp, so it had been hand delivered.

Nimbus tugged backward on the leash and grumbled softly. I stopped and looked up. Davin's truck rumbled up to the curb. I'd been heading for the parking lot, but somehow, I knew he was here to see me. Or maybe that was wishful thinking? I jerked my hand down to my side after I caught myself smoothing my hair. Tall, muscular, blond, powerful, kind. What was not to like?

Maybe there was another store I needed to hit if there was a good toy shop in the city, because holy hell, my body was feeling needy.

"Hannah," Davin called, getting out of his truck. "Do you have a moment?"

That was incredibly polite and aware, I thought. He didn't just call my name and expect me to wait, he actually asked if I had time. He got hotter by the moment. My stomach fluttered.

"Yes, of course, Davin."

He hurried over.

"I didn't know you had a puppy." He kneeled and held out his hand. Nimbus cautiously approached.

"Yeah, Nimbus and I found each other last night."

Davin glanced up at me, raising an eyebrow, but he didn't question me when I didn't offer more details.

"Well, congratulations. I wanted to check with you and see how your new vehicle was treating you?"

I grinned. He was totally flirting with me. "You pay personal visits to everyone who buys a car from you?"

He smiled, maintaining eye contact. "No. Just the ones I might be considering asking on a date."

Direct, too. Confident.

"I might be convinced." My mouth said it before I even had a chance to think. *Was I safe enough here to date? What if I let something slip?* In theory, the bad guys were all behind bars or dead, but there was still enough danger that the government had decided to erase my past and transplant me, anyway.

"I sense a bit of hesitation?" Davin's tone was not unkind at all.

"Oh, I just, uh, have a shitty ex, so I'm interested, but a little hesitant." *Good story.* I'll add that one to my list. I fingered the fancy envelope in my hand, drawing Davin's attention.

"Ahh, the—" He cleared his throat. "I see you've caught Katsuro's interest."

A thrill of shock sent electric tingles through my chest, not unpleasantly. "Is this something he does often?" I held up the card.

"No. I just recognize his scent, uh, style." Davin shrugged. "He's not a terrible sort, and it certainly wouldn't hurt to have him as an ally, uh, friend." Davin frowned and glanced at the apartment with an irritated look on his face before looking back at me with a grin.

37

I had no idea what to make of that.

"When and where?" I brought us back to his second question. "Oh, and the car is great. Thank you."

His expression turned pleased. "Excellent. Is tonight too soon? I thought maybe, first, I'd introduce you to more of the town, show you around some. If you agree to a second date, then I'll take you over to Mayday Hills and treat you to a fancy dinner."

"Well," I replied with a grin and a stronger flutter in my stomach. "How can I refuse?"

"I'll pick you up here at four. Nimbus can tag along tonight."

"Oh, a man who lets the children come. Even better," I joked.

I swear Davin blushed a little. "I like dogs."

Nimbus wagged his tail.

He gestured at the envelope in my hand. "Seriously, make friends with Katsuro. It's in everyone's best interest if you two get along. I'll see you tonight."

I watched as Davin left, stomach tingling. I hadn't expected to get asked out so soon, but I was really looking forward to it.

"Crap," I muttered. "I don't have anything to wear."

Okay, I'd make a few stops while I was in town.

I looked down at the envelope and considered Davin's words. Why on earth would it make a difference to *everyone* if Katsuro and I got along? I pictured his longer dark hair, and his dark, piercing gaze, and the warm feeling inside strengthened. If nothing else, he'd said Nimbus could come to the coffee shop any time, and that was certainly something.

I slid my finger under the edge of the envelope and pulled it open.

Dear Ms. Miller,

Had I given him my last name? I couldn't remember. But it seemed like everyone in town knew everything about everyone else already, so I guess I shouldn't be surprised.

I request the pleasure of your company tonight...

Dakota Brown

Chapter 7

"Tonight? Why tonight?" I stared at the invitation in my hand, rubbing the expensive paper with my thumb and biting my bottom lip. What did I do? Cancel on Davin? Put Katsuro off?

I released a long breath and put the card in my pocket. How did I even tell Katsuro yes or no? He owned the coffee shop. I could probably leave a message there.

"Damn it."

First off, I needed to head over to Mayday Hills, look into the job at the bookstore Jaz had mentioned might be available, and do a little wardrobe shopping. Actually, first I needed to go to the pet store.

"Well, Nimbus, ready for an adventure?"

He rooed at me, wagging his fluffy curled tail. The anxiety that had threatened to take up residence in my chest dissipated at his adorableness. He trotted along at my side with a jaunty little swagger to his gait. I chuckled and went to my car.

The little guy jumped in the back like he'd been riding in cars his entire life. Which, since I knew nothing about Nimbus, other than that he was adorable and a puppy and fluffy beyond belief, and soft, and okay… anyway— maybe he had been in cars quite a bit in his brief life.

I put the pet store in my GPS, turned on some tunes, and headed out.

The pet store was a cute local place not too far into Mayday Hills and they had everything I needed. Little Nimbus won over everyone in the store. Conveniently, the bookstore was right next door. If I did get a job, I might be able to bring Nimbus to the pet store. They had a small play and boarding area. For today, I was going to take him inside with me. I'd been told it was pet friendly.

The bells on the door jingled when I went inside, and the mingled scent of old books and coffee eased a tension in my shoulders I hadn't realized I'd been carrying. Though I'd never considered books as any sort of career in my old life, now the idea was all I could think about. Even if I never actually wrote anything good, maybe I could be surrounded by them and sell them. I wasn't being negative about my aspirations to be an author. It was simply a new skill, and I wasn't sure how it would go for me. Courtesy of the government buying me out of my old life, I had the time to give it a try, and the leeway to take a lower-paying job. It was also so radically different from what I'd done before that it was unlikely to trigger any suspicions should there be any surviving members of the trafficking ring out there.

"Hello!" A woman popped up, nearly literally, from behind the counter.

It took an act of will to keep from yelping. She looked like an owl had mated with a goblin and produced a somewhat human offspring. After the last few days in Beechworth, I was almost willing to believe she wasn't human, and it startled me.

"Hi." I made myself smile back. She certainly sounded friendly enough.

"Are you here for the séance?"

"The what?" I glanced around, wondering if somehow I'd gotten confused and gone into the wrong store.

"We summon dead authors and ask them about their books once a month. This month we're summoning Chaucer."

I raised my eyebrows. "Uh. No, actually I came about a job?"

"Oh?" She narrowed her eyes and peered at me. Squinting, she removed her glasses, cleaned them, and looked at me again. "Ahh, I see. You're hired."

"Wait, what?"

"Yes, stand here." She gestured to her spot behind the counter.

"Okay?"

Nimbus rooed, and she leaned over the counter.

"Yes, of course. You're hired, too. Now, have you ever worked a register before?"

"It's been a few years. Do you want to see my resume?"

"No. You're the chosen one. I'll show you the basics now, and if you have any questions, they'll have to wait until after the séance. Just do the best you can."

"Of course, Miss…?"

"Clare. Now, what's the dog's name?"

"Nimbus."

"Excellent. Nimbus, you sit here and look adorable. It'll increase sales." She pointed to a spot next to the counter. "We'll get you a bed."

For all the world acting like he understood, Nimbus sat where she indicated and gave us his fiercest puppy dog eyes. My heart melted into a puddle.

"Perfect." She turned her attention to me. "We have fifteen minutes. Let's get started."

Completely confused, but willing to go with it for now, I let her show me how to work the register and the basics of selling books in her shop.

Exactly fifteen minutes later, the first patron of my employment entered. She was every bit as esoteric as Clare.

"Anita!" Clare came around the counter and held out her arms. They hugged and air kissed, and she took the younger woman's coat. While Clare had to be in her sixties, Anita was closer to twenty-five. She was a tall, thin Black woman and wore a beautiful gray shawl that someone had skillfully made, and she had the brightest pink hair I'd ever seen.

Clare introduced her to Nimbus, who got a great deal of cooing and kisses, before she waved vaguely in my direction, and led Anita to the back room.

I couldn't even be offended. Nimbus' cute little roo roo of greeting totally stole the show.

Before I could process that interaction, an older Asian man came in. Suspenders stretched over his ample belly, holding up linen slacks, and his tweed jacket was a touch threadbare around the cuffs. He doffed his flat cap before bowing to Nimbus and making his jolly way toward the back. And those two were the least strange appearing of the crowd.

Every single one of them made a big deal of Nimbus, greeted me like I'd always been there and headed to the back.

By the end, I just waved and accepted that my job was going to be as odd as anything else about this place. I hadn't realized the strangeness surrounding Beechworth extended out to Mayday Hills. Still, it wasn't going to be boring.

After about twenty minutes, one more person walked in. He was tall, portly, wore a long jacket of some really old style, and had a well-manicured white beard.

"Ahh, hello. Is this the Chaucer séance?"

"Yes."

"I'm Geoff. Nice to meet you." Oh, he was British. Too old for me, but cultured sounding, and seemed like he had a good sense of humor by his tone of voice.

"Hannah." I offered my hand, which he shook.

"Roo!"

"And Nimbus."

He kneeled and gave the puppy a good scratch behind the ears.

"I suppose I'd better pop back there. Good day." He doffed his cap and sauntered into the back of the shop.

"Nimbus, what on earth have we gotten ourselves into?"

He wagged his fluffy little tail and rooed happily.

***

After no one came in for a bit, I shifted my feet and looked around for something obvious to do. Nothing presented itself, so I turned my attention to my dilemma about tonight. Maybe I could let Davin take me out to dinner, but tell him I had to see Katsuro, too? He had told me I should accept the coffee shop owner's invitation, after all.

Scenes from romantic comedies flashed through my mind about having dinner with both of them in the same place and taking lots of "bathroom breaks" to dash between one table and another. I knew that wouldn't work regardless, but it was a fun thought exercise for a few minutes. Then I had to move on to figuring out what to wear. For that, I'd have to go shopping.

The time stretched, and I finally pulled out my phone and started looking up clothing stores. I doubted Clare would get mad at me when I hadn't intended on staying. I'd have to interrupt soon if I was going to go shopping and meet up with Davin on time. Not to mention figure out what to do about Katsuro. Hell, maybe I'd ask Davin's advice. Or Oliver's. That was a thought.

He might even have an idea what Katsuro wanted. Bridger had claimed he was flirting with me. Surely not.

Finally, I decided direct was best. I pulled out Davin's business card, put his number in my phone, and sent him a text.

Davin, this is Hannah. I guess Katsuro wants to meet tonight.

I wasn't sure what else to say, so I left it at that. He'd understand the context.

It didn't take long before he replied.

Hannah, that's no problem. I can make sure you're at the coffee shop just after dark. He won't show up until then, anyway.

Great, thank you! I sent back.

After dark? What the heck? It really was strange here.

Embracing the vampire image a bit much? Or just a night owl?

I hoped I didn't regret sending that somewhat joking text.

Davin's reply took a little longer, and I started to get anxious again when the others came out of the back room full of laughter and good cheer at how successful the séance had been. Their departure was nearly the same as their entrance. They showered Nimbus with love, waved at me like they'd known me for years, and left.

Sometime during that, my phone dinged, but I couldn't spare a second to look at it because Clare came over with a huge grin on her face.

"You're perfect. What hours can you work? Part-time? Full-time? Ahh, part-time to start with?"

I raised my eyebrows. That was exactly what I'd been hoping for but hadn't had the opportunity to say it aloud.

"Yes, of course. We'll see how it goes," she said before I could reply.

"If you don't mind a bit of an early morning, we can meet here at nine am tomorrow before the shop opens, and I'll get you up to speed. Probably should do all that pesky paperwork, too. Discuss pay, all that."

"That's great, Clare. Thank you."

She smiled and patted me on the hand. "Let's call it three hours today. I'll add that to your timecard. See you tomorrow."

She kneeled and gave Nimbus a good scratching. He rooed and gave her a soft nose kiss before trotting over to my side.

"Oh, go to Francine's for clothing. Some new, some used, you'll find exactly what you're looking for." She waved me toward the door before I could ask how she knew all that. Was she telepathic?

Not a hundred percent positive I should be taking clothing advice from my new boss, considering her style and mine were very different, but willing to at least give it a try, I pulled out my phone and typed in the address. It was within walking distance. Excellent.

The text reply button flashed at me, and I chewed at my lower lip as I hit the icon while I walked.

See you at four.

Well, that was a non-answer if I'd ever seen one. What did that mean?

My puppy brushed against my leg as if trying to reassure me while I shoved the unreasonable anxiety away.

Had I screwed up?

I pulled my glasses off and cleaned them on my shirt.

Backward pressure on the leash and a quick bark were all that saved me from plowing into someone on the street.

"Oh, sorry!" I shoved my glasses back on my face.

The man that stared back at me gave haughty a textbook definition.

"You should be."

Every warning sense I'd developed over the last couple of years dealing with the trafficking ring went off, and I backed away, hating myself for retreating, but not at all interested in making myself memorable to this person. Besides that, there was something vaguely familiar about his voice and his profile, though I was certain I'd never seen him before now.

I pulled Nimbus into the nearest store, heart racing.

"We're closed," a familiar voice said.

I spun around, noticed I was in more of a dance club type setting than a store, and widened my eyes when I saw Jaz behind the bar.

"Jaz?"

"Hannah, you shouldn't be here. It's not at all safe."

"This guy—" I pointed at the door just as the bell chimed and "this guy" followed me inside.

Jaz's eyes narrowed. "She's under Katsuro's protection. Leave."

The guy smirked. "She's not in his territory, Jaz. She's in ours. As are you. Best you remember that." He sauntered past, his gaze lingering on me before flicking toward Nimbus. He widened his eyes in surprise.

Nimbus had his lips drawn back in an impressive display of teeth for a puppy his size.

"I'll discuss this with you later, Jaz." The man went deeper into the club.

Jaz turned toward me. "Leave, now."

I figured I could get answers later, so I split. So much for not making myself memorable to whoever that was.

I hurried on to the clothing store, heart racing. Nimbus trotted along at my side, tail curled up over his back, but an alertness to his expression I'd not seen before.

Chapter 8

I stared in the mirror and hoped that I'd dressed up enough for the evening, while still remaining casual. Davin had said this wasn't a fancy date, after all. I was so not ready for this. What if I slipped up and said something I shouldn't? While I'd been able to keep my face out of the news, the trial and aftermath had made the national news. There had been some big names involved.

This was a mistake. I went to pick up my phone and tell Davin I needed to reschedule, but Nimbus placed a paw on my phone and snuffled me with his adorable little snoot. I got the feeling he was telling me everything would be okay.

The cool draft I'd felt every day since I moved in swirled around me. I couldn't pin it down and it never seemed to be tied to any one location.

Grumbling, I took the phone after Nimbus moved his paw, grabbed his leash and my bag, and headed out of my apartment.

One of the doors down the hallway clicked shut just as I stepped into the hall. Nimbus perked his ears, and I took a step in that direction, but no one was there. It was the first real sign of any neighbors that I'd seen. I never heard anyone. Packages showed up in the entry where the mailboxes were and eventually vanished, but otherwise, Oliver was the only one I saw here. He said that was normal. I thought it was weird as hell, but then, so was everything else.

Starting to wonder if I'd gotten in over my head choosing Beechworth, I shivered and went down the stairs. Oliver wasn't in, but Nimbus got his hackles up at a particularly dark shadow in the stairwell behind us.

Uneasy after a long day, I hurried outside.

Nimbus found his favorite tree to potty by, and I let him take care of business. I'd brought water and a bowl for him, as well as his dinner.

Davin pulled up in his old truck just as Nimbus was finished sniffing around.

Hoping I could hide my unease with a smile, I went over to the curb where he'd parked while he got out.

"Hi, Hannah. How are you tonight?" Davin's grin was genuine, but I thought I caught a hint of wariness in his eyes.

Shit, was the vampire joke too much? In this town? I wouldn't have thought it would be, but maybe I'd been wrong.

"It's been a weird day," I admitted.

"Anything you want to talk about?"

"I got a job at that weird bookstore in the next town." I didn't feel like elaborating more.

Davin smiled. "Clare is a character. Harmless, mostly. Congrats on the job."

"Thanks. So, where are we headed?"

"Let's go for a drive, then I'll feed you." He led me back over to his truck and offered me a hand before scooping Nimbus up and putting him on the bench seat next to me.

We drove for a bit, with Davin doing his best tour guide impression. I was interested, but I couldn't help being distracted by everything that had happened that day.

50

The forest that bordered the northern edge of town was particularly beautiful in the late afternoon sun.

Davin interrupted telling me about some of the lakes hidden away in the trees, trailing off and glancing at me. "What's wrong, Hannah? I can take you back any time you want."

"Oh. Uh. Sorry." Apparently, my distraction was obvious, or Davin was uncommonly good at reading people. "I don't know.

He pulled over and put the truck in park before shifting so he could face me.

"Hannah, if you're not comfortable, I'll take you home."

"It's not you, Davin."

His shoulders eased when I said that. It was completely true and, somehow, he believed me. I couldn't help noticing the way his shoulders stretched his shirt as he twisted to look at me. The powerful muscles in his arms and the shine in his eyes. I wondered what it would be like to be held by someone like him. Kissed. Loved.

A faint smile played across his lips, as if he could read my thoughts. There was no way, though.

"I just had a weird encounter after a weird couple of hours at the bookshop. It's nothing."

"Tell me?"

I shook my head and relayed my story.

Davin's brow furrowed, and he looked grave. "Hannah, are you planning on staying in Beechworth for long?"

"I'd hoped to stay here indefinitely," I admitted.

He took a deep breath. "We need to get a mark or two on you as soon as possible."

I raised my eyebrows. "What, now?"

"Were you joking in your text earlier about vampires?"

51

"Yeah, of course. Despite what Bridger seems to think, vampires aren't real. Humans are evil enough without having supernatural creatures, too."

He massaged one of his temples before sighing. "I'm going to let Katsuro handle that one. Okay, well, for now, let's finish the tour and get some dinner. I'm starving." He smiled at me.

"Did I do something wrong?"

"No, Hannah, not at all." Davin took my hand and kissed my knuckles.

My pulse sped, and I bit my lower lip, enjoying the attention, but nervous at the same time.

"You are quite intriguing and very charming. I'm still hoping you let me take you out again, but I don't want to push you and you've had a stressful day. Let's eat. Burgers okay?"

"That sounds amazing."

Nimbus rooed and wagged his fluffy tail.

"Kibble for you, young man." I waved my finger at him.

The little guy just grinned at me.

Before Davin could get us moving again, the truck jolted, and I heard a pop and a loud hiss before the truck settled oddly.

"Fuck," Davin muttered softly.

"What happened?"

"Somehow we lost a tire." He tilted his head as if listening, or maybe sniffing the air. Nimbus sat up and looked out the window, lips drawn back from his teeth.

"Would you mind staying in the car, Hannah?"

"Sure. You don't want help?"

"Let me check this out first."

I was a strong, independent woman, but I knew evil was real and felt safer in the truck cab with Nimbus. At least it wasn't dark yet.

Davin got out, slammed the door, and walked around the truck, paying more attention to our surroundings than he did to the vehicle itself. He pulled out his phone and sent a quick text before turning to the damage.

Something moved in the shadows. I banged on the window just as Nimbus barked a warning.

Davin spun around, but nothing was there.

I rolled the window down. "I swear I saw something in the shadows."

"I believe you, Hannah. Help is coming."

Howls in the distance chilled me. Nimbus added his own *arwoo* to the calls.

"Wolves?"

"They won't hurt us," Davin assured me. "The thing in the shadows, however... Shut the window."

Before I could get it all the way up, a shadow detached from the trees and crashed into Davin, driving him down and out of view. A very familiar-looking six-legged shadow.

"Davin!" I threw the door open, not sure what I could do, but not willing to hide. I did manage to shut the door on Nimbus so he would be as safe as possible, though he shrieked and pawed at the partially closed window.

I stumbled out of the truck in time to see the creature go flying. Davin staggered to his feet, shirt torn and bloody.

He put himself between me and the creature. It turned, pink tongue flicking out of its black, shadowy mouth, licking gleaming white teeth. It very clearly wanted Davin and me dead.

It growled, a sound that vibrated through my bones and rattled my eardrums.

I whimpered, stomach clenching in fear.

Wolves howled in the distance as the creature leaped, teeth aimed for Davin's throat.

Dakota Brown

Chapter 9

I screamed.

A gray streak blurred past us, slamming into the thing's side and throwing it off course, so it crashed into the front of the truck instead. Metal pinged as the thing's claws rent the steel. It screeched and I covered my ears, hoping they weren't bleeding.

The new creature tumbled into shadows along with the nightmare attacking us.

"Fuck!" Davin exclaimed.

"Are you okay?" I looked around for the creature. "What is that thing?"

"A shade," Davin answered tersely as he stared into the shadows, ready for another attack.

I wanted to ask him to explain, but the creature slipped back out of the shadows and stalked toward us.

Nimbus's frantic scrabble of claws against the window and his high-pitched barking intensified. I stared at the six-legged, shadowy dog-looking creature and took a step back. The metal door of the pickup was cold against my back. I tried to reach behind me for the door latch but couldn't get it without turning, and I did not want to take my eyes off the thing in front of us.

Davin kept himself between me and the being, but I could see the gleaming white teeth it licked with an impossibly long tongue.

This time a gray streak and a brown streak dove into the shade.

Davin grabbed me around the waist, tugged open the door and shoved me inside the truck with Nimbus. The little floof crawled into my lap and bared his teeth at the scene outside. I buried my fingers in his fur and winced when Davin slammed the truck door.

The new creatures turned out to be huge wolves, and two more, a golden-colored one and a brown wolf had joined the first. The shade shrieked again, tail lashing cat-like as it weaved back and forth. The movement reminded me of videos I'd seen of cobras.

The golden wolf lunged forward, and the creature turned and vanished into the shadow. The three wolves remained, swarming Davin, rubbing against him.

That was crazy. This whole thing was crazy. Hell, this town was freaking nuts. Clearly the rumors I'd read online barely brushed the surface.

I didn't realize tears were running down my face until Nimbus licked my cheek.

"Hey, buddy. I'm okay." He tucked his muzzle under my chin and rooed softly, lessening my fear a little.

As crazy as this was, I was probably still safer than I had been with the traffickers.

After a few minutes of quiet conversation with the wolves, Davin came over and opened the truck door.

"If you want to meet the local pack, they're friendly."

"How is that possible?"

Davin tightened his lips for a moment before shrugging. "How about this. Let's get through the rest of the day, chat with Katsuro, and I'll answer any questions you have tomorrow."

"Not now?"

"Not now. I promise, they're friendly, though."

I glanced at Nimbus, and he licked my cheek again. So far, he'd seemed to have pretty good instincts, so I set him on the truck seat and let Davin help me exit the vehicle.

"Do I hold out my hand?"

"If you want. You can touch them if they come over to you."

The golden wolf came right up to me and pressed its head under my hand. I gave him? Her? A few scratches before the gray one came over and I repeated the gesture. The brown one huffed and trotted off into the woods. I didn't take offense, though.

While I was petting the wolves, Nimbus stared around me at them, eyes wide but not acting afraid or even aggressive. That, more than anything, helped me relax.

"Davin, are you okay?" I asked while I marveled at the wolves rubbing against me.

"I'm fine, Hannah, don't worry about me."

Another truck pulling up behind us interrupted any more questions I might have asked. Two women and a man piled out of the newer truck, all built like muscular tanks. They brushed past the wolves, obviously familiar with them, running hands along fur before doing similar with Davin, touching his arm as they came to the front of the truck.

"Wow, that's shit, Davin," one of the women said. "Let's get this tire changed."

"Thank you, Rachael. Everyone, this is Hannah. Hannah"—he pointed at each person—"Rachael, Jamie, and Maggie."

"Hi."

They all acknowledged me, friendly enough but a touch wary. I swear I recognized at least one of them from the grocery store. Nimbus jumped from the seat to the foot well and, before I could stop him, onto the ground. I was still somewhat surrounded by wolves and couldn't grab him. He trotted calmly to my side, pausing to sniff noses with the two wolves.

My heart was in my throat, however neither wolf acted aggressive at all. Their heads were bigger than my puppy, but they treated him gently.

I had a lot of things to ask Davin tomorrow.

The newcomers had the tire changed in no time, hopped back into their own vehicle after again brushing their hands against Davin and the two wolves, and left. The wolves also left, and I wondered if I'd meet them again.

"Wow, that was efficient roadside service," I said.

Davin chuckled. "Yes. Let's get you something to eat."

I bent over and scooped Nimbus up, then climbed into the truck.

Davin went around to his side, opened the door, and leaned his seatback forward, grabbing a small bag from behind his seat. "I should probably put on a clean shirt."

"Are you sure you're okay? That looked nasty."

"I'm fine, Hannah. Just a scratch." He turned his back as he took off his shirt, but holy hell the view... I couldn't help staring at all that defined muscle he briefly exposed.

Fuck me, I thought and hoped I didn't say it out loud. He seemed to have uncommonly good hearing.

As soon as he was dressed again, he climbed into the truck and fired it up.

I had myself under control by the time he pulled back onto the road.

"So, things like that happen often around here?"

"No." Davin sounded troubled. "Beechworth is a pretty quiet town, believe it or not."

"I've seen that creature before. Once over by my apartment."

"Are you sure it's the same one?" Davin glanced at me with a frown. "There's a friendly one in the area."

"Really?" I blurted. "Of course, there is." I sighed.

"Hannah, if you want to stay in the area, you'll have to get used to the strangeness. Oh, and you'll have to agree not to tell anything to Bridger. He's an outsider."

"Bridger? Wait, are you telling me he actually knows what's going on here?"

Davin laughed as he pulled into a parking lot. The scent of hamburgers made my stomach growl, and Nimbus perked up from where he lay on the truck bench next to me.

"No, Bridger has no idea what really goes on here, and it needs to stay that way."

"Are you telling me I'm going to know? And why do I get to be an insider when I've only been here a few days and he's been here much longer?"

Davin leveled a serious look at me. "Somehow, you're already mixed up in whatever is going on."

"And you're going to let Katsuro explain it?"

"Yes. He's much better at that sort of thing."

"I do believe he's been flirting with me. Just saying."

Davin smiled, not looking terribly bothered. "If you tell him to back off, he will. Likewise, just so you know. You know I'm interested, but I'm also happy to simply have you as a friend."

"Seriously?"

Davin nodded.

"You'd be the first man I met like that."

He shrugged. "I'm glad I'm not like all the other guys, then." He hopped out of the truck and came around to open my door before I could reply.

"Nimbus can come in." He helped me out of the truck.

I must have still been a little shaky because I tripped and ended up in Davin's arms.

"I swear that wasn't on purpose," I gasped out, mortified. My entire face had to be bright red. Though, being pressed up against his firm chest, with his strong arms wrapped around me was certainly not terrible by any stretch.

"Mmm, I don't mind." Davin took one arm from around me and tilted my chin so I could meet his gaze. "Not one bit."

He leaned forward, his lips mere inches from mine, his expression soft.

My heart pounded in my chest and my hands shook for a different reason. I wanted to close those last few inches between us, but I held back. I needed to know what was going on before I made any more commitments.

As if sensing my decision, the heat left Davin's expression and he pulled me into a soul-healing hug instead.

Tears sprang to my eyes. I hadn't been hugged like this in… well, a long damn time.

"Are you okay?" he asked.

"Yeah, just been a while. Thank you."

"You may fall into my arms any time, Hannah. For whatever reason."

Nimbus rooed, and I laughed and helped the little dog out of the truck, though he hadn't needed it earlier. I was anxious for dinner.

***

Dinner was tasty, and I finally managed to focus fully on Davin and what he was telling me about the town. We'd been seated on the back porch and the puppy had gotten his way with a little hamburger of his own along with his kibble.

We talked until the sky darkened. I didn't want the night to end, unfortunately Davin was keeping track. When he helped me back in the truck, I almost recreated the trip from earlier on purpose so I could have an excuse to kiss him, but I held off. There was a lot I needed to know first.

He was quiet on the drive to the coffee shop, though it didn't seem to be a tense silence, at least from him. I was nervous, but my fingers curled in my puppy's soft fur helped a great deal.

When Davin stopped, I made it out of the truck before he could come help me. That didn't stop him from taking my hand—a little possessively, I thought—and walking me into the coffee shop. Nimbus trotted happily at my side.

Katsuro was there when we arrived, and Jaz stood behind the counter. Her lips tightened when she saw me, but I didn't think it was from any sort of dislike toward me. Hell, maybe she was looking at Davin. I wasn't sure. Katsuro looked ravishingly handsome in a deep-red dress shirt and black slacks. He had his black hair tied back and the friendly smile on his face almost reached his eyes. He looked troubled, not angry, though he did spend a long moment studying Davin before his gaze flicked back to me.

"Hannah, my dear, I hate to start our evening like this, but you are in very grave danger."

Like an ice-cold bucket of water, his words both chilled me and set my heart racing. I didn't stop myself from looking for the nearest exit, though Davin's hand on mine kept me rooted in place.

Nimbus rooed softly and pressed against my calf, possibly the only thing keeping me from a full-blown panic attack.

"Oh hell," I muttered softly. "What now?"

Chapter 10

Katsuro came forward and stepped to my other side, putting a hand on my shoulder. "Hannah, let's go to the back and we can discuss it. Davin, please join us for a bit."

Davin nodded curtly.

"Jaz, dearest, a drink for all of us, please, and water and a treat for the nimbus."

"Yes, sir." She dipped her head in a bow and turned to her work while I let Davin and Katsuro lead me toward the back.

By the time we got to a comfortable sitting room in the back that must have been overflow for the coffee shop, I had managed to get my breathing under control. The room was cute. It had a few tables with chairs and a couch and loveseat with a coffee table by a gas fireplace and looked well used, but in a homey sort of way.

Katsuro sat me down on the couch. Nimbus jumped into my lap and Davin sat next to me, putting his arm around my shoulders. I leaned against his solid warmth, grateful for the support. Our host shut the door before joining us. He sat on the coffee table and put a cool hand on my knee.

It was certainly more familiar than I would have expected from someone I barely knew, but the contact comforted me, and I didn't pull away.

"Davin, why were you bleeding earlier?"

My date had a spare shirt in his car, and he'd changed after the fight. How on earth did Katsuro know?

Davin tightened his lips for a moment before he sighed.

There was clearly a power dynamic here that I didn't understand, and I didn't think Davin was completely happy about it. Yet he had encouraged me to, at the very least, make friends with Katsuro.

"I was giving Hannah a tour of our town. I pulled over at one point near the edge of our forest and a shade slashed my tire, though I didn't know it was a shade until I got out and was attacked. We drove it off."

Katsuro's eyes narrowed and his hand tightened on my knee. "A shade?"

"Not *our* shade," Davin clarified. Well, at least the other man seemed to understand what he meant. I was still lost.

Nimbus pushed his head up under my chin and rooed softly.

Before I could ask for any further information, we were interrupted by a soft knock on the door.

"Come in," Katsuro said without raising his voice.

I was impressed that Jaz heard. She opened the door and pushed in a small cart with drinks, a few pastries, and a water bowl for Nimbus, along with a small bowl with some dog treats.

Once Jaz left, after she gave Nimbus a quick scratch under his chin, Davin took a breath.

"Are they after Nimbus, or are they after Hannah?"

"I'd say that it is one and the same, at this point," Katsuro answered.

"Wait, why would they be after a puppy? He's cute, and obviously special, but he's a dog."

Both Davin and Katsuro shared a look before fixing their gazes on me.

"Hannah, you've found a nimbus, or a cloud puppy. He's not a dog but a supernatural being. They are typically full of good humor and occasionally mischief. They're rare, but if they choose a person, they're quite loyal." Katsuro took his hand from my knee and petted Nimbus.

"What the fuck?" I buried my fingers in my puppy's fluffy fur and tried to process what they were saying.

Nimbus rooed and turned his big brown eyes on me, widening them and flattening his ears in concern.

"Hey buddy, it's okay, I'm just confused."

He wagged his tail and gave me a soft nose kiss before settling back onto my lap, apparently satisfied.

"How do I take care of a supernatural puppy?"

Davin ran his finger along my cheek and wiped away a tear.

"And why is a shade after me? And what is going on?"

Katsuro smiled, and this time the emotion reached his eyes. "It says a lot about you, Hannah, that your first thought is how you care for the creature you've rescued. As to the rest, we'll do our best to explain. This is not how I had hoped to spend the evening, but I feel you need this information."

"First off, Davin is a werewolf." Katsuro smirked at the man sitting next to me, who growled softly in response.

I was grateful I hadn't picked up my drink yet because they would have been performing the Heimlich after that statement.

"And I am a vampire."

"Right—" I gasped, trying to catch a breath.

"And no, we do not normally tell a human we've just met any of this. You would not have been chosen by a nimbus if you weren't worthy of this information. Please do not share it."

"Gah." I cleared my throat and tried again. "You're serious?"

Katsuro inclined his head. Damn, but the man was elegance incarnate.

"So, is like, Clare from the bookstore some sort of gnome because…"

Davin laughed. "Clare is actually human, though I can see why you might think so. She is psychic though."

"Well, that explains how she knew what I was going to ask before I even opened my mouth." I was managing to not panic or hyperventilate, but only barely, and only because I'd already faced terrible men and these two men were clearly not evil.

"Beechworth is a sanctuary of sorts for those of us who wish for a relatively peaceful existence. For the most part, we werewolves and vampires maintain our boundaries and keep those within as safe as we possibly can from outside influences that might try to bring danger to our small town."

"Davin said things were relatively peaceful here."

Katsuro nodded and Davin tightened his arm around my shoulders, probably meaning to offer comfort.

"And then I show up and throw everything into chaos."

"Arguably, Nimbus did that," Katsuro said. "Your friend is magical and rare, and they are often captured and sold. When you found him, how was he secured to the lamppost?"

"A golden lead that somehow got lost at the vet clinic. I wasn't worried about it, though. I didn't like it."

"Yes, that is one method of capturing them. How he ended up tied to a lamppost, well, that may be something we will never know. You rescued him and I'm sure the people who captured him would like to recover him. We must devise a plan to keep you and Nimbus safe until he comes fully into his powers, and then they will not be able to contain him, and he will no longer be useful. The magic they use to contain these creatures keeps them young and undeveloped. Once he grows to adulthood, he will be safe."

"How long will that take?"

"They grow quickly. A few months to a year," Katsuro explained. "I do not know much more, and I only know this much because I've done a bit of research since I met him."

I took a deep breath, absurdly grateful that whatever was going on, it wasn't related to my past. Though, how it could have been, I had no idea. The people I'd put behind bars were human. Well, I assumed they were, anyway.

"Okay, can we back up to the part where the supernatural is real and you two are a werewolf and a vampire, because that's nuts." I held up my hand at Katsuro's look of protest. "The whole thing is nuts, but, clearly, I have to try to believe all this. I think I met the other shade in town, too."

"Yes, it's likely you caught his interest." A bit of heat entered Katsuro's expression as he locked eyes with me. "You have certainly caught mine."

I licked my lips and tried not to react to the intensity in his gaze, but my heart was racing again and not from fear this time. Hell, I should be afraid. He'd literally told me I was on the menu, but if he wanted to hurt me, I felt we'd be having a different conversation, or I'd already be lunch. Or dinner, or whatever.

"Not too many single women in town?" I tried to deflect.

Katsuro smiled. "No. Not many we'd be interested in, either."

I laughed nervously. "Um, did Jaz tell you about what happened earlier, too?"

"She did." Katsuro leaned back, taking some of the pressure off me.

67

"Katsuro, we need to protect her," Davin growled, his arm still tight around me.

"Yes, Davin. I agree. If she's going to be leaving Beechworth and going to Mayday Hills on a regular basis, we must claim her so she is safe."

"This, uh, claiming, what does that…entail?" I cleared my throat again.

Katsuro smiled, and it was impossible to miss the predatory glint in his eyes this time.

"One or more of us needs to put our mark upon you, to declare to the supernatural world that you are under our protection. Both Davin and I are powerful enough that our mark alone should keep you safe from anyone in Mayday Hills. This will also help protect Nimbus, though we will need to take additional measures for his safety."

I blinked, then blinked some more, at a loss for words.

"But, I barely know you," I finally protested.

Katsuro touched my leg again, gently but with a touch of ownership. "You don't have to decide right now, Hannah, and we will protect you to the best of our abilities without this step, but you should consider it."

I bit my lower lip and Katsuro's gaze fixed there for a moment before he met my stare again.

"While you decide, you must promise you won't share anything we've told you with anyone. Most of the people in town know all of this, but a few don't. None of them should know of your situation."

"Don't want more competition?" My heart was racing again as I was trapped by his intense stare.

Katsuro reached forward, brushing delicate fingers along my cheekbone before tucking some hair behind my ear and lightly running his fingers down my neck. His touch sent jolts of electricity through my nerves, to settle in my core and leave a warm, needy feeling there.

"No." He smiled and leaned back.

"It's more than that," Davin said with a grumble. "Katsuro and his vampires, as well as I and my pack, can protect you."

"And I have to choose between vampires and werewolves?" My voice squeaked and I didn't like it.

"No," Katsuro replied. "You simply have to choose to allow us to protect you to the fullness of our abilities."

My hands trembled, and Davin cleared his throat. Katsuro finally looked away, a hint of amusement in the faint smile on his lips.

"I think I need a minute."

"Of course. We're keeping you from your coffee." The vampire got up from the coffee table he was sitting on and handed me a drink. "Decaf latte."

He handed Davin something before he took a drink. Davin took his arm from around me and grabbed a pastry, too. Nimbus got up and hopped onto the coffee table, taking a drink and selecting a treat from his bowl. I didn't have the energy to tell him to get on the floor, but if he was a supernatural being, should I be making him eat on the floor? I didn't know.

"Wow, this is… so much." I gulped a long drink of the latte before leaning back on the couch.

"Why did you come to Beechworth, anyway?" Katsuro asked.

Suddenly, I wanted to tell him absolutely everything. Nimbus grumbled and gave the vampire a dirty look before he hopped back on my lap. The feeling eased slightly, but they had trusted me, and I wanted to trust them. Still, this was my new life and there shouldn't be any need to bring up the past. The past was dead or behind bars.

"Wait, did you just use some sort of vampire mind power on me?" I glared at Katsuro.

He winked but didn't answer.

Shaking my head, I took another drink before answering. "Yeah, so, I came here because the rumors about this place caught my interest. I wasn't sure what I thought I'd find, but this is certainly not it."

Davin laughed, but whatever he was going to say was interrupted by another sharp knock on the door.

Jaz entered. "You have an urgent visitor, m'lord," she said stiffly, bowing and stepping aside.

My blood ran cold as I recognized the man I'd almost run into earlier today. His hawk-nosed profile was unmistakable.

Nimbus growled, teeth bared, and his little claws dug into my thighs as if he was getting ready to launch himself at the newcomer.

I clutched at my mug and prepared to use it as a weapon.

Chapter 11

"**W**hat brings you to Beechworth, Drake?" Katsuro stood, putting himself between me and the newcomer.

A low rumble thrummed through Davin's chest, matching Nimbus's growl.

"You have something of ours."

Though Katsuro was blocking the view, I could tell this Drake guy was staring through him, speaking directly to me. I didn't answer.

"That nimbus is spoken for."

Okay, I wasn't about to ignore that. I surged to my feet, dislodging Nimbus and storming up to Katsuro's side. I wasn't dumb, I stayed well within the vampire's reach.

"Oh, are you the one trying to enslave supernatural creatures?" I demanded.

"The nimbus—"

"Listen right here, asshole. This nimbus chose me after I rescued him from whatever evil plans you had for him. You can go fuck off if you think I'm handing him over."

Drake seemed taken aback.

Whatever Drake was, and I had no doubt he was supernatural too, I was not nearly as scared of him as I was of the people I'd helped put behind bars.

Katsuro put a hand on my arm when I took a step forward.

"The nimbus is mine as long as he chooses to stay with me. I'll protect him, with my life if I have to, and I'm sure as hell going to make it so people know that if something happens to me, they should connect it to you." I pulled out my phone, snapped his picture, and showed him—after a quick glance to make sure the picture actually took. "Just say a threatening word and I'll send this to my BFF in D.C." BFF was a stretch, but my contact in witness protection was in D.C., and I'd been instructed to maintain a bit of contact.

Drake cleared his throat, and his gaze flicked to Katsuro before returning to me.

"I suppose we shall see if you are that brave when you don't have a vampire and a werewolf standing at your back."

I showed him my teeth. "Fuck off."

Drake smiled, the unfriendly expression twisting his features and showing a hint of the evil I'd learned to look for over the last couple of years. "Good day, Hannah." He nodded ever so slightly to Katsuro and ignored Davin as he turned abruptly and left.

Jaz's eyes were wide as she bowed and followed Drake out.

"Are you *sure* she needs our protection?" Davin said softly once Drake was gone.

Katsuro burst out laughing. "That was unwise, my dear spitfire, but entertaining."

Nimbus rubbed against my leg and rooed, his fluffy tail curled over his back and wagging.

"Shit, I'm going to have to start carrying a gun, aren't I?" I pulled my glasses off and cleaned the lenses before shoving them back on my face.

"Do you know how to use a gun?" Katsuro asked, not unkindly.

"Yeah, I do." I crossed my arms and rubbed my hands on my biceps. Fuck, I'd never wanted to have to carry one again.

I could see the questions in the vampire's eyes, but he left me alone for now. Lots of people used guns, but I was sure the tone in my voice had clued him in that I hadn't learned for sport.

Davin touched the small of my back. I took a deep breath and let him ground me with the contact.

"So, what do we do?"

"Tonight, we get you home safely. Davin and I will get our people to keep an eye on you. And, we will come up with a plan for when you go to Mayday Hills."

"I don't want bodyguards following me everywhere." I was so done with that, too.

"Necessary to help protect Nimbus," Katsuro insisted. "You did say you'd do whatever it took to protect him."

I glared, annoyed that he was using my words against me, but he also had a fair point. "And what do you get out of this? No one does this kind of thing for free."

Katsuro shared a glance at Davin before turning his attention to Nimbus.

"The good favor of a nimbus is payment enough. They are powerful, and when he has come into his own abilities, perhaps he will find a way to return the favor."

Nimbus rooed and sat next to Katsuro, putting his paw up. The vampire kneeled smoothly and took the little fluffball's paw before giving him a scratch behind the ears.

"It certainly doesn't hurt that we may also win your good favor, Hannah. You are intriguing, in more than one way."

Katsuro's direct regard was intense, and I made myself remember to breathe. "Do I get to know what Drake is?" I asked to deflect his attention.

"Drake is an unfriendly shade. Though I doubt he's the one that attacked us. He doesn't like to get his hands dirty," Davin replied.

"Right." I hugged myself. "Okay. I need to go home and freak out now. Thanks for the lovely evening." I shuddered and headed for the door. The men let me go, probably the right decision, though for a moment I hoped one of them would follow me.

Nimbus stayed right by my side, dragging the leash I'd put on him. "I suppose I don't really need this, do I?" I bent over to pick it up, but when I went to unclip it from the cloud puppy's collar, he danced away.

"Leave it?"

Nimbus wagged his tail and sat next to me.

"Okay." Whatever he wanted, I supposed.

I got to the door of the coffee shop before Jaz caught up to me.

"Are you my guard for the night?"

She smiled. "You'll be safe once you get to your apartment. Oliver is more than sufficient to keep you safe while you're within his domain."

"Oh, fuck. What is Oliver?"

Jaz held the door for me, and I went outside. "Ask him."

I wanted to ask her what her story was, but right now I'd had more than enough for one evening and hopefully I'd get time alone with her again, soon.

"Why me?" I blurted when we were halfway back.

Jaz studied me before shrugging. "Why me? Why anyone. Wrong time, right place. Snuggle that nimbus and hopefully this will blow over."

"You work for Katsuro or Drake?"

She frowned. "Depends on who you ask." *Later,* she mouthed, and I recognized my mistake. If I only had to worry about humans, we would have been safe to talk quietly, but who knew what was out there now, listening, able to hear from any sort of distance or lurking in nearby shadows.

We walked, in silence, through the darkened streets until we got to my place.

"Well, here you are. Stay inside for the rest of the night if you can." Jaz's voice was cool and professional, a bit aloof.

We'd reached the brick building that had once been a school but was now an apartment complex full of mostly supernaturals, I imagined. That I hadn't seen any of my neighbors now made a lot more sense.

"Thank you, Jaz."

She winked, but her tone was at odds with her expression. "Don't thank me yet, Hannah. Katsuro and Davin might be all over you, but I'm certainly not your friend." *Later*, she mouthed again.

"Well, for the company on the walk, then," I replied tightly. I didn't know what would be safe for me to say in reply. Her back was to the street, mine was to the building. Anyone could see if I mouthed something or winked or whatever. I'd have to trust that, for now, she understood. Of course, I didn't know her story yet, either. I'd seen her in Mayday Hills working for Drake, and I'd seen her here working for Katsuro. Where were her actual loyalties?

Hell, could I trust anyone?

That comforting thought followed me through the vestibule where our mail was and into the keypad-protected main entrance. I would check my mail in the morning. Right now, I just wanted inside.

Where I nearly ran into Oliver.

A soft roo of greeting was all that saved me from plowing into him.

"Fuck." I jumped back, almost smacking into the doors.

Oliver grabbed my arm before I could hurt myself.

"Hannah, are you all right?"

His smell of cinnamon wafted over me, reminding me of the pastry I had sadly left behind in the coffee shop.

His light blue-gray eyes were narrowed in concern.

I tried to say yes, that I was fine, but I couldn't force the words past my lips.

The attack earlier and the confrontation with Drake caught up to me, and I started to shake.

Chapter 12

"**W**hat did they do to you?" Oliver frowned, his normally mild and friendly expression darkening.

"Other than tell me the truth?" I hugged myself, grateful that Nimbus was pressed up against my calf.

"I see," he replied hesitantly.

"Oh, uh, sorry." I shook myself and tried to stop my reaction. "I'm not especially freaked out about the whole vampire—werewolf thing, though I probably should be. When I was out with Davin we were attacked, and then Drake paid us a visit while I was at the coffee shop, trying to get Nimbus." Talking about it helped some, though my hands still shook. I shoved them in my pockets to see if that would help.

"Can I make you some tea? Perhaps you want to talk about it somewhere other than the hallway?"

"Oliver, that would be great. Thank you." I'd thought I wanted to be alone, but his offer felt like exactly what I needed.

He held out his hand. After a moment's hesitation, I took my hand from my pocket and placed it in his. His hand was warm with light callouses, and his grip was firm, comforting.

Oliver led me to one of the lounges that I knew existed but had yet to visit. It was just down the hallway from the entryway.

"Please wait just a moment. I must get more acceptable tea." He led me to a padded chair by the counter.

"I'll be right here."

That made Oliver smile. He turned and hurried out of the room, and I took a moment to look around. The lounge had a couch, a love seat, a long table lined with chairs, and several bookshelves overflowing with books. The furniture was all well used, but not shabby, giving the place a homey feel. The counter was the boundary between the kitchen and the rest of the room. Even the kitchen had decent appliances, though everything was generic, no actual personalization to the equipment. I also spied an electric teakettle. I removed Nimbus' leash, and he trotted off to explore the room while I grabbed the kettle and filled it with water. At this point I didn't even care if the tea Oliver brought back was caffeinated. I wasn't entirely sure I'd sleep tonight, anyway.

Oliver returned just as I was adjusting the settings on the kettle.

"So, Katsuro and Davin filled you in on the town's secrets?" He came over, placing a couple of containers next to me, two tea balls, and two large mugs.

Nimbus trotted over and rooed enthusiastically. Oliver gracefully kneeled and pet the little guy.

"Yeah. With everyone apparently after Nimbus, he felt I needed to know."

"And you are not bothered?"

I took a deep breath, leaning both hands on the counter and staring at the ground. "I've seen evil, Oliver. Davin and Katsuro are not evil. Drake, yes. I promise I never expected anything like this, but hell, I wanted something different. I got it."

Oliver chuckled.

"Oh, Jaz told me to ask you what you are. I hope that's not rude."

"It could be rude under different circumstances, but I am not offended. Especially as you were told to ask by the right hand of one of the two unofficial leaders of our town."

"Who's the official?"

"Mayor Henrietta Clifton. She answers to Davin, however. And, of course, no one would cross the vampires. Henrietta is also a werewolf and is quite skilled at administration."

"There's a lot to untangle." I sighed and grabbed one of the jars of tea. I was still waiting on Oliver to answer my other question, but I'd asked it and I'd let him answer in his own time. The tea was herbal, and a beautiful blend of colors. I popped open the lid and knew immediately that this was the one I wanted. Chamomile mixed with lavender and maybe something else already soothed my senses and it wasn't even steeped.

Oliver handed me a tea ball before he let out a soft breath. "I am also a shade."

"Ah. You're the *friendly* shade?"

"Yes. Friendly enough, anyway."

I glanced up at Oliver. His brow was furrowed, and he studied the tea he measured out of the other canister. Something mint by the smell.

"You're the only one of the three I've now run across that smells like cinnamon."

He actually blushed. "Ah." He cleared his throat before continuing. "I had a run-in with a pixie. She was convinced she was doing me a favor."

I laughed. "Seriously?"

He nodded.

"Wow. That's kind of hilarious."

"At least it's not offensive." Oliver shrugged. "Would you like to tell me about your day?" He poured the hot water and put the tea balls in the mugs to steep. "If you want any sweetener, it's in the cupboard."

"Thanks. I'll see how it tastes before I add anything." I cradled my cup and took it back to the couch. Nimbus jumped up on the cushion next to me, and Oliver sat on the loveseat. Once we were all comfortable, I launched into the details of the day.

Oliver was an attentive listener, though his face darkened into an expression I never wanted directed at me when I described the attack. When I got to Drake, he shook his head in disgust.

"So, now I have to keep Nimbus safe."

The puppy snuggled into my leg and rooed softly.

"Yes, of course we do. I suspect the entire town will be involved in this mission before long. He will be quite the benefit to Beechworth. Not to mention it's the right thing to do. He chose us after all. You more than any of us, of course, but he came here and that makes him our responsibility."

"Well, I appreciate the help. I don't know how to deal with supernatural danger."

"That implies that you're used to dealing with regular danger?"

I cursed myself but shrugged. "What woman isn't?"

"Sadly true," Oliver agreed.

The tea was well steeped by the time I finished my story and tasted divine. We sat in silence for a while, enjoying the drinks.

Once I'd finished mine, I set it down and glanced at my phone for the time. It was truly late.

"Leave your mug. I'll take care of it. Can I walk you to your room for the night?"

"Yeah. I should probably walk Nimbus, first, though."

The little guy sat up next to me, his leash in his mouth.

I swore I'd left that over on the counter, but maybe I hadn't. Or maybe Nimbus had teleported it somehow.

He wiggled happily while I took the leash, rubbed his soft ears, then clipped it to his collar.

"I'm surprised he wants to wear this," I said as I stood.

Oliver joined me as we went into the hallway and headed back outside.

"I suspect to him it is a symbol of being under your protection."

"That does make sense."

It had cooled considerably since I was last outside, and I shivered after the warmth from the lounge. Fortunately, Nimbus was quick. No one bothered us, and we were back inside in minutes. Oliver walked just behind me up the stairs and Nimbus led the way. When we reached my door, I turned.

"Will you hug me?" That probably sounded weird, but I didn't know how else to ask, and I wanted some sort of human-style contact.

"Of course, Hannah. Anything you want."

As Oliver wrapped his arms around me, enclosing me in a tight, comforting hug, I got the idea that he really did mean anything. Katsuro had mentioned I'd probably caught Oliver's attention, too. Something else complicated I had to navigate, but that problem was for another day. Right now I just wanted to be held for a minute. I held him tightly in return, leaning my head against his chest and breathing in his cinnamon scent.

After a moment, I remembered he was my landlord and was mortified especially when I recalled a flash of my shower-time fantasy from the other day. Heat colored my cheeks. Still, I'd needed this.

"Thank you," I said, loosening my grip.

"Any time, Hannah." Oliver released me.

His voice was extra soothing at that moment, and I instantly regretted the inches that were now between us as he stepped back. I looked up and met his light blue-gray eyes. The tenderness they held nearly undid me.

He brushed his finger along my cheek, wiping away a bit of moisture. "Is there anything else you want to talk about? Just because it's late, doesn't mean we need to part ways if you need me. I'm nocturnal. You aren't keeping me up." He smiled kindly.

"Uh." Fuck, I wanted to tell him everything, but it so wasn't safe. I'd been warned about this, too, and told if the need to talk ever arose, to call my contact in D.C. and talk to him. It wasn't the same though, and Oliver was a good hugger.

"No." I finally said. "It's just been a long day. A long week. A long year. I'm just tired. Sorry."

"Nothing to apologize for, Hannah. I'm here for you."

"Thanks." I turned away, opened my door, and reluctantly went inside. I almost didn't shut the door, and I kicked myself mentally while I took off my shoes and hung my jacket on the hook. Then I kicked myself some more and went back to check. Oliver had left, the hallway empty now.

"Damn it," I muttered. Sure, he was my landlord, but also, damn it. I ran my hand through my hair and tried to decide if I needed a hot shower or a cold one.

Nimbus pressed against my leg and grumbled softly.

"Thanks, buddy. I suppose I really should be concentrating on keeping you safe, anyway. And I probably shouldn't be completely exhausted for my first day at work. Or is that second? I don't know. Today was kind of weird, anyway." I gave the cloud puppy another scratch and hoped my day at work would be relatively uneventful.

Chapter 13

Making it to work without anything strange happening, other than one of the werewolves waving at me from a parked truck—did they all drive trucks?—and following me into Mayday Hills, was a huge relief. I wasn't sure what she was going to do while I was working, but I supposed that wasn't my problem. I recognized her from the store but didn't know her name.

I parked behind the shop, let Nimbus out, and took the leash he held in his mouth.

Before long, we were inside. Clare popped up from behind the counter, much as she had been the other day when we'd come in. Her owlishly-wide eyes and slight goblin appearance was still a little startling, especially now that I knew such things were real, but I took Katsuro at his word that she was human.

"Ahh, Nimbus, your post is there." Her smile, however, was genuine and very comforting.

The cloud puppy wagged his fluffy curled tail and trotted over to the soft bed Clare had placed next to the counter for him. He had his own bowl of water and a bowl of treats sat on the counter. I laughed, shaking my head before unclipping his leash and placing it on the ground next to him.

"And Hannah, can you help me with this box?"

I went around the counter and helped Clare lift the box of books, placing it next to the register. She proceeded to tell me how to check in books and other details of my job.

The morning passed in delightful peace. The slightly musty scent of old books mingled with the sharper aroma of new ones and combined with the light incense smell the shop had in a soothing manner. Customers came in at a reasonable pace, and I didn't have to worry about anything but working the cash register correctly and learning a few names of the regulars that stopped in that day. When Clare sent me out to stock shelves, I kept my eyes open for anything on the occult or supernatural that might help me learn more about my current circumstances. Even a history book about the towns might help. I might have to hit the library, too. I needed information.

When lunch came, Clare got me started on paperwork and we settled on my hours. I didn't want a lot to start, and she was content with morning help four days a week with an occasional Saturday thrown in. She kept the bookstore closed on Mondays and Tuesdays since her other part-time help had quit a while back.

After I finished the technicalities, I browsed and found the books I wanted to buy and took them to the counter. Clare gave me a knowing look but didn't outwardly comment on my selections. When I turned toward the door and got ready to head back out into the real-world, Nimbus put on the brakes and backed away from the door, lips wrinkled and a low growl rumbling from his throat.

Clare turned her attention to the door, trusting Nimbus's instincts as I did.

Drake walked in, a smug expression on his face.

"You are not welcome here." Clare grabbed her phone.

I took a few steps back to stand next to my growling nimbus, not sure what else to do.

"I've simply come for the creature. You're no longer in protected territory, and I will have what is mine."

"I already told you, you can't have him. He's not yours." I stepped in front of Nimbus, heart speeding, adrenaline coursing through me.

"And he certainly doesn't want to go with you," Clare replied, putting her phone down and pulling something else out from under the counter.

"It's not his choice." Drake stepped toward us.

I took one of the heavier books out of the bag and dropped the rest. "Seems he's intelligent enough that it should be."

The shade ignored my statement, apparently done with talking, and came over to me.

I lunged forward, slamming the book into his throat, spine first, just as Clare tossed something powdery at the shade.

Drake gargled out a shout of pain as he clutched at his throat. We'd surprised him, but I wasn't sure it was enough. If he'd been human, the book to the throat would have dropped him.

Nimbus howled, and a whirl of air stirred up the powder Clare had thrown, pelting the shade with it and driving him to the door. The door slammed open, and Drake was shoved out, still batting at the remnants of whatever Clare had tossed at him.

"I forgot to tell you, dear," Clare said once the door clanged shut behind the shade and Nimbus's howl quieted. "There's a sort of repellant in this bag under the counter. Anyone supernatural comes in and makes a scene, throw it at them. It nullifies their powers to a degree. You're allowed to defend yourself."

The werewolf who had followed me to work slammed through the door a moment later. I didn't know her name, but she had clearly been running. Her hair was disheveled, and a bruise faded on her cheek.

"Sorry. He had friends."

I blew out a breath between my teeth. "Fuck. Clare, I don't know if it's safe for me to be here. Not if this is going to happen."

"Nonsense." She waved away my concern. "This problem will be dealt with soon enough."

"You think so?"

She shrugged. "I sense it. Until then, we'll just do the best we can."

I wondered what 'soon enough' meant to Clare, but she seemed disinclined to elaborate, so I let it go.

"Nimbus, you did good." I kneeled and rubbed his fluffy cheeks. All the fear I thought I'd left behind was creeping back up my spine, quickening my heart, sending tendrils of adrenalin through my veins.

The cloud puppy rooed and leaned into my touch. I got a very distinct image in my mind of him sitting in front of me being a very good boy and me feeding him hotdogs.

"You want hotdogs?"

He wagged his fluffy tail and grumbled happily at me.

I laughed. "I'll see what I can do." His happy attitude dispelled some of the darkness trying to overtake me. I thought back to the conversations we'd had last night. What could I do against vampires and werewolves and shades?

I didn't know, but I had to keep Nimbus safe. Even if it meant hiding in a coffee shop for months until he got bigger and was no longer of interest to Drake.

"Let's get you home, Hannah," the werewolf said.

"I didn't catch your name," I said as I followed her outside.

"Kerin."

"Thank you, Kerin."

"I'm just sorry I couldn't help with Drake."

We reached my car, and she stopped me before I put my hand on it.

"Hold up, smells funny."

Nimbus growled.

The old anxiety from dealing with the traffickers came crashing back down on me all at once. My throat closed, and my lungs stopped working. I sucked in air, trying to hold the panic back while Kerin sniffed around the small SUV.

If they were pulling tricks the humans had, I knew how to deal with it, but I'd never wanted to be in this situation again.

Nimbus leaned against my leg.

"Yeah, maybe we better take my truck. I'll drive." Kerin tugged on my elbow.

I glanced down at my puppy. His ears twitched as if he were listening to something, but after a moment he followed Kerin to the truck. Though uneasy, I followed. She was one of Davin's wolves, and he said they'd protect us.

I got into the old-style bench-seat truck and pulled out my phone. I hadn't checked it all morning and I didn't have any messages. I shot off a quick text to Davin letting him know about my SUV and the incident with Drake. Then I checked but didn't have any email.

When I looked up, I frowned, not recognizing the roads or surroundings. We were driving on a two-lane road through some hilly neighborhoods. The houses were set back into the trees on large lots. They looked older, but nicely kept-up large family homes.

"Where are we?"

"I didn't want to be followed," Kerin said.

Nimbus rooed, sounding concerned.

My phone chimed. It was a text from Davin.

I'll come get you.

Too late, I sent back. *I went with Kerin.*

Where are you?

I don't know.

"Something wrong?" Kerin glanced over at me.

"No," I lied.

I pulled up my GPS app and took a screenshot and sent it to Davin.

After I sent another one a few minutes later, Kerin glanced at me, frowning. Before I could react, she snatched my phone away and tossed it out her window.

"What are you doing?" I'd been nervous before, but now I knew something was wrong.

"Just sit still."

My hand went to my seatbelt. She growled softly and slammed on the brakes, throwing me and Nimbus forward. I was restrained. He shrieked when he hit the dash.

Still disoriented, I undid my seatbelt. Thanks to my past, I'd had some training in dealing with situations like this, and the training took over while my brain tried to catch up. I spun on my butt, slammed my feet into her head, and scrabbled at the door. It was locked, but I wrenched it open. I snagged Nimbus by the fluff and dragged him out of the truck after me. He shrieked again but didn't struggle.

As soon as my feet hit the pavement, I ran.

Chapter 14

I got an image of Nimbus on his own feet, so I paused long enough to let him down. He sprinted ahead of me, and I followed, hoping he had an idea of where to go.

I'd dashed up one of the large house's driveways and then crashed through their side yard into the wooded area that ran behind the houses. Branches and leaves snapped and cracked under my feet, and the tree branches tugged at my clothing. Nimbus raced along, but just as I wasn't used to sprinting long distances, he was young, and I sensed his energy flagging.

There was no way we could outrun a werewolf, anyway.

Nimbus came to a creek and turned to run alongside it.

I didn't hear any pursuit, but if Kerin had shifted, I probably wouldn't until it was too late.

A whiff of cinnamon caught my attention just as shadows swirled from the depths of the trees and solidified into a now familiar six-legged, dog-like monster. Hopefully, from the cinnamon, it was Oliver.

Nimbus barked his high-pitched bark then kept running. The shade ran back the way we'd come. I chased after Nimbus until he slowed. I stumbled to a halt, clutching my side, gasping for breath, trying to stay alert, but wanting to fall to my knees until I regained the ability to breathe.

Wolves dashed out of the trees and surrounded us, setting my heart racing again. They faced outward in a ring, and I guessed they were friendly. Either that or they, rightly, knew I couldn't run and were keeping me in one spot.

I heard yelping in the distance followed by ominous silence. The cries had sounded canine, not the eardrum-destroying cries of a shade. Before long, the creature dragged an unconscious, or dead, wolf into the clearing and dropped it at a large gray wolf's feet.

The six-legged creature flowed back into the shadows before fluidly shifting into a familiar human shape.

"Oliver!"

He nodded and approached the circle of wolves. The big gray glanced at me, huffed, then began his own shift.

I watched, fascinated, as bones popped and cracked, fur receded, and before long a man kneeled where a wolf had stood.

It took me a moment to realize that, unlike Oliver, Davin had not shifted with his clothing.

I blushed furiously and looked away, though I'd mostly gotten an eyeful of his muscular backside.

"Are you okay?" Davin rose to his feet.

I finally let myself drop to my knees. Nimbus came over and pressed his fluffy face against mine and rooed softly.

"No," I answered. "But Nimbus is safe, so there's that. What happened?"

"Apparently Kerin isn't as loyal as we thought. We'll question her, and she'll face pack justice." Davin didn't sound happy about that. I hadn't stopped staring at the ground, so I couldn't see his expression.

"If you like, I will walk with Nimbus and Hannah," Oliver said. "While you deal with your rogue wolf."

Davin's pause made me think that perhaps he wasn't thrilled with that idea, but he finally agreed.

"If that is all right with you, of course." Oliver kneeled next to me.

"Yes, please."

He held out his hand and I took it, letting him pull me to my feet. "Let's leave the wolves to their business. Davin can find us later."

"Thank you for coming for me and Nimbus," I said in Davin's general direction. "You too, Oliver."

Nimbus rooed as if agreeing.

"Of course," Davin replied. "Any time. Hannah, I'll catch up with you and Oliver in a while. I'll make sure I'm wearing clothes, too. Sorry about that."

"Uh, yeah, sure, it's fine," I stammered.

He chuckled. "It would be far more convenient if our clothing shifted with us, or we could talk in wolf form. Unfortunately, we have to deal with nudity instead. We're all used to it. I'm sorry for subjecting you to it before we had a chance to discuss it. I'm shifting back now. Thank you for texting me when you did, or we might not have caught up in time."

"Thank you," I said again.

I let Oliver lead me away, cheeks still flaming.

Nimbus trotted ahead of us, nose working, as if staying alert for trouble.

Once we were out of the clearing and heading back toward the road, the reality of what had just happened hit and I started to shake.

"Fuck." I hugged myself.

Oliver put his arm around me, and I leaned into his touch.

"We've got you, Hannah."

I turned and buried my face against his chest. Oliver put his other arm around me and held me while I shook. "I thought I'd be safe here."

Nimbus came back to my side and leaned against my leg.

Oliver stroked my hair. "I feel there's more to that statement than the current circumstances."

"I can't talk about it," I muttered into his chest. That helpless feeling brought more tears to my eyes. I wanted to talk about it. I wanted to be safe. I wanted to be held and loved and not to have had to walk away from my old life.

For his part, Oliver simply held me. He didn't protest my silence, try to get me to talk, just kept me close while I soaked his shirt with tears.

"We will figure something out, Hannah."

I leaned back and tilted my head up so I could look at Oliver. He brushed his fingers along my cheek.

I licked my lips when I met his gaze and considered that maybe I didn't care if he was my landlord anymore.

His grip tightened before he took a breath and broke eye contact.

I remembered to breathe and took a step back. He turned and I followed quietly, though I did take his hand. I needed some reassurance and his hand in mine helped a lot.

Nimbus trotted along beside us.

"Did you drive?" I finally broke the silence between us.

"Yes. I'm parked near where your last screenshot showed you. The wolves ran. Davin will take care of retrieving your car from the bookstore, if that's okay. He'll make sure it's clean."

"Thanks." I took a breath and started thinking of all the things I'd learned about avoiding trafficking. My car was certainly something I needed to be aware of. I had to have it, but it wasn't difficult to drug me with a contact drug, or disable it, or any number of things I'd been trained to look for. Training I'd hoped to leave behind.

The grass was springy and lush under my feet as we cleared the woods and cut through someone's yard.

Nimbus dropped his shoulder and flopped over onto his back, wiggling around and grunting a little in enjoyment.

His simple delight pushed back some of the darkness threatening to overwhelm me.

Oliver chuckled. "If only your fluffy dog staining his white patches green were all we had to worry about."

"Yeah."

Once Nimbus finished his roll, we continued to the street. A sedan crawled past. I recognized the driver immediately. Drake glowered at Oliver and me. His passenger looked vaguely familiar in a way that sent chills down my spine. I knew I hadn't seen that person since moving to Beechworth. Did they just look like someone I'd known once, or were they actually someone I'd encountered in my past life? The man peered at me, and I stared back, knees trembling. Things had just gone from bad to worse.

"Hannah," Oliver said. "He won't hurt you while I'm around. Let's go."

I let my landlord lead me down the road and got into his car in a daze. Nimbus hopped into the back seat.

"Are you sure you don't want to talk about it?" Oliver asked after he got into the car.

I wanted to tell him everything. Almost did. But I held back.

"I just want to get back," I finally replied.

"Of course."

The car started and I breathed a sigh of relief that they hadn't messed with his vehicle, too.

"Oh, she threw my phone out the window. I don't know where it is."

"We'll find it," Oliver assured me.

I fidgeted the entire drive back to the apartment complex, no idea what I should do. Did I move again? Take Nimbus and hide away until he was older? Hide at the coffee shop and in my apartment until the outside world was safe again?

Though my mind reeled, I had not come up with any answers by the time we got back to the apartment complex.

Oliver stayed right with me while I let Nimbus take a potty break and then he walked me inside and to my room. The cool, dark hallway contrasted so sharply with the afternoon sunlight, and though I'd grown used to Oliver's aroma of baked goods, it tickled at my nose now, making me hungry. Hungry for the lunch I hadn't had, and hungry for touch.

He offered a hug and I stepped into his embrace. This time I tilted my head back and met his eyes. I wasn't sure he was breathing, and I certainly held my breath. Was I going too far? Asking for too much? And what about Katsuro and Davin? It was all too much, and I pushed those worries away.

Hesitantly, Oliver cupped my jaw and brushed his thumb lightly over my cheek. My pulse raced as I leaned into his touch.

"Hannah..." he trailed off, instead lowering his lips until they were a breath away from mine. "I don't want to take advantage," he finally whispered.

"Maybe I'm the one taking advantage," I replied, and closed the distance between us.

Chapter 15

It was almost like a very first kiss. Hannah, the person I'd had to become, had never been kissed after all. I'd certainly never kissed anyone like Oliver. Monster, man, he held me gently and followed my every lead. I pressed with my tongue, and he opened for me, letting me take what I needed and giving everything I asked for.

Oliver's fingers dug into my back, gently, possessively. He made an appreciative sound, and I briefly wondered how long it had been since he'd kissed anyone. Maybe he needed this as much as I did?

A door clicked open and Nimbus rooed softly. I could practically feel shock radiate down the hallway, and the hairs on the back of my neck stood up.

Oliver broke off our kiss with an annoyed grunt and turned to look, but by the time we responded, no one was there.

My landlord took a deep breath before turning his attention back to me.

"I should…" He cleared his throat. "I should probably go."

I was on the verge of asking him to stay when he turned and hurried away.

"Fuck me," I whispered, hugging myself. What a crazy day it had been, and it wasn't even over yet. I had no idea what was going to happen when the vampires woke up, but I expected I'd hear from them.

Until then, I was going to hide in my room and try to figure out what the hell I was going to do. I touched my lips once I was inside. I'd felt the need for physical contact before, but kissing Oliver had awakened the desire and brought my need to a whole new level. And now I had to navigate that business, too. Three men I was interested in, and none of them I wanted to alienate.

Ugh. Maybe I should just move. Hiding away until Nimbus was older was beginning to seem like the best choice. I didn't want to hide, but I wasn't sure if I had another encounter with this sort of danger in me.

The first one had been bad enough. Uncovering the trafficking ring had saved countless lives, but it had taken almost a year to manage all the arrests. A year of undercover work I wasn't qualified for but was the only one who could do it. A year of stress, of looking over my shoulder, of wondering if I was next. I was an accountant. I'd taken a new job looking for higher pay, and it had been great, until I'd started finding discrepancies.

After a little digging, I'd gone to the police instead of my employer. That had probably saved my life. An astute sergeant had put a few pieces together and called the feds. They'd enlisted my help with the rest of their investigation. Not that I'd had a lot of choice. I'd been in danger since I'd taken the job. I just hadn't known it.

Now I was Hannah, and living in Beechworth, a small town apparently inhabited by supernaturals, instead of the beach town I'd loved. And I was in danger again. Possibly because of the adorably floofy cloud of fur that was currently following me around with his ears flat and his tail down instead of curled over his back. It was entirely possible I would have ended up in trouble regardless and I didn't regret rescuing him. I just wished I could have had the quiet and peace I'd been after.

A cold draft chilled me. I stopped my pacing and stared around, trying to figure out where it came from. It was warm outside, but cool enough in the building that I didn't have any air-conditioning going.

Nimbus gave a high-pitched bark before jumping up and snapping at the draft.

I could almost see it swirl away, as if the temperature difference briefly caused mist.

"Okay, what was that?" I kneeled and Nimbus came over to me. I buried my fingers in his fluff.

Of course, I didn't get an answer from the little guy, but I got the idea he was tired. I couldn't imagine why. It's not like we had a busy day or anything. I sighed, a little tired myself as the adrenalin faded.

"Let's get you some food and we'll have a nap. How about that?"

He curled his tail over his back and wagged it happily.

***

Hours later, I was woken from a deep sleep by a firm knock on my door.

"Coming," I muttered, not sure if whoever it was could hear me or not. I supposed it depended on what variety of supernatural stood at my door. Considering I'd never met the neighbors, it was probably Oliver. Taking a quick moment to look in the mirror and swish a little mouth wash after my nap, I made it to the door in a reasonable amount of time considering whoever it was had woken me. Nimbus sat by the door, and I suspected whoever it was, still waited.

Glancing out the peephole confirmed my suspicion that Oliver waited, though he wasn't alone and that surprised me.

"Sorry," I said as I opened the door. "I was asleep."

"My apologies for waking you." He smiled gently.

I glanced at his companion and raised my eyebrows. "Bridger? Hi."

The hunter grinned. "Seems you need a bodyguard."

If anything, my eyebrows climbed higher. "What?" Choosing Bridger after everyone had told me he couldn't know anything about what was going on in Beechworth made no sense to me.

"If you're comfortable with Bridger accompanying you outside of Beechworth, he has agreed to be your shadow when I cannot," Oliver continued.

"What do Davin and Katsuro think?"

"I have not consulted them. Undoubtedly, they'll disagree, but so far they've failed to keep you safe."

I had some doubts about what having Bridger around would accomplish. Maybe if everyone were desperate enough to keep their secrets from him, it would make them think twice about revealing any powers they might have.

"Uh, yeah, sure, that's great."

Bridger grinned. "Oliver told me that some thugs over in Mayday Hills took an interest. Real low lives. Resorted to poison. I bet it was the vampires. Hoping to knock you out until dark so they could catch you."

I glanced at Oliver, who had a hand over his mouth, hiding a smile.

"Yeah, maybe," I agreed.

The thing was, Bridger sounded excited about having this opportunity. He was practically jumping up and down. Did he not have better things to do?

"Okay. So, I have to be at work by nine tomorrow morning. Does that work for you?"

"Absolutely! I'll meet you at the front door. We'll sweep your car before we head out, or we can take mine. I'll keep watch while you work and run errands, then I'll get you back here. Sounds fantastic."

"Are you sure?"

"Yes, Hannah. Anything I can do to keep you safe from the bad guys."

"Okay. Thank you." I meant it.

"If it's all right, I need to go prepare a few things. I'll see you in the morning." Bridger beamed at me and ran off.

"Oliver, what the fuck?"

The shade chuckled. "He's perfect. He actually knows quite a bit of useful information about fighting the supernatural, though we've managed to keep any solid knowledge from him. The people in Mayday Hills also know who Bridger is and will likely try to avoid any confrontation while he's around, and he lives for this sort of thing."

"Doesn't he have a job or something?"

"Not that we can tell." Oliver shrugged and turned his shoulder as if he were thinking about leaving.

"Hey, uh, about earlier. I'm sorry if I pushed," I said.

Oliver glanced away for a moment before turning back to me. "I did not feel pressured. Quite the opposite. It was a nice kiss." His smile brought his blue-gray eyes to life.

Suddenly feeling a little mischievous, I grinned back at him. "You do know that Bridger has been flirting with me, right?"

"I'm not surprised." Oliver didn't sound overly concerned.

"And that Katsuro and Davin are practically drooling on me?"

99

"Wolves do drool, though vampires are far too refined for that sort of thing." The skin around Oliver's eyes crinkled into laugh lines.

"And what do shades do?"

"We're patient." He winked at me. "Sometimes too patient." His expression shuttered for a moment before lightening again. "It's not always beneficial, I suppose."

This made me laugh gently. I sensed a story behind that last bit, but I wasn't going to push just yet.

"I've been alone too long," I admitted. "It's making me reckless. And restless."

Oliver focused on me, his gaze turning intense. "Why did you move to Beechworth, Hannah?"

The deep breath I took failed to calm the anxiety that curled through my chest. I took another. I'd never had anxiety, or panic attacks, until the last couple of years.

"I did not mean to cause distress." Oliver backed off the intensity, obviously sensing something from me, though I'd developed a pretty good poker face, too.

I held out my hand, taking his loosely, in case he wanted to pull away from the touch.

"It's complicated, Oliver. Something I'm supposed to be leaving completely behind. Unfortunately, everything that's happening is bringing all of it back. It's nothing I did, just something I found. I chose Beechworth because it was completely different from my old life and full of tantalizing rumors."

He brought his free hand up to my cheek, and I leaned into the contact.

"I will not hold it against you, if you should tell me you're not interested," Oliver said. "I promise you and Nimbus will be safe in these walls no matter what happens between us on a personal level. I do not care for all my tenants, but unless they are themselves a danger to others here, they are welcome. I just wanted you to know that. I do not want things to be awkward between us."

"You're not making it any easier for me to have restraint."

"That was not exactly my intention." He glanced away for a moment, as if embarrassed.

Need raged through me. Desire for my sexy landlord and his gentle ways. Curiosity at the monster that lurked beneath the surface combined with the way he made me feel safe, respected, and desired. I tugged gently on his hand. "Oliver, do you want to come in?"

"I do. Very much."

Dakota Brown

Chapter 16

Heart thudding in my chest, anticipation swirling through me, I stepped back, allowing Oliver into my apartment. He let the door shut behind him, then took my hand and gently tugged me into his arms. There was no point in pretending we weren't both here for some physical contact. I readily went into his embrace. The feel of his hands on my body reached deep into my soul and touched me in a way I hadn't felt in ages. I pressed closer and met his lips with mine.

This kiss was less restrained. We were both starving for affection and touch. Oliver's fingers dug into my back, and he cupped my head with his other hand. I had no hesitation about digging my fingers into his ass. He didn't wear particularly tight pants, so I was a little surprised at how firm and muscular it felt. Though I didn't let that exploration distract me much from the skill with which this shade was kissing me. The way his tongue danced with mine made me desperately want to know what else he could do with it.

The need I felt traveled through my center and settled deep inside me, heating me. The nearly embarrassingly needy moan his touch pulled from me came straight from that heat and spread tingling threads all the way to my fingers and toes. I was uncomfortably wet, and I squeezed my legs together, needing relief.

Oliver's cinnamon scent intensified, and he broke off our kiss for a moment. The shade took a deep breath. "You smell amazing," he whispered against my neck.

"You smell like baked goods." I couldn't help joking a little.

He chuckled. "Sorry about that."

"There are worse things," I replied before nibbling gently on his neck.

He rumbled softly in his throat and let me tug him farther into the apartment. Then I paused.

"What's wrong?"

"I, uh, was not expecting to be entertaining. I don't have condoms. After the last time I had sex, which was forever and a half ago, I did get tested, and I don't have any stds. I don't have the paperwork though, to show you." I couldn't show him even if I'd had it. It had my old information on it. Shit.

"I believe you, Hannah. Also, shades are immune to most human diseases including all but the worst sexual ones. The same goes for humans. I don't know about procreation though. While I have not undergone any sort of testing, as there isn't that sort of facility for my kind, I would know if I had anything transmittable to a human, and I do not. Nor do I believe I have any other diseases. They are very rare among my kind. Also, it's been an age and a half for me, as well. There are plenty of things we can do that won't put us at risk for procreating though." He smiled gently at me.

"Sweet!" I tugged more urgently, practically dragging him to my bedroom.

Nimbus had retreated to his spot on the bed, and I wrinkled my nose while I thought. He saved me from having to evict him, however. He gave a happy grumbling roo, hopped off the bed, and left us alone in the bedroom.

"I like what you've done with the place," Oliver said.

Snorting, I glanced around. There was absolutely no décor. "Uh, yeah. The space-themed comforter was a whim. Don't hold it against me please."

"I like it."

"Great!" I grabbed the top and pulled it back. "Then you'll love the spaceship sheets."

He full-on belly laughed. "They're marvelous." It even sounded like he meant it.

Oliver turned his attention back to me. "You are in charge of how far we go today. Are there any boundaries you want to discuss?"

"I've never been with anyone who wasn't human. Anything I need to know?"

"I'm a shape shifter." He shrugged. "Other than that, pretty normal."

"Then I think we'll be fine. If we want to get creative later, we can get more in depth in our discussion."

His eyes lit up when I mentioned the future.

Fairly certain we had covered the basics—Oliver was far more considerate than anyone I'd ever been with before—I hooked my fingers under the bottom of my shirt and pulled it off.

Glancing up, I caught a flash of pink as Oliver licked his lips before he pulled his own shirt off.

I bit my lower lip and stared, taking him in. Lean, but well-defined muscle just begged me to touch. I reached out and gently traced the muscles over his ribs. Oliver sucked in a breath, eyes shuttering as he enjoyed the touch.

While I was there, I took his hand and placed it on me. He didn't hesitate to return the favor, fingers sliding up over my bra—I'd have worn the lacy one if I'd known I was going to be taking my clothing off for someone—and gently pebbling my nipple.

He stepped closer, his hands going behind me. After a quick glance and my nod, he slipped the catch on my bra, and I let it fall to the floor. My heart thudded and my pussy ached for attention, as he explored my skin.

"May I?" Oliver asked, his hands going to the button on my jeans.

"Yes, please."

He unbuttoned them and slid my pants off, ending up on his knees in front of me as he did so. Oliver rumbled again, a pleased and primal sound, that turned me on even more. My panties were soaked, and I wanted out of them. I put my hands on the waistband, and Oliver took the hint, helping me slide them off.

I stood bare in front of him. Oliver looked pleased, kneeling with his hands on my hips and his gaze roaming my body. I let him look. Then, before long, he stood, the motion smooth and a touch hurried. He backed me up gently, giving me all the time to object then laid me down on the bed. I thought about trying to get the rest of his clothes off, but then suspected my resolve not to go all the way—as it were—would fail. That might actually be why he hadn't shed his pants yet, either. Still, at some point, I was going to get my mouth on him.

Oliver seemed to be on the same wavelength. He kneeled over me, first kissing my lips, then moving down my body. I reveled in the feeling of having a man, especially someone like Oliver, over me, kissing me, tasting my skin, rolling my nipple in his lips and nipping gently down my stomach until he reached my aching pussy.

His tongue was every bit as talented down there as it had been when he was kissing me. Before long he had me writhing on the bed, clutching at my spaceship sheets and keening his name. He undid me hard when he slid a finger inside me and curled it just right.

"Ohmygod, Oliver," I cried out, almost kicking him by accident.

"Good?" he said mischievously.

"Yes," I gasped.

"More?"

"Oh, please," I practically begged. He had no idea how glad I was that he wasn't stopping at one. That fast orgasm had only served to whet my appetite after so long on my own.

Fortunately, Oliver seemed to be enjoying me shattering all over his face. He kept going until I was completely wrung out and satisfied. Then he crawled up next to me and held me close while I floated in an endorphin-induced haze.

"Fuck," I murmured.

"Perhaps you should get some sleep," I heard him say through a fog. That jerked me awake.

"Oh, hell no. Not until I get you in my mouth."

Oliver raised his eyebrows, but a grin danced on his lips. "If you like."

"Yes, please."

My shade got off the bed and undid his pants. I watched as he pushed them off his hips and let the slacks fall to the ground. He'd been going commando, and I further enjoyed the view, mouthwatering at the thought of wrapping my lips around his delicious-looking cock.

I flicked my finger at him, gesturing him toward me.

Oliver obliged, coming to me. We got situated on the bed, and I straddled his legs. I took his cock in my hand and stroked his velvety length, getting a groan of pleasure in response.

Leaning forward and taking his length into my mouth, I ran my tongue around, getting a feel for his responses. He gasped out a breath as I gave an experimental suck.

I swirled my tongue across the head of his cock and tried not to snort laughter. "Did you know you also taste like cinnamon?"

"I…" He looked at me, eyes wide with surprise. "No, I had no idea."

"It's different, but certainly not bad." Before he could reply, I went back to work, doing my best to bring him pleasure.

He bucked, thrusting gently into my mouth. He curled his fingers in my hair, but didn't try to control me, his groans becoming more urgent.

"Hannah," he warned me.

I kept sucking, and he shuddered and went rigid as he spilled into my mouth. I swallowed the cinnamon flavored cum down, not at all minding the taste.

This time when we curled up together, we both drifted off, content in each other's arms.

Oliver's phone ringing woke both of us some time later. He cursed but made no move to get up.

"Do you need to answer that."

Grunting in annoyance, he shifted out of the bed. "Probably. It's Davin."

"How do you know?"

"His ringtone," my shade muttered and stumbled over to the pile of his clothing.

Sleepy, just woken grumpy Oliver was adorable.

He answered the phone with an annoyed grunt, listened to what Davin had to say, then his gaze slid toward me with a not entirely pleased expression settling on his face.

Unconsciously, I pulled the sheets up to cover my chest and wondered what had happened now.

Chapter 17

"**W**hat's wrong?"

Oliver sighed. "Let's get over to the coffeehouse. Davin's interrogation revealed some interesting developments."

Not reassured in the slightest, I stayed in bed. Nimbus, perhaps sensing my mood, jumped up on the bed and settled next to me.

Frowning, I glanced at the bedroom door. It was shut, and I swore he'd left the room.

"Am I in danger?"

"You were already in danger," Oliver pointed out.

"Right, but not from any of you."

Oliver paused, his eyes widening. "Hannah, I'll do anything in my power to protect you. You are in no danger from me or the others."

"You're sure?"

He nodded and came over to me, taking my hand and sitting next to me on the bed. Nimbus watched him, but didn't object, so I relaxed.

"My annoyance was at the extra danger, not at you. My apologies. I should prepare you. I think you're going to have to tell us about your past, but it's also possible we've discovered it inadvertently. We'll know more when we meet with the others."

"Fuck." I shuddered, and Oliver put his arm around me and kissed my forehead.

"It's all right, Hannah. We'll figure it out."

I leaned against the shade and hoped no one would be mad.

Nimbus rooed softly and leaned against my other side.

"One other complication," Oliver said.

I huffed out a breath. What else?

"Vampires and werewolves have excellent senses of smell. They will know what we've been up to."

"We showered. Also, so?"

"A shower is not enough. And I just thought I'd warn you. They are, after all, both interested in having you as a mate."

"Well, they can suck a dick." I buried my face in his shoulder. "Let's just stay here. I was having a nice nap."

He chuckled. "While I tend to agree, I think we do need to address the danger. It impacts more than just you. Also, while werewolves are notoriously bisexual, I'm fairly certain Davin is straight. The same applies to vampires and also Katsuro. I doubt that suggestion will appease them."

"Kinda my choice, isn't it?"

"Ahh, my dear," Oliver kissed my forehead again. "You don't have to choose."

"I don't have to what? I don't understand."

"Should you desire it, date all of us. Mate with all of us, or none of us, or choose. It's your decision."

"Is that… normal?"

Oliver shrugged. "Sometimes yes, sometimes no."

"Do you think Katsuro or Davin would go along with it?"

"If you tell them that it is your desire, they will. If you don't want all three of us, you will eventually have to make a choice, but know this, however you choose, I will still protect you and Nimbus and you will always be welcome here, as I said before."

I rubbed at my eyeballs. "That's a lot. I think I'll go back to dealing with the people trying to kill me. Much more straightforward."

"Are you sure they want you dead?"

"If it's the same people as before, yes."

"Unfortunately, there are far worse things than death. Let's go see what Davin has discovered."

Chilled by Oliver's statement, I crawled out of the sheets and let him help me get dressed. Nimbus stayed glued to my side.

***

Jaz, hair dyed a vibrant green today, handed me a latte when I walked in. Her eyes widened, and she flicked her gaze toward Oliver, who ignored her scrutiny.

"Thank you," I said, also ignoring her rare expression of emotion.

"This one has caffeine in it. You're going to need it."

"Great. So, they're keeping you filled in?"

She curled her lips. "It's excessively complicated, but know this, I am on your side. Even in the times when I might appear that I am not."

"You can trust her," Oliver said, touching my shoulder and gesturing toward the back.

I took a calming breath and nodded. "Cool. Thanks."

Nimbus trotted along at my side as we headed into the back room with the comfy couch. Katsuro lounged in a chair and Davin sat on the couch arm. They both stood when we went in. Katsuro's eyes narrowed, and he glared at Oliver. Davin's nose twitched, and I swear he lifted his lip as if he were going to growl at the shade. For his part, Oliver managed to keep his expression neutral.

111

"So, what's up?" I asked to forestall any posturing. I wasn't interested.

Katsuro dragged his attention from Oliver back to me.

"I understand why you were reluctant to share your past. I'm assuming this is related to you?" He picked up a paper from the table and handed it to me.

I took it and gave it a quick scan, but I knew it was. I recognized the picture from a news article about shutting down the trafficking ring. They'd kept my picture out of the media, amazingly enough, but I'd seen this article a few times. I sank down onto the couch. Oliver leaned against the doorframe and Nimbus sat at my feet.

"Yeah. What brought this up?" I gave it back.

"Kerin had a lot to say," Davin admitted. "She won't be a problem any longer." His expression turned to sorrow. "However, it appears that there was more depth to this trafficking ring than the human authorities knew."

I buried my hands in my face. "Fuck."

"They were apparently blood suppliers for a less ethical group of vampires, along with their other unsavory activities," Katsuro added. "The human authorities shut down the operation, leaving the supernatural side of the equation extremely displeased. I suspect Drake is involved with that, but I don't know. Jaz will do her best to discover more."

"Do they not know she is loyal to you? I'm confused."

"They know. They also think they can win her away from me. Her story is one she should tell, but I trust her." Katsuro steepled his fingers and studied me while he talked.

"Old debts, etcetera," Davin added.

There was too much to untangle, and in the end, it didn't matter. I hadn't been able to leave my past behind as I'd hoped. Somehow, I'd arrived in the very worst place possible and come to the attention of vampires who wanted blood slaves. Oliver was right; there were worse things than getting killed.

"Okay." I couldn't think of what else to say. Clearly, Nimbus and I had to leave. Now. I'd have to figure out what I could tell my contact in Washington as to why I was moving again so quickly. A few tears burned in my eyes. I really liked it here.

"Something else."

I looked up, and Davin held out my phone.

"It's been ringing off the hook, as it were."

I glanced at the caller ID. Max. My contact in D.C. had called half a dozen times in the last hour.

"That's weird." I took the phone.

"Hannah, perhaps you should answer it where we can all hear. If you think that activity is strange, perhaps one of us can hear something you can't," Katsuro suggested gently. "I understand if you want to call in private, but it may not be wise."

"Think they hacked my phone?" It wasn't out of the question.

"Call your friend," Katsuro said instead of answering.

I hit the button to dial.

"Hannah?" Max—that wasn't his real name—picked up on the first ring. "Are you all right?"

"Yes, of course. I'm allowed to sleep, right?" I couldn't help the edge of irritation that colored my tone. It might even make the discussion sound more realistic.

"Are you alone?"

"Uh, no, my dog I just got is with me. Why?"

"Just making sure. So, something came up and we need to move you. Same as before, we'll replace everything. We can have a car there in a few hours. I'm really sorry about this, Hannah. We'll get you to D.C. and get you a new identity."

Even to me, he sounded a bit strained.

113

I glanced around at the men in the room. They all had small frowns, as if concentrating hard. Perhaps listening to things my merely human ears couldn't hear?

Nimbus whined softly and laid his chin on my knee. Wait, since when was he tall enough to do that? Little guy was growing fast. That revelation distracted me from the fear twisting my gut, which might have been his point.

"Yeah, okay, Max. I'll see you all in a few hours."

"Great, Hannah. Stay inside until we get there."

"Will do." I hung up and dropped the phone on the table. "Okay, even I thought that was weird."

"He was not alone," Katsuro said. "The being with him was not breathing, but I could hear the faint rustle of cloth, and it was not from this Max person."

"Well, I'm fucked. I have to leave. Now." I stood abruptly and hurried toward the door.

"Hannah—" Davin said.

"No, I have to go. The only thing I can do is run." I was out the door before the men could stop me. Oliver, for his part, didn't try, which I thought wise.

"Call Bridger," Oliver said as the door shut. "She needs a vehicle."

"Bridger?" Katsuro replied flatly. Then I was out of earshot as I ran toward the exit.

Jaz followed me, and I hoped they were right that we could trust her. We didn't speak. I just ran toward my apartment complex, Nimbus and Jaz keeping pace.

She waited at the entrance while I went inside and sprinted up the stairs, fighting tears. I'd just found a place where I might belong, and now I had to leave again. And this time, I couldn't even rely on the government and whatever protection they might have been able to give me.

Nimbus stayed glued to my side while I threw a bag of essentials together and hurried back down the stairs.

I hadn't intended to go with Bridger, but then I remembered that the bad guys knew my vehicle now. They might know Bridger's, but somehow I thought that might still be safer. He stood there twirling his keys in his hand and staring at Jaz when I came back down. Jaz bared fangs at Bridger before vanishing from view.

"Where the fuck did she go?" I glanced around.

"Vampire." Bridger shrugged. "I told you. They're quick. I hear you need a ride?"

He sounded way too calm about this. Especially since they'd clearly just let him in on the truth about Beechworth.

"Yeah."

"Great! Let's go!"

He headed for his car and, feeling miserable and swallowing around the lump in my throat, I followed.

Dakota Brown

Chapter 18

"**S**o, where are we going?" Bridger asked after driving west, away from Mayday Hills, for about an hour.

I'd spent the time with my face buried in Nimbus's fluff and fighting tears. Not only because I was in danger from something I thought I'd left behind, but because I'd grown to love my new life. Not to mention the men I was leaving behind. Of course, I barely knew Katsuro, but Davin and Oliver were very nice, and I hadn't been opposed to getting to know Katsuro better. About the only good thing about fleeing was that I didn't have to untangle that knot of attraction. Hell, I needed to figure out what to tell my boss.

That thought brought more tears to wet down Nimbus's fluff.

"I don't know," I said, voice thick. "What did they tell you?"

"Merely that you needed to escape a group of supernatural beings that wanted to kill you and do bad things to your puppy."

"Wait, that's it?" I glanced over at Bridger.

"There wasn't a lot of time, Hannah. I didn't even know Katsuro had my phone number." He frowned at that.

"You're not excited that you got confirmation the supernatural existed or anything?"

This time Bridger glanced at me with an eyebrow lifted. "I know the supernatural exists, Hannah. I have since I was a boy. Werewolves killed my mother. I saw the whole thing. Saw them shift, saw them tear her to shreds, saw them feast. The only thing that saved me was a shadow creature whisking me away. They subjected me to therapy for years, trying to convince me it was bears or something. We were camping in a public campground."

"Oh. I'm sorry."

Bridger shrugged. "It was a long time ago. I am a hunter. I've killed supernatural beings before. The people in Beechworth are just beings trying to live their lives. Mayday Hills, on the other hand." He winked at me. "Not that I know what everyone is, but I've got a pretty good idea."

"Do any of them know your history?"

"Not that I'm aware of." Another shrug. "Anyway, what's the story with Nimbus? Why do vampires want him?"

"I don't actually know that it's vampires. Drake is a shade."

"It's always vampires, Hannah."

"Oh. Well, okay. You know more than I do. I guess Nimbus is a cloud puppy, or nimbus. Some sort of supernatural dog that, when they're older, become very powerful. Right now, we have to keep him safe until he can defend himself. If they capture him while he's a puppy, they can control him and his magic forever."

"Well, we can't let that happen." Bridger sounded so confident, so intense, that while some might have taken his comment as flip, I could tell he was deadly serious.

"And apparently the human trafficking ring I helped put behind bars was also trafficking blood slaves to the vampires, and they figured out that I was involved with all of that, so they're after me for two reasons now."

"Fuckkkk," Bridger drew out the word. "Well, that's some shit. We'll keep you safe while Katsuro and Davin figure out what to do. Do you have any idea where you want to go?"

"I don't." I grabbed for my phone to search for something and remembered I'd left it behind. "Um, no phone. So, just pick something."

"Honestly, why don't we just go to my place? It's well defended. Safe. Stocked with food. We could stay there for a year and not have to leave."

"Sure." I had a vague worry that Bridger was actually secretly working for the enemy, then banished it. If he was, I was screwed, and that was all there was to it. I also doubted he was.

"I'm fairly certain we haven't been followed, but I'm going to take a roundabout way of getting there. It'll take a couple of hours, but in the end, we won't be too far from Beechworth."

"Okay."

Bridger gave me a look full of sympathy. I buried my face in Nimbus's ruff and tried not to cry.

***

By the time we made it to Bridger's house, I'd worn myself out, and it was dark, so I didn't pay any attention to our surroundings, other than to note that we were deep in the woods. It seemed like a lifetime ago that I'd enjoyed a pleasant spell with Oliver and woken in his arms.

Bridger drove through a gate, stopped to watch it close behind us, then drove into a garage.

I just sat in his car, clutching Nimbus. He came around the side and opened the door for me. Nimbus rumbled softly and licked my damp cheek.

"What can I do to help, Hannah?"

119

"I don't know."

"How about food and a drink? Alcohol or non, your choice."

Sniffing, I rubbed at my nose with my sleeve. Nimbus, after one more quick nose kiss, hopped off my lap. He was definitely growing. Not that I wanted him to get big too fast, but the sooner he was no longer in danger, the better. One less thing I would have to worry about.

Nimbus wasn't on a leash. I hadn't taken the time to grab one before rushing over to the coffee shop earlier and he truly didn't need one. I only used it when he insisted. I guessed it had something to do with his nature and the protection I'd offered. He didn't wander, however. I could tell he sniffed around and paid particular attention to things I couldn't even notice. I knew I should have been paying strict attention to my surroundings, cataloging exits, making sure I knew places I could hide and things I could use as weapons, but I just couldn't bring myself back to that headspace. My body rebelled after spending so long existing in fear. Now I just felt exhausted, heart-sick, and numb. I knew once I got over the initial shock, I'd find a way back to the alertness needed to survive while in actual danger, but right now I followed Bridger and felt defeated.

"Have a seat. I'll bring you something. Anything you don't eat? What do you want to drink? I can accommodate most anything."

I sank down onto a comfortable couch and curled up into a ball. Nimbus hopped up next to me and laid his chin on my shoulder. Yeah, definitely growing.

"I eat most things. I'll take some water. And maybe some whiskey if you have it. Nimbus could have some meat and water, if you don't mind."

"Not at all. Make yourself at home."

With that, Bridger left me alone.

Trying to pull myself together, I took stock of my surroundings. The walls were concrete, painted different colors, but clearly concrete. This room was a soothing sky blue. I vaguely recalled some white walls and some greens. The floor had been carpeted in a plush brown that would hide dirt and be easy to care for. The furniture seemed like normal couches and recliners and end tables. Nothing that stood out, but all well made. I didn't see any windows from the room I was in, which was probably some sort of living room. A large TV hung on one wall with a game system nearby and a computer sat over in one corner.

The air had a bit of a chill to it that basements often held. A blanket lay draped over the back of the couch, and I pulled it over my lap.

It wasn't long before Bridger came back with a tray containing food, water, and a golden liquid that had to be whiskey.

Nimbus dug into the plate of meat Bridger had brought, and I gratefully ate the ham sandwich. He sat with us, munching on some chips and not talking while I ate.

Once I was done, he whisked away the food while I sipped on the whiskey.

"So what's next?" I finally asked.

"You get some rest. I'll check the cameras and stay up for a while and keep an eye on things. If nothing goes wrong, I'll catch a nap. Tomorrow, I'll give you a tour. And we'll go from there. One day at a time, Hannah."

I took a deep breath and nodded. "Okay. Thank you."

"Sure. Besides, this gives me a chance to hang out with you more." He winked. "Seriously though, I want you safe."

Laughing, I shook my head and finished my whiskey.

I nearly dropped the glass when Bridger's phone rang.

"How did you get my number?" Bridger answered.

I couldn't hear the reply, but Bridger rolled his eyes. "Right, vampire things. So what's up, Katsuro?"

"Yeah." He glanced at me. "Okay if I put him on speaker?"

I nodded.

"Hannah, we have more information. I would like to come speak with you." Katsuro's soothing voice reached out through the speakers.

Bridger arched an eyebrow, and I shrugged. "It's your house."

"Can you guarantee you won't be followed?"

"Yes," Katsuro said. "Obviously, I'll come after dark."

"Come alone. Don't get followed, and you can visit."

"Agreed."

"Do you need my address?" Bridger mouthed, *please need my address.*

"No, of course not."

Fuck, Bridger mouthed.

I would have laughed if the situation weren't dire.

"I suspect your general location is safe from most, but you are in the werewolves extended territory and Davin gave me the address. Hannah, Oliver sends his regards."

Was it just me or was his tone just a touch flat when he delivered that message?

"Thank you," was all I could think to reply.

"I'll see you both tomorrow an hour after sunset." Katsuro ended the call.

Bridger looked put out that his location wasn't as secret as he had thought.

I did smile briefly at his expression.

"Well, we're still safe here, even if they know where I live. It's shade proof, werewolf proof, and vampire proof, unless I let them in the front door."

"I sure hope you're right."

"It's been tested."

He didn't elaborate, and I almost didn't want to know, so I let him bring me to a bedroom that definitely wasn't up to code. There was no window. Just then, I really didn't care. The bathroom had everything I needed, the bed looked soft and inviting, and I was ready to let someone else handle things for a little while.

Tomorrow, Katsuro would be here, and hopefully he would have a plan. Thoughts of the sexy vampire chased me into a fitful sleep.

Dakota Brown

Chapter 19

I stared into the mirror in the bathroom attached to my borrowed bedroom and pushed my glasses up my nose. I hadn't grabbed makeup. Did I need makeup? Why was I so nervous?

Well, okay, Katsuro was an extremely powerful supernatural being, and I hadn't even known vampires existed until just recently, so I had a pretty valid reason for being nervous. That wasn't it, though. My stomach fluttered and I cursed myself for a fool.

Pulling off my glasses, I put them on the counter and turned on the water. I splashed the cool liquid on my face. Damn it, he could smell emotions, right? I was so out-classed. I should just get over it and turn myself in. There was no way I could run forever from the supernatural.

As if sensing my distress, Nimbus pressed against my leg and rooed softly. I reached down to pet him, and barely had to bend to scratch his head. Little dude wasn't so little anymore. Kneeling, I buried my fingers in his soft fluff and pulled him close.

"Hey, buddy. It's going to be okay, right?"

He grumbled softly and gave me a quick nose kiss.

"I'll take that as a yes."

He dropped his jaw in a doggy grin before his ears perked and looked toward the door.

"Shit," I muttered. "He's here, isn't he?"

Nimbus trotted over to the door then vanished.

"Fuck!" More startled than alarmed, I hurriedly opened the door. My fluffy dog waited on the other side, his curled plumage of a tail wagging back and forth over his back. That explained a few things. Why hadn't anyone told me nimbuses could teleport? Was I the only one who knew?

It seemed like only a few days ago my puppy was just that, a puppy. Now he was taller, fluffier if that was possible, and teleporting. As much as I'd rather enjoy his puppyhood, the sooner he was old enough to defend himself completely, the better off we all were.

"I told you to come alone," Bridger was saying to Katsuro.

When I walked into the entryway, the sexy vampire stood there looking just as amazing as ever. His longish black hair was pulled back like normal, and he wore a deep red button-down shirt that looked like silk, along with black slacks. I wanted to find out if his shirt was as silky as it looked. Shaking my head, I tried to banish those thoughts. Now was not the time. Would there ever *be* a time?

Next to him stood Clare, my boss, the awkward-looking woman who I liked so very much. She stared at me owlishly for a moment before grinning.

"Hannah, my dear, let's get you fixed up." She held up her arm, drawing attention to the basket looped over her forearm. She ignored Bridger, instead taking my arm and leading me into the complex like she'd been here before, which, from Bridger's reaction, I was guessing she hadn't.

"She showed up at the coffee shop and insisted she was coming along. Have you ever tried to tell that woman no?" Katsuro sounded a touch astounded.

I laughed as my boss led me out of earshot. Nimbus kept right at my side, bumping into me occasionally. I let my fingers trail in his soft fluff.

"So, the biggest problem right now is that you have no way to defend yourself against the supernatural. Therefore, we're going to unlock your potential," Clare said as she opened the door to the inner courtyard and led me outside. Bridger and Katsuro had caught up to us by this point, but she shut the door in their faces.

"My what now?"

"Your potential, dear."

"Potential for what? Shit luck?"

Clare laughed. "Magic. Many people have the ancestry and genes necessary, but few have the right triggers early in life to unleash this power and therefore it is never realized. But you are lucky in that you know me. And more importantly, I know Anita. She's very powerful, and she gave me exact instructions."

I recalled the young black woman with the pink hair who wore a knitted gray shawl every time I saw her, regardless of what she wore for clothing.

"I hadn't realized she was a magic user."

"Yes. Her family is very wise in the old lore. She descends from hedge wizards who have kept their magic alive all the way back to prehistoric times. It's quite rare to find a family with so much continuity. Especially with all the turmoil in the world. Part of their secret is their ability to commune with their ancestors. I believe they learned it from Asian mystics." Clare carried on while she set a circle of candles on the ground and put a small brazier in the center with a tiny clay pot over it. "Now, the unlocking happens right away, but the unfolding and your discovery take time. I've brought a book for you to read that will help you understand what is going on inside of you as this develops, and once you've fully bloomed, Anita will train you. Until then, she suggests you work on instinct."

"That sounds dangerous."

"Less so than you might think. Your instincts are to protect yourself and those you love or care about. The magic will react appropriately. Your nimbus is also growing stronger by the day, and between the two of you, it will go well. Perhaps not always easily, but at least you'll have the ability to protect yourself. Then you can come to your men as more of an equal, despite their burning desire to protect you."

I laughed at that, startled. Then sobered. "Men?"

"Oh, honey, you are so fortunate. Four good men. Most of us are lucky if we find one." She patted me on the arm. "Now, let's begin."

I wanted to question her further, but she'd moved on to the ritual.

"This is actually not terribly complicated. Sit in the circle cross-legged there." She pointed, and I did as instructed.

Clare sprinkled a packet of herby-smelling leaves in the small clay pot, then took a long match, lit it, and touched the flame to the fuel in the brazier. Using the same match, she lit all the candles around me and stepped back.

"I'll be right over here, dear," Clare said. "When you're ready, pour the water into the clay pot and drink the contents, leaves and all. Then stay calm and quiet until the door opens."

"The water?" She hadn't put any water in the circle, I was sure of it.

Clare grinned at me, her owlish eyes gleaming with mischief.

Nimbus rooed softly, then trotted back a short distance and lay down, his eyes fixed on me. I took a deep breath and glanced at the brazier. Sure enough, a clear glass full of water sat next to it. What the hell?

Steam rose from the clay pot, though I had no idea how that was possible. Hands trembling slightly, I picked up the glass. The light from the candles filtered through the impossibly clear container, seeming to pool in the water within until the glass appeared to contain liquid flame.

Getting the feeling that I shouldn't wait too long, I carefully poured every drop into the clay pot, though on a normal day this might have caused the clay pot to crack. Still, I did what I was told.

The aroma from the pot intensified, curling into my nostrils and seeming to seep into my pores and flow through my veins. It was a scent I couldn't even identify, though it contained hints of cinnamon, iron, earthy loam, and a smoky scent that reminded me of a touch of Bridger. It also carried the musk of my cloud puppy and a lighter, fruity scent. These scents shouldn't combine so wonderfully, but to me, in that moment, it was the aroma of my life and the best thing I had ever smelled. I inhaled deeply and forgot my last fear that the clay pot would burn me when I picked it up off the brazier.

It was cool to the touch and the liquid within the exact perfect temperature. I drank the contents down and my consciousness seemed to follow it until I was focused on a spot deep inside myself, all other concerns forgotten.

For a time, I simply floated there, basking in the aroma of my life and the feeling of safety and contentment. Everything was dark, but I was not worried, simply happy to exist.

Moments or days might have passed in that dark bliss, but after some time, I gradually became aware of a new feature in the dark. I turned my awareness and beheld a door. It had a stone frame and solid wooden planks banded in iron. The handle was a simple iron loop, and the outline of a familiar-looking dog was burned onto the planks. I took the iron ring in my hand and, on impulse, said "Friend."

The door creaked open easily when I pulled, and I stepped through.

"Have you considered what you are doing?"

A masculine voice startled me, and I whirled around, but the door was gone. In its place stood the most magnificent animal I'd ever seen. He was clearly a nimbus, but his markings were different from *my* nimbus. His overcoat was long and lustrous, a mix of white and the deep gray of a storm cloud. His tail was curled over his back, and it was long and heavily feathered. He regarded me with electric blue eyes. I desperately wanted to run my fingers through that feathery fluff but didn't dare.

"Excuse me?"

"The ritual you are undertaking. Have you considered the consequences of unlocking the magic within you?" He padded forward until he was standing in front of me, then sat. The dog's mouth moved when he spoke, though how he managed human words, I didn't know. Magic, probably. When he sat, his head was level with my chest so that we looked at each other nearly eye to eye. My fingers again twitched with the need to bury them in his fluff.

He huffed laughter. "Go ahead, friend of the nimbuses. You may touch."

"Thank you." I indulged myself, trying to be respectful of his person, while also giving him a good scratching. He was grinning, and his magnificently plumed tail wagged.

"We do so enjoy humans," he said once I'd finished, though I kept my hand on his shoulder and hoped he didn't mind.

"I'm glad."

"We are grateful you found the little storm cloud you call Nimbus. He was in dire need, and you more than rose to the occasion. We find you worthy and will aid you should you truly wish to unlock your potential. But be aware the path will not always be easy, and you will have to study hard to master the power you hold."

"Will it help me keep him safe until he is in his full power?"

"Yes." The adult nimbus leaned his head against my arm.

I could feel the power he contained, but also his playful and soft spirit. It was as if there was a spark of connection between us.

"Do you think I will regret it?"

He huffed playfully. "No, I do not. There will be times you wonder what you were thinking, but overall you will be content with the decision. Perhaps even happy with it. However, you have other paths. The men will protect you and Nimbus and keep you both safe if you submit to them. You have others in your life now that will keep you safe without submission, but the peril will be greater. You may choose to run, and that may also be an answer. Nimbus will protect you when he reaches his full storm. But this path gives you the greatest power. Power is not always the answer, however. You must choose to take on the responsibility with the power. Any road you take from this point will be the correct answer, but this is a branching and the branch you travel now will change your life completely, no matter which direction you take."

I shivered, and he leaned into me. "There is only one option for me," I said. "I must be able to protect the ones I love and care about, along with myself. I'll willingly take help, but I don't want to be helpless."

The adult nimbus touched his nose gently to mine before stepping back. I reluctantly took my hand from his fluff.

"I am Twister," he said with a regal bow of his head. "Nimbus is too young to be your guide on this journey, so I will aid you. I'm one who has gone on from the mortal world and no longer has a physical form. But I exist within the storm, and I choose to join your path if you will have me. I've already spoken with Nimbus, and he approves."

"Twister, I'm honored. Thank you. I accept."

Twister's doggy grin widened. "Then go through the door and we will meet again soon."

I turned to look where his attention directed me and beheld another door. This one seemed to be grown from an apple tree. The tree was in full fruit, and I touched one of the red-gold apples in awe. It came away into my hand and, unbidden, I took a bite.

The explosion of sweet, crisp, wonderful flavor gave me strength, and I touched the round knob on the door in its trunk.

It opened, and I stepped through.

Chapter 20

I opened my eyes later, unsure how much time had passed. The candle wicks still burned, though the wax was completely melted. A moment after I opened my eyes, the flames winked out. The clay pot I'd drunk from, and the brazier had vanished. The only remains of the ritual were the puddles of wax.

Nimbus trotted forward and pressed his nose against mine, rooing softly.

"Hey, buddy. I talked with Twister."

He perked his fuzzy ears and sat back, curled tail wagging.

"Who is Twister?" Katsuro asked, voice soft but filled with curiosity.

"A nimbus who has fully joined the storm," I answered, and buried my fingers in Nimbus's fluff. He leaned against me.

"Did the ritual work?" The vampire rose smoothly to his feet.

"Yes. I have no idea how long it will take for my powers to unfold, however."

He came over to me, standing outside the ring of wax puddles, and offered me his hand. When Nimbus didn't object, I took it and let him help me to my feet.

The vampire pulled me close, raising his other hand and brushing his fingers along my temple.

133

"You are radiant."

I took a deep breath, then everything that had happened in the last few days hit me. I'd come to a new town, gotten a dog—as it were—met new friends and gotten a new job. I'd also apparently found four men who wanted me, been rediscovered by the group of traffickers I'd thought I'd helped put behind bars, been almost kidnapped, had to run again, and they'd gotten to my D.C. contact. Now I was hiding in a compound in the woods with beings I hadn't even realized existed until a short time ago.

Seeming to sense my mood shift, Katsuro turned down the intensity and pulled me into a comforting hug.

He was the last person I would have expected that from, but I accepted the affection and rested my cheek against his chest.

"All will be well," he murmured.

Nimbus pressed up against my leg and rooed softly as if in agreement.

***

We found Clare and Bridger in the kitchen a while later. I'd stayed in Katsuro's arms far longer than I'd expected, and he had held me patiently, kindly, and with great compassion, not letting go until I'd finally stepped back.

Clare's enormous eyes widened, and she smiled. "Well, dear, how do you feel?"

I took a breath and shrugged. "I don't know if I feel different or not."

"That is perfectly fine. It takes time for the unfolding. Now, let's eat something." She glanced pointedly at Bridger.

The hunter obediently got up and went to the pantry.

It didn't take long for him to procure drinks for everyone and a quick meal of stew from a can for those who wanted something to eat. Though it was canned, it tasted like a feast. I hadn't realized how hungry I was until the first bite of food passed my lips.

Bridger's phone beeped as I was polishing off my stew. He frowned as he stared at the screen.

"We're going to have company soon." He massaged his forehead as if easing a headache before sighing. "This place is secure against the supernatural, but apparently they're adapting to modern times, finally. They brought assault vehicles. The walls will take a lot of damage, but they'll get through after the wards are broken. Katsuro, there's a tunnel that hits an old mineshaft. In the mineshaft there's an ATV that you can take. Get Hannah out of here. Clare and I will distract them by running in your car. If they don't capture us, we can meet up in Redmont. You should be able to make it before sunup. If you get there, go to the Redmont Inn and tell them you're friends of mine. As long as the owner doesn't figure out you're a vampire, he'll believe you and hide you away until I show up. If Clare and I don't show up, wait a few days and make another plan."

"Bridger, we'll make it to Redmont," Clare assured him with a pat on his arm. "I brought plenty of dust."

I assumed she referred to the substance she'd used on the shade back at her bookshop.

"The three of you might take longer than one night to make it, however. Your unfolding makes the visions less reliable. Take your time. We will wait."

Not completely comforted by Clare's words, I still let Bridger lead us to the hidden door that let us into the escape tunnel. It was well hidden and even Katsuro thought it would remain secure unless it took physical damage.

135

On impulse, I gave Bridger a quick hug, but he put his finger over my lips when I tried to apologize.

"This is an excellent test of my defenses. If any of them fail, it gives me a chance to make them better in the future. I do admit, I hadn't planned for assault vehicles, but I should have. I was thinking of supernatural attacks."

"Well, okay then. Clare, be careful." I gave the psychic a quick hug, and then Katsuro, Nimbus, and I descended into darkness.

Total darkness, as far as my human eyes were concerned, anyway. I froze as soon as the thick door shut behind us. My breathing was harsh in my ears, and it was quiet enough that I could hear my heartbeat. Nimbus pressed against my leg before I could panic, and a soft whisper of cloth, then a gentle touch on my arm, let me know Katsuro was there.

"I can see, Hannah," he said.

I jumped as his quiet voice seemed to shatter the surrounding stillness. I desperately wanted to be able to see instead of relying on the vampire to guide me.

"We're going down steps. They are even. You shouldn't have any issues."

I squinted in the darkness, but let the vampire lead me.

"Why are you interested in me?" I blurted out. I couldn't figure out why any of the men were interested. I wasn't unattractive, but I certainly wasn't the sort of eye candy that caught men's attention as quickly as I had these powerful beings.

"There is something about you that calls to me." He hesitated, then continued. "Calls to all four of us, I guess I should say. Even the human hunter feels it. A resonance, if you will. Not to mention, you are intelligent, interesting, compassionate, and your scent reminds me of apple spice."

"Apple spice?"

"Yes. Very compelling." He squeezed my hand, and I couldn't tell if he was joking or not.

"Do you feel a draw to any of us?" He continued.

"I assume you mean Oliver, Davin, you, and Bridger, right?"

"Indeed."

"Well, obviously, I'm attracted to Oliver." No use in pretending I hadn't practically had sex with the shade already. "And yes, there's something that catches my interest about all four of you. I just don't know what to do about it, and I haven't really had time to settle in."

He squeezed my hand again. "Hopefully we can conclude this unfortunate business quickly and then you can take more time to get to know us."

"Are you all serious that you'd share me?"

"All of our fates are intertwined," he said. "It would be unwise to ask you to single one of us out."

"Did Clare tell you that?"

"Yes, but on reflection, it is also obvious. At least to me."

As we walked farther down, my knees starting to ache at the descent, the darkness lightened and gradually, I could see again.

By the time we reached the bottom, I realized that my ability to see wasn't because there was a light source.

"Katsuro, I can see."

"Good. Perhaps your powers are awakening already."

A thrill of terror chilled me, followed almost immediately by exhilaration. I'd accessed my new abilities and used them to help myself in a dangerous situation. And by helping myself, I made myself less dependent on Katsuro in case something happened, and he needed to act.

Nimbus bumped me with his nose, and I scratched his head.

The ATV waited as promised, provisioned with supplies for an extended camping trip in case I needed food. Katsuro's only real concern was shelter from the sun. He'd told me it wouldn't kill him instantly, but it certainly wouldn't do him any favors.

"Do you know how to drive one of these?" I asked the vampire.

"Yes. Do you?"

I nodded.

"As you can see, perhaps you should drive. Your nimbus can lead the way. That will leave me free to watch for trouble and react if necessary."

"Okay." I glanced at Nimbus, and he trotted out in front of the ATV as if agreeing.

I got on and Katsuro climbed on behind me. He put one arm lightly around my waist, though there were handholds in the back, and his thighs pressed against mine as he slid into a comfortable spot behind me.

"This okay?"

"Yep." My voice squeaked, and not in fear. Warmth flushed through me at his proximity.

"Hannah." His breath tickled my ear.

"Yeah?"

"Perhaps you should turn the vehicle on."

I shook my head and jerked my attention away from the vampire's closeness and the heat flooding through me. "Right. Sorry."

He laughed, a low sound that completely scattered my brain again. "I'm certainly not offended, nor am I unaffected by your presence, but we do want to get out of here. That is the priority, unfortunately."

That he was having similar reactions made me feel marginally better. I turned the key and got the ATV going.

I kept the headlights off since I could see reasonably well, and Nimbus didn't seem to have any issues in the dark either. The sound of the engine echoed in the close confines of the tunnel, and I found myself wishing the engine was quieter.

"That power of yours is useful," Katsuro said.

"What?"

"You turned the engine noise down somehow. I'm grateful."

"Huh. Cool."

He tucked himself close against me, tightening his arm around my stomach and making sure I was well aware of every inch of him that pressed against me.

"I thought getting out of here was our priority."

"We're in very little danger at the moment."

I shivered as his breath tickled my neck.

"And we are moving forward."

His free hand slid down my thigh.

"And I can't help myself. Unless you want me to stop?"

"Uh." My mouth stopped translating my thoughts into words, and I could only shake my head. No, I didn't want him to stop.

"Just don't wreck the ATV," he murmured as his lips touched my neck.

The strangled noise that came out of my mouth was a confused mix of pleasure and fear. His low chuckle didn't help.

Nimbus barked sharply ahead of us, a sound he rarely made, and Katsuro laughed again.

"Quite right, little one. Quite right."

Whatever Nimbus had said to the vampire, he eased off his distracting touches a bit. I was still extremely aware of him behind me, the tension building in my chest nearly painful. The ground grew uneven, and I had to concentrate on where we were going. Grateful for the distraction, I tried not to think about how much I wanted him to keep running his hands over my body.

"Did Bridger say how long this mineshaft was?"

"No, but I sense a difference in the air. I believe we are coming to the end." His voice had lost the playful tone from earlier, and he had clearly focused on our problems and not on tormenting me.

Nimbus slowed and turned a bend in the shaft. I hadn't realized we were rising up an incline, but apparently this was an old enough mine that they'd had rails going in and out instead of an elevator system and we'd come to the surface.

We left the confines of the mineshaft and entered the forest. My vision adjusted to the increased light, and Nimbus raced off down an overgrown two-track while I tried to keep up.

In the distance, wolves howled.

"Those are not Davin's wolves," Katsuro said, voice tense.

"Fuck," I muttered.

"Indeed. We're not going to make it to Redmont before sunrise. Nimbus, perhaps you could find us some shelter where we might have a chance to fight off the wolves and shelter from the day."

Nimbus rooed and raced down the trail.

I hoped he'd grown enough that he'd be able to keep up the pace ahead of fully grown werewolves. Hell, they could probably outrun the ATV.

"We are ahead of them." Katsuro apparently sensed my fear. "We should have time to reach shelter if there is some close. There are a lot of natural caves in this region."

Another set of wolves took up the howl.

The vampire tensed. "Those wolves are a lot closer."

"Double fuck."

He kissed my neck, arm tensing around me as we hit a bump on the track. "Perhaps you can go a touch faster."

I opened the throttle as much as I dared and prayed the mineshaft had given us enough of a head start to get away.

Branches cracked in the distance, and I wished for invisibility.

.

Chapter 21

Katsuro shifted around on the seat behind me, probably looking in the gear as best he could while we bounced along through the forest. His vampiric nature gave him an edge, and he didn't fall off even though I hit a rock or something and nearly dumped us over. He probably saved us when he shifted his weight, and I kept going as fast as I dared down the track.

"Bridger left us a gun. Werewolves in the forest are notoriously hard to hit, but I believe I have a chance, and I do know how to use this. It has a suppressor, so it shouldn't deafen you." Katsuro's breath tickled my skin as he spoke, leaning forward so I could hear him over the muted noise of the ATV.

"Great," I replied through gritted teeth. My arms and shoulders ached from wrestling the vehicle, and a dull throb had formed behind my eyes. I suspected it was heading toward migraine potential, though I didn't typically get migraines.

To make it worse, my glasses were sliding down my nose and I didn't dare take a hand away from driving to push them back up. I might be able to see in the dark, but that didn't make my vision any sharper. I wrinkled up my nose and tilted my head back, but gravity was stronger than my contorted face muscles and the glasses stayed low on my nose.

143

"Problem?"

"My glasses are sliding down. Because, of course, they are."

The vampire kindly pushed them back up my nose for me, startling me but returning my normal range of vision.

"Thanks."

He didn't reply, instead twisting around and firing the gun. I jumped at the muted sound of the suppressor. I was unfortunately very familiar with the way a suppressed gun sounded, but that didn't mean it wasn't startling.

An answering yelp, followed by an enraged roar, had me twisting the throttle as far as I could, even though there was no way I could make this even sort of safe. We were still ahead of them, but not by much.

"Fuck," I muttered, then swerved as something huge crashed past us, racing toward the approaching wolves. Sensing that the giant thing was Nimbus, I skidded to a halt. That Katsuro didn't question me, only confirmed what I'd thought.

"What the fuck?"

"Your nimbus has discovered a new power."

My nimbus was huge. He still looked like himself, just the size of a buffalo or an elephant or something. I immediately thought of the cuddle possibilities as I stared at his fluffy, feathered legs. He crouched as several wolves came out of the forest on the other side of him.

They stopped, clearly startled, heads tilted dog-like.

Nimbus lowered his tail, bared his teeth, and shrieked.

The trees bent away, leaves quaking, and the dried litter on the ground blasted into the air, scattering under the onslaught. The wolves collapsed, howling in pain as my dog destroyed their eardrums. He didn't do mine or Katsuro's any favors either, but at least we weren't on the receiving end.

"Holy crap," I said, belatedly clapping my hands over my ears.

Katsuro rested his forehead against my back, and I faintly heard him cursing in another language. Well, I thought he was cursing, anyway. I would have been if I had vampire senses.

Nimbus wagged his giant fluffy tail where he'd curled it over his back, pleased with taking out the wolves, before trotting back over to me and lowering his massive head to touch his nose to mine. Except his nose was the size of my head, at least, and I almost ended up in his nostril.

"Buddy," I said, caught between laughter and pain and a little worry that the puppy wouldn't know his own size.

Nimbus seemed to understand the hesitation in my voice and backed off, peering at me.

"Good boy, Nimbus. Now, how about that shelter?"

He rooed softly—though at his size it was still a rather large roo—and trotted off into the woods, crashing through the underbrush like an elephant.

Katsuro grunted but put his arm around me when I maneuvered the ATV to follow.

"Are you okay?" I'd lost the sound suppression on the ATV, however I'd accomplished that, but I could still see, though perhaps not quite as well as before. The headache had blossomed into epic proportions.

"I will survive," he answered loud enough for me to hear.

"Even if we find shelter, how will we stay safe? They can follow our trail."

Katsuro pointed at Nimbus, and I had to concede his point.

By the time we reached the shelter Nimbus had found for us, Katsuro had to take over driving, and I lay against his back, exhausted and head pounding. I'd lost my night vision, but that I'd even managed as much as I had after

145

literally just unlocking buried powers had me ecstatic despite how bad I felt at the moment.

Katsuro drove the ATV into the cave, and Nimbus backed his fluffy bum into the opening and laid down, effectively sealing off the entrance. The vampire helped me get off the ATV, then picked me up and carried me over to the bed of fluff Nimbus's curly tail had made and laid me down in it. The giant fluffy bed was everything I ever could have dreamed of and more.

"Wow," I murmured.

Nimbus wagged his tail as much as he could with me laying on some of it, letting me know he was happy to have me there.

"I just hope he doesn't fart," I murmured. "We'd need a gas mask to survive."

Katsuro burst out laughing, probably not something the vampire did often.

"Let us hope. Do you require anything?"

"Something to drink, a massage, aspirin, and a solid cuddle." I blurted out the last before I could stop myself.

"A giant fluffy dog ass isn't enough to cuddle with?"

I snorted, then winced as pain lanced through my head. Groaning, I pulled Nimbus's tail around me. Katsuro moved away for a few moments, returning with a bottle of water and some painkillers. I downed the water and pills, then glanced over at the vampire when he sat down behind me.

"You wanted a massage."

"Seriously?"

He nodded, expression solemn. "I'll even behave myself."

Shocked, I rolled over onto my stomach, head rested in fluff, while Katsuro's powerful hands kneaded my muscles into submission. It was as near to a professional massage as I thought the vampire could give. His touch was a bit more than professional, but not by a lot, and he didn't once try to make any sort of suggestive move or comment. That and the soft bed of nimbus tail feathers were as close to bliss as I was going to manage, especially once the pain in my head eased.

"Thank you," I murmured as I drifted toward sleep once he'd turned my body to jelly.

"Of course."

Then he shocked me further by pulling me into his arms and holding me while I drifted off to sleep.

Waking curled up with Katsuro and surrounded by my dog's fluffy tail was so comforting, I almost forgot the danger we were in, and I wasn't talking about the possibility of a giant fart from my currently enormous dog.

The vampire curled his fingers in my hair and stroked gently as I worked my way to full consciousness.

"Did you hold me the entire time I slept?"

"Of course. We're safe enough with Nimbus keeping watch. I felt comfortable indulging both our desires to be touched."

I shifted in his arms until I could look up at him. "You like to be touched?"

"Very much. I simply have few opportunities to indulge in that desire. I'm picky about who I let close enough."

It had not occurred to me that such a powerful man would have needs that weren't being met. Surely he could have anything he wanted, including someone to cuddle with that he trusted. I got the feeling he wasn't talking about being touched sexually, either.

"Werewolves are very unconscious of their need for physical contact. You may have noticed that Davin touches you quite a bit and doesn't seem conscious of personal barriers. Believe it or not, he is more restrained than many of his kind."

"I had noticed. Now that you put it like that, it makes sense. Canines are very tactile."

"Yes, I believe they tend to sleep in giant puppy piles, even when they're not romantically involved."

"That almost makes me jealous."

Katsuro kissed my forehead. "Yes."

I very briefly allowed myself a fantasy of my own version of a puppy pile with the men I was beginning to care about, then banished it. There was no way they'd ever want anything like that. I supposed they'd all have to be okay with Nimbus, however. No way would I kick him out of my bed for a man. Not unless we were having sex, and the nimbus had already shown that he would leave the room for that.

"What about Oliver?"

"I believe shades are quite physical, as well, if significantly more reserved than werewolves. I don't know about Bridger's preferences."

I returned my head to his shoulder and held him tightly. "How long until the sun goes down?" A little sunlight filtered around my dog's rump where it blocked the entrance to the cave.

"A couple of hours."

Shifting around, I rose up on my hands and leaned over Katsuro so I could look at him.

He gazed back at me, one eyebrow arched curiously. "Yes?"

Screw it, I thought, and pressed my lips to his.

Chapter 22

Katsuro's eyes widened, and he went still for a moment, as if he'd not expected me to make any sort of move right now, possibly ever. I stayed where I was, giving him a moment to decide how he wanted to react. After a small eternity, his lips curled, and his eyes crinkled into a smile. He ran one hand up my arm, fingers tickling along my skin before cupping my shoulder.

He gently cradled me with his arm, applying just enough pressure to let me decide if I was going to let him change my position. I yielded to his strength and let him roll me until I lay on my back on a bed of Nimbus's tail fluff with the vampire over me.

"Are you sure?" His voice roughened.

"That I want to kiss you? Yes."

He touched his lips to mine, hesitantly at first, but more confidently as I responded. His lips were smooth and firm. I opened at the press of his tongue, his hungry groan going all the way to my core and sending tingles of heat through me.

"Your skin tastes like apples smell," he murmured as he kissed along my neck. "Sweet, crisp, delicious."

"I'm sweaty and gross," I protested.

"Also that," he agreed, barely pausing as he continued to examine my available skin.

I laughed, but my humor didn't ruin the moment and, clearly, he didn't mind the sweat. I dared to slide my hand up his arm. His muscles were firm under his silky shirt and the contrast felt good under my palm. He rumbled in appreciation and worked his way back up my neck with his kisses until his lips found mine again.

For a time, we simply kissed, exploring each other. I enjoyed the feeling of his weight pressing me down, and the almost delicate way he touched me. It was as if he savored a fine wine.

It could have been only minutes or maybe hours of us touching and kissing and holding each other, before Nimbus huffed and shifted his tail. As I was lying on top of his tail feathers, this got my attention. Katsuro smoothly rose to his feet and helped me to mine so we could free Nimbus's tail.

Once unrestricted, he stood and shook.

I covered my face as dirt from the forest floor that had caught in his fluff pelted us.

"Okay, so some disadvantages to having a giant dog. I swear he got bigger." I shook off the dirt and peered out into the twilight.

The sound of rushing water, then the pungent aroma of urine made me wonder what exactly he was drowning in giant-sized dog amounts of pee. I almost felt sorry for whatever it was.

And then the trees groaned, and the underbrush crackled as he trotted farther away, and after another moment an even more pungent smell wafted back toward us.

"I can't decide if my eyes are watering because I'm trying not to laugh, or because I need a gas mask."

Katsuro chuckled, though it sounded a little pained. "It is a good thing he didn't fart while we were sleeping.

Perhaps we can get him to shrink down again before we have to feed him?"

"Yeah, he's probably starving." I scrubbed at my face, trying to figure out how we could even feed a giant cloud puppy.

Katsuro put his arm around me and pulled me close. "If we have to, I'll take down a deer for him. I also need sustenance before we rejoin the others. I'm sure Nimbus would share."

It took me only a moment to understand Katsuro was talking about the blood. He could drink deer blood, good to know.

"Yeah, if he doesn't shift back soon, that may be necessary. Thank you for the offer."

The vampire bowed slightly.

Nimbus returned at a jaunty trot, tail curled up over his back and wagging happily.

"Feel better, buddy?"

He rooed softly.

I caught Katsuro's wince out of the corner of my eye. A few disadvantages to having a giant dog, but the cuddle opportunity still outweighed them in my mind.

"Do you think we have time to go back to our cuddle session?" I glanced around as the sky darkened into true night.

"As much as I would like to say yes, I sense the wolves in the distance, and I suspect we were simply lucky the enemy didn't bring human weapons to bear during the day. I did my best to shield our presence with my powers, but they aren't the best under the sunlight. Nimbus may have assisted."

"Why didn't you hide us last night?" I tried to keep all blame out of my voice. I was sure he had a good reason.

"Bridger's wards interfered at his property, and by the time we were free of them, they were already well on our trail. By myself, I could have gotten away. However, I certainly wasn't going to leave you."

"Thank you for that."

He stepped in front of me, his hands going to my shoulders. "I will not leave your side until I'm well satisfied you can protect yourself."

"That'll make it difficult to pee," I pointed out.

Katsuro smiled. "You know what I mean."

I thought I did, and I smiled back. "Thanks."

He kissed my forehead before releasing me. "We should find the others."

Nimbus play bowed in front of me, which put his massive head at my level, and sniffed my nose like he often did, except he was huge, and I thought I'd get blown down. His wet exhalation wasn't exactly unpleasant, but I was a little concerned about his giant size.

"Hey, any chance you can return to normal, buddy? We need to get caught up to the others."

Nimbus sat on the ground with a thud and cocked his head to the side as if he were thinking. Then he shut his eyes, ducked his head, and... grew.

"Wrong way, buddy."

Now he towered over me, the tips of his ears even with the tops of some of the mid-sized trees.

He huffed.

"Well, just think about it."

Katsuro started the ATV and pulled it over to me. "How about I drive for now, as I can see without magic?"

"Sure." Happy enough to let the vampire drive, I hopped on behind him. It wasn't hard to convince myself to mold my body to his and put an arm around his waist, though the ATV had handholds in the back. He certainly didn't complain.

Nimbus trotted along behind us, crashing through the trees.

I didn't even worry about how loud the ATV was. The dog was louder.

The reality of our situation came back to me, and I sobered. Having myself wrapped around Katsuro was extremely pleasant, but we were in danger, and I had no idea how we were going to get out of this.

The sharp bark of a high-powered rifle and a spray of dirt pulled a scream from my throat.

"Nimbus, hide!" I shouted as Katsuro gunned the engine on the ATV.

We were so fucked.

Chapter 23

The engine sputtered and died with a rending screech. I didn't even think, just launched myself off the back and ran toward my giant dog, hoping he would run if I did.

Strong hands grabbed me around the waist, and I shrieked, but it was Katsuro. He tossed me into the air. I flailed, not understanding what the hell he was thinking, until I landed on Nimbus's back.

The cloud puppy woofed in surprise before I sensed his assent. Reacting, more than thinking, I wrapped my hands in his fluff and hoped if I pulled, it didn't hurt him. He wasn't like a horse that wouldn't feel much when I tugged on a mane. His fur was so thick, I was practically buried in it.

It took a moment for Nimbus to move, but once he did, he was fast. Even faster than when he'd been running with the ATV. Maybe even faster than the werewolves that chased us. Certainly better able to navigate the woods than the human-driven vehicles.

I leaned down, not able to see over Nimbus's fluff, and having no idea where to go, anyway. Katsuro hadn't joined us, and I hoped he'd be okay. As my thoughts strayed to the vampire, it occurred to me just how far he'd tossed me, like I'd weighed nothing. Yeah, if he could avoid the guns, he'd probably be just fine in a fight.

Nimbus ran, and I held on, concentrating on breathing, staying balanced on his back, and keeping my grip on his fluff.

Finally, the cloud puppy slowed to a halt. He flopped on the ground, and I hastily let go, sprawling away from him. This was certainly nothing like the handful of times I'd ridden a horse.

"Are you okay, buddy?"

I sensed weariness and hunger.

"Shrink down, and I'll see if we can get you fed." I didn't have any food. It was all with the ATV. But maybe I could use my magic to find something for him.

This time, Nimbus wearily shrank to his normal size and curled up, his tail over his nose.

"We can't stop right here, buddy." I picked him up, grunting a little in surprise. Not that I hadn't just seen him in giant dog form, but he had certainly grown in his normal size as well.

The only thing I could think to do was ask my magic to show me a source of food for the cloud puppy. Clare had said to work on instinct, and it felt like I should be able to find something to eat with my newborn abilities. Reaching out into the forest with my thoughts, or whatever it was, focused on food, I sensed something off to my left. Hoping I wasn't making a mistake, I followed the feeling.

Gunshots sounded in the distance, but they were far away. They trailed off and were punctuated by an explosion before the relative silence of the forest returned. I listened, holding my breath and praying we were alone. Well, Katsuro could certainly show up and I wouldn't mind.

Nimbus grew heavy in my arms, and I found a somewhat hidden spot to put him down by the small pool my intuition had brought me to. The water was certainly fresh enough for him to drink, and I cupped my hands and brought him water. He tiredly lapped it up and wagged his tail gratefully. Then I went back to the small pool and sat, wondering what to do. I thought several fish slept in its depths, but not only did I not have any way to get them, but I wasn't sure how good night fishing was. I'd been a beach bum, not a fisher.

The puppy really needed food, though, so I put my hands in the water and thought about how much I needed the fish for him. A silver flash of light darted between my hands. If magic hadn't been guiding me, I would have missed the creature. As it was, I barely got hold of it and jerked it out onto the shore. Still, I'd managed.

Nimbus perked up when he saw the fish flopping.

"It's for you, buddy. Do you want it cooked?"

The thought of food rejuvenated him, and he pounced on the fish and tore into it before I could even wonder how I was going to cook a fish.

I wrinkled my lips but left him to his meal while I went back to try to get one more for him.

Once Nimbus had eaten the second fish and had a little more water, we moved away from the stream a short distance and curled up together on a bed of pine needles with a boulder to our backs. He was unconscious instantly. I was so uncomfortable that, even if I had wanted to, I couldn't have slept. I did rest, though, and I listened.

A werewolf would be able to follow our trail, but maybe not human trackers. At least not until daylight. I held my slumbering puppy and tried to stay alert. Time had no meaning in the depths of night, and I had no idea what time it was, or how long we had until daylight. We couldn't stay here much longer, but Nimbus needed rest.

"Hannah," a familiar voice whispered. "We're safe for now."

"Katsuro?"

"Yes." He stepped into a ray of moonlight near my hiding place.

I gently pet Nimbus. "Buddy, we have to get up now."

He grumbled and tucked himself more firmly against my side.

Katsuro laughed and kneeled by me. "I'll take him."

For a moment, I stared at the vampire. Had they somehow captured him? Made him switch sides, or even worse, mimicked him so completely that I was fooled?

"It's okay," I finally said. "I'll carry Nimbus."

He didn't argue, which was certainly a point in his favor. But if he had been taken over by the enemy, slowing me down with Nimbus could be useful to him. I shook my head. If they'd somehow gained control of Katsuro, I was fucked anyway.

The vampire put a gentle hand on my shoulder. "I think we can safely attempt to rejoin the others," he said.

"You know where we're at, right?"

He glanced around, then sighed. "I am not a werewolf with instinctive knowledge of my surroundings in the forest. I knew where you were because I could sense you and Nimbus specifically. I can sense settlements in a few directions, and I believe we need to go that way." He pointed. "But I'm not positive."

"Do you have your phone?"

"No signal." He fished out his cell, unlocked the screen and handed it to me.

I fiddled with it one-handed for a bit before shrugging. "Well, let's go then."

Nimbus could have told us where to go, but Nimbus was unconscious, and I doubted he'd wake for a while.

So, we walked.

***

"Is it safe to talk?" I asked sometime later.

"I believe so."

"Tell me about yourself?"

It was dark, but I saw him give me a measured look. I'd managed to use my power to enhance my vision again. Not as good as last time, but it made wandering around in the woods at night a lot easier. My arms ached from carrying Nimbus and I thought about turning him over to Katsuro but couldn't quite make myself do it.

Finally, he answered. "As much as I've lived a long life, I don't know how much of it is truly interesting. The history, maybe, but I've had to live so much of it in the darkness." He sighed and remained silent for a while. "I used to enjoy sword work. I still do, I suppose. My father had fought in a war and one day I found his sword. He taught me a little when he had time and energy. We were farmers, and I was an only child. The rituals and customs of my people were quite rigid. I do not think you would like it very much, but the rituals had their beauty, too. This was long ago, of course. In Japan. I thought being a mere farmer was boring and desired more, hence the sword practice. It was my life's ambition to go to war and be a hero." He snorted. "Now I would give it all up to return to the farm of my youth."

"All of it?"

"I rule Beechworth alongside Davin. We do our best to make it a sanctuary, as you know. But the weight of the years, and the responsibility for the lives I protect, does wear me down." Katsuro glanced at me again. "Though, I must admit, you've brought a fresh breath of life to our town. Despite all this." He gestured broadly, and I knew he was referring to the current conflict. "And truly, it is an honor to use the power I've amassed through the years to protect others. Please do not misunderstand. While it is within my ability to do so, I will protect the beings of

Beechworth. That does not dispel the longings for my relatively carefree youth. I didn't know it until much later, but we had great privilege. My father had chosen the life of the farmer after all the honor he had won in the wars. Even in a hard year, we never went without because of that privilege, and he always made sure the people of his village had what they needed, too. He was a good man."

"What happened?" I hoped he didn't mind me asking after he trailed off again. I could see it being a sensitive topic.

"Ahh, forgive me. Lost in memories. As with most stories like this, war happened. Eager for adventure, I answered the call. I never returned home."

"Boohoo."

We both started at the derisive voice.

"Never returned home. Didn't end up in service to a powerful vampire lord. Didn't amass his own power base. Don't let this one fool you, human. Katsuro could buy a large country and have money left over. He's not hurting for luxury after his departure from human life." Someone stepped into view.

"I never said I was," the vampire replied with quiet dignity, as he sheltered me with his body. "Simply that I now find the value my father did in a quiet life as a farmer."

Belatedly, it seemed, some sense in the back of my mind lit up like an alarm bell and adrenalin shot through me. How had they snuck up on us?

"Well, your girlfriend cost us a lot of money and power. And unlike you, we don't want to be no bleeding farmers."

"On the contrary, that's exactly what you were doing, farming blood," Katsuro pointed out.

"Shut it."

I didn't recognize the voice, or the face, but I had noticed a weapon pointed in our direction before the vampire had stepped between us. Who the hell was this, and how had he snuck up on us?

I had to get Nimbus out of here. He was still out cold.

Something rustled, and I turned around just in time to hear a quiet pop and feel a sting. I knew what had happened, even as I tried to protest. Tranq guns were all well and good in movies, but in real life they were a terrible idea to use on people.

My vision blurred and my limbs went numb, and I fell to my knees before I could drop Nimbus. Shouts and the sounds of fighting chased me into darkness, my last thought on how badly I'd failed my cloud puppy and desperately hoping he'd wake up and run before he could be captured.

Dakota Brown

Chapter 24

The raging headache let me know I was awake instead of in some sort of nightmare. My mouth felt like cotton, and the rest of me felt gripped in some sort of sleep paralysis.

The last time I'd dealt with the traffickers, they'd not known I was on to them, and that I was working with the feds to get them taken down. I hadn't had to deal with this side of things, other than learning a thing or two about what I could do to stay alive until I was rescued.

I stifled a groan and tried to look around. Was I tied? Or still affected by the tranquilizer. I couldn't make out shapes, but I also couldn't move my hands to touch my face and see if I was blindfolded.

Trying for patience, I lay there and listened.

It was hard not to struggle against the lethargy that weighed my limbs, but I managed. My breathing was loud in my ears, overshadowing my heartbeat. Once I calmed, I could hear it, too. That, and not much else.

Slowly, feeling returned, and I almost wished for the oblivion from before. Along with the headache and the dry mouth, my nerves were now screaming at me, running hot fire through my limbs, and yet, I still couldn't move.

I didn't think I was blindfolded. It really was that dark. The lack of sounds and sight might have had me panicking, but honestly, at this point, that was the least of my worries. At least if there was no sound or sensation, there was nothing around attacking me. And if the light returned and showed me in a vat of snakes or something else terrible? Oh well. On the other hand, if they were already shipping me off to get trafficked, well, I had a vague hope of some supernatural rescue.

I wondered what had happened to Katsuro.

I was trying really hard not to think about Nimbus. He was my biggest concern, but also, panicking about him wasn't going to help me escape.

A soft, feather-light brush against my thoughts pulled my attention inward. My mind's eye resolved an image of an ancient apple tree, limbs spreading, and laden with young green fruits, not yet large or ripened. Beneath the tree sat Twister, expression solemn. Though he dropped his jaw in a doggy grin when he saw me.

"The storm is intense this day," he acknowledged me.

"Very." I came over and sat next to him. He tilted his head the same way Nimbus did when he wanted pets. I was happy to oblige. Sinking my fingers into his soft fluff and leaning against Twister. "What do I do?"

"Your powers must move to their full fruit." He looked up at the apple tree. "Make the fruit mature, and you will have the power you need to escape."

Before I could ask him how I was going to do that, the ground trembled, and I was thrown to my side.

I blinked, and the tremor came again. It wasn't the ground; it was someone shaking me awake.

When I finally got my eyes open, my vision was blurry, and it took a while for the blur to resolve into a face. Not one I recognized, and my last, distant hope that I'd been rescued while I slept dissolved. The person shaking me was a guy. Younger. He had dark eyes, dark hair, light skin, and a short growth of stubble. At least, I thought that's what he looked like. I tried to clear my vision.

164

"Get up!"

It took a minute to comprehend what the man was saying. My brain was as fuzzy as my vision. At least there was light now, though I was having trouble making out the rest of my surroundings.

"Get up!" he shouted.

The noise sent daggers through my brain.

When I didn't reply, he grabbed my arm and jerked me to my feet.

I didn't even try to stand. It wouldn't hurt them to think I was more helpless than I was. Also... I actually couldn't make my legs work yet, anyway.

"Dumb bitch," he snarled, as I failed to keep my feet.

The pain of hitting the ground was a distant thing. So was the kick to the ribs. I desperately tried to regain the peace of the apple tree and Twister's presence, but it was like trying to hang on to grains of sand. Everything slipped through my fingers and blackness took me.

The next time I struggled awake, I was alone. I lay sprawled on hard ground, as if the guy who had tried to get me to move had just left me where I'd crashed to the floor. In fact, that's probably what had happened.

My mouth was just as dry, and my bladder raged at me.

I struggled to my hands and knees and looked around. I was in a small room with two doors, ugly beige walls, a wooden floor, and a pile of blankets where I'd probably been tossed before dickhead had dragged me off them, then left me in the middle of the room. The window had been boarded over, and a little light seeped in around the edges.

One of the doorknobs had a lock. One did not.

I really hoped the one that did not led to a bathroom.

The effort of getting there almost left me unconscious again, but I made it and sighed with relief. A bathroom.

Relieving myself, then cleaning up in the sink and drinking water helped drastically. By the time I left the closet-sized room, I was only staggering a little. I tried the handle on the other door, just in case.

It didn't turn, but moments later, I heard the lock click and someone shoved it inward. I jerked back with just enough balance left to not fall on my ass, but it was a near thing. I cursed the dumbasses who had hit me with tranquilizer. They were lucky they hadn't killed me. Well, okay, I was the lucky one. They probably didn't care. They had Nimbus, and while I'm sure they were really pissed off at me, having me dead likely wouldn't break their hearts. It wasn't like I had information they needed or anything. My use to them was likely purely revenge.

I just had to figure out how to stay alive long enough to rescue Nimbus and Katsuro if he was captured.

The dumbass from before was the one staring at me. I was pretty sure, anyway. My brain was still a little fuzzy.

"Come on."

I let him grab my arm and drag me out of the room, staggering more than I needed to, though I was far from steady.

We looked to be in a house of some sort. A big one, judging by the hallway dumbass pulled me down. The floors were old wood and creaked under our feet, and the dark wooden paneling seemed like it should have been decorated with tapestries and paintings, but the walls were bare like the floor. The lighting fixtures were oddly cheap-looking compared to how expensive everything else seemed.

It was a puzzle that didn't really matter. Likely, the current owners of the house had nothing to do with the light fixtures.

Dumbass jerked me to a halt and shoved open another door.

166

I wanted to bitch about the treatment, but right now, I kept quiet.

What I saw on the other side of the door stole any words I might have had, anyway.

Katsuro lay sprawled on the floor, a stake shoved through his chest. I could only assume he was still alive based on the little real information I had on vampires and a wealth of lore. He lay in a tangle of limbs. His lovely black hair was no longer contained in a tail and obscured his face. His shirt was ripped, and his pants stained with dirt.

I covered my mouth with my hand to keep my gasp from escaping.

Even worse, Nimbus was in the room. I'd have been happy to see him, but he was still curled up in a little fluffy cinnamon roll, trapped in a glass cage with air holes. He was unconscious, and a golden leash tethered him.

I could nearly feel his torment, though his eyes were shut and his breathing even and slow.

Rounding on my captor, I balled my fists.

He just laughed. "Careful, or we'll wake the vampire up and lock you in here with him."

I couldn't help myself, throwing out a clumsy punch to his face. I knew how to hit people, but my body still wasn't responding right.

Dumbass just laughed and shoved me to the ground. "We don't really need you, bitch. Boss wants to play with you a little before we feed you to your boyfriend, but if you make too much trouble, I don't think he'll care if we end you early."

I didn't get up, defeat draining any energy I had left.

"Gonna leave you here, but just so you don't go getting any ideas, I wasn't lying about feeding you to fang face over there. They wake up hungry and out of control. You pull that stake out of him and you'll do us all a favor. And that cage, well, if you touch it, you won't live long enough to enact any of those escape plans I'm sure you're forming." He leered. "Now be a good girl and sit and stay until we're ready for you."

Speechless, I watched as he turned and slammed the door behind himself.

I didn't get the impression he was lying about anything he'd told me, and I suspected the only reason I was in here was to torment me awhile.

The room didn't give me a lot of options. No windows, only one door, and Katsuro and Nimbus were here.

Well, it didn't give me options, but an ancient vampire?

Fuck it. If he killed me, well, hopefully, he could at least rescue Nimbus. I went over to Katsuro and kneeled next to him. It didn't take much to roll him onto his back, and I brushed some of his long, silky hair off of his face.

Taking a deep breath, I wrapped my hand around the stake and hoped he'd forgive me for dragging him into this mess. There was always the possibility that he wouldn't kill me, after all.

"Just make sure you rescue Nimbus," I said, hoping he heard me as I pulled.

Chapter 25

"**W**hat are you doing?" someone hissed.

I froze at the familiar voice and glanced over my shoulder. "Jaz?"

"He'll never forgive himself, or me, if you get killed." She kept her voice low as she crept around the cage containing Nimbus.

"So, what do we do?"

Though I'd often seen Jaz with bright lipstick that set off her porcelain skin, now she was just wearing a gloss and very conservative clothing. Her eyes darted around nervously, and her head was tilted slightly as if she listened hard to what was going on around us.

"Just watch for your opportunity. I can't do anything until we're assured of success, but if we find our opportunity, I'll wake Katsuro. You'll have to do the rest."

"How do we rescue Nimbus?"

Jaz gave the cloud puppy a dismissive look and shrugged.

Clearly, she was more worried about Katsuro than anything else. I supposed I understood. I was more worried about Nimbus than the vampire. I hoped Jaz really was on our side, though. For whatever reason, the enemy seemed to trust her, and I just couldn't help but worry that they knew something we didn't. Katsuro trusted her, too, but since I didn't know her story, I couldn't judge for myself.

The room we were in appeared to be some sort of large study. A massive solid wood desk sat in front of a fireplace. Bookshelves lined the walls, and another fireplace was on the other side of the room with a dark leather couch and loveseat arranged in front of it. Neither fireplace was lit, which, considering the time of year, made sense. I rubbed my arms, still having a hard time regulating my temperature after being drugged. Though I looked, I didn't see any smaller chairs. I could have used them as a weapon, and that might be why they were missing. If the bad guys had considered that, anyway.

The rug Katsuro lay on looked Persian, though I wasn't an expert. Generic art, mostly pastoral scenes, plastered the walls. Heavy black curtains covered the windows, no light leaking in.

While Jaz watched, I staggered over to the desk and looked around for anything. A letter opener, a paperweight, something.

Either this room wasn't used for its apparent purpose, or my kidnappers were smart. There was nothing, and the drawers were empty. The only thing potentially useful that I could find were the books. The cloud of dust that rose up when I pulled one off the shelf made me think they hadn't even remembered they existed, despite being obvious.

Interestingly enough, the book I pulled out was a tome on varieties of apples.

Apples... Make the apples grow.

How?

Clutching the book, I went to the fireplace and sat on the couch. I tried not to look too closely at the cage they'd put Nimbus in. I had to rescue him, but if I couldn't touch the cage, I'd have to use magic. Also, I didn't want to accidentally hurt the cloud puppy in the process. So. Magic.

Which meant I needed to make my magic work.

170

I cradled the book like a talisman and tried to capture the feeling I remembered from my initial unfolding. In my mind's eye, an orchard formed around me, a crushed stone path at my feet. I followed it, feeling the pain of Nimbus's absence. He should be at my side, helping me on my journey as I helped him.

Instead, another presence joined me. Twister pushed his fluffy head under my hand as he stepped close to me. We didn't speak. I simply walked, my hand tangled in his fluff.

All the trees were in various stages of growing fruit. The first ones we passed were barely buds. As we continued, the buds matured into full flowers, then the beginnings of fruits were on the tree. Our path stopped, and the vision simply seemed to end in a fog.

Clearly, I needed to do something to proceed. Reaching inside myself, I tried to pull the warmth of the magic out and feed it into the vision.

The fog swirled, and I moved forward. It gave way, revealing trees with apples still green but much larger than any I'd yet seen.

Before I could try again, the vision dissipated with the sound of a banging door, and I snapped open my eyes.

I recognized the hawk's nose and sharp features of the first man to walk into the room. Drake. The shade that had originally been after Nimbus. The vile man glanced at the cage that held the cloud puppy and the smile that crossed his lips promised nothing good.

The second man I didn't recognize. He was taller, like Drake, had short cropped black hair, and pale skin that had clearly not seen the sun in centuries.

Well, shit. Maybe this was the man on the supernatural side of the trafficking ring I'd helped put away.

"Ahh, Ms. Miller, I believe you're going by that now, yes?"

I didn't reply, and he didn't seem to be waiting for one.

"Your friend in the FBI was quite helpful after a bit of persuasion. Unfortunately for him, he was just strong enough to break away, and we had to put him down. Can't have that kind of person around. Too troublesome." His voice was smooth, low, and oily. I already wanted to scrub myself with lava soap just to get the feeling he gave me off. Not to mention the way his eyes traveled my body. My breath caught, but I otherwise remained as calm as I could. My FBI contact had been a good guy, and he'd had a family. These people didn't care, though. Obviously.

"You've caused us quite a bit of trouble. First cutting off our blood supply, and second, stealing our creature. Either one of these would be a death sentence, but both? Well, we might need to get creative. Death, I think, is too easy."

I avoided glancing at Jaz. She couldn't help me. At least not yet. Katsuro was out of the picture, and I had no idea if the others would find me in time to save me. I had to save myself, because I could well imagine what sorts of things this man might have in mind for me, and none of them were good. If it came down to it, I'd make him kill me, but I hoped my magic and my friends would come through in time.

The vampire stalked toward me. I made the mistake of looking into his eyes. Their endless depths promised pain, and worse, but they held me, and I was unable to look away. Something whispered in the back of my mind, telling me it wouldn't be so bad to submit, but a greater part of me screamed a warning.

"On your knees, bitch," the vampire whispered in his smooth, oily voice.

An apple tree sprouted between me and the vampire's deadly gaze. I focused on it, forcing it to grow, to spread, to save me from this creature.

With a shout of rage, I jerked myself away from the vampire.

He snarled and his fist lashed out, catching me across the jaw and sending me tumbling backward over the couch.

My neck ached from the whiplash motion, but at least he hadn't broken my neck.

"I suppose we'll have to have other sorts of fun together." He'd regained his composure, and I managed to get back to my feet in time to see Drake whisper something to the vampire.

They turned and left without another word. I glanced around but Jaz was gone, too, leaving me alone with an unconscious Katsuro and Nimbus.

I had to save Nimbus, no matter what, so instead of curling into a ball and crying like I wanted to, I sat on the floor and focused on apples.

Dakota Brown

Chapter 26

The sharp pain of my hair being yanked on jerked me out of my meditation. I snapped my eyes open but didn't fight back. The same man was holding me, and he didn't look happy about it.

Before I could change my mind, he twisted my arm up behind my back.

"Just watch. The master wants to play with one of his new toys."

"How very Renfield," I muttered under my breath.

Either he didn't hear, or he ignored the comment.

The same vampire as before sauntered into the room, the oily grin on his face as he surveyed us. Me, basically helpless in his servant's grasp, Katsuro unconscious on the floor, and Nimbus trapped in that awful cage.

"You almost made it, too," the vampire said. "He almost escaped with his magic, but we were just in time. These things are too dangerous to leave wild and on their own. There's no telling what mischief they would get up to." He waved at Nimbus.

While I hadn't exactly avoided looking at my poor cloud puppy, I hadn't spent any great time viewing his prison. I knew it would take magic to free him, so I'd focused on that.

I was forced to look now. As before, he seemed peaceful, but that golden leash attached to his collar, that thing, was evil regardless of how pretty it was. That was the thing I needed to destroy. If I could get that, Nimbus would be able to escape the cage, regardless of how clever it was. I suspected it was more to keep people from stealing the nimbus than it was to prevent him from escaping.

How he'd gotten away all those weeks ago with a leash still attached, I might never know.

The apples on my mental apple tree hadn't fully ripened yet, but we were out of time. I found the threads of magic that bound Nimbus and started picking at them.

The vampire turned toward the cloud puppy and took a step closer. I guessed it was that toy he wanted to play with.

I needed to distract him. I didn't want anything to happen to Nimbus, and we needed to get him away.

"You know, it's polite to introduce yourself when you're torturing someone."

"Is it?" He turned back to me, his smile gone from oily to downright malicious.

The first thread on the leash unraveled, but there were so many more to go.

The creature stalked toward me, grabbing the front of my shirt, and slowly bunching it up into his fist before jerking me out of his minion's grasp.

"You can call me Master."

I snickered, more to piss him off than because I was amused. Terror turned my limbs to ice and curled through my gut, but another strand unraveled in Nimbus's golden shackles, and so I kept at it.

"We don't have that kind of relationship."

His lips twitched as if he were fighting a laugh. "We could."

I felt his willpower brush against mine, digging into the shields protecting me, and trying to dominate me as my joke had suggested.

Splitting my attention between protecting my mind and picking away at the threads of Nimbus's prison was actually easier than I would have expected, but I couldn't do much else, and when the vampire—I refused to call him master, even in my head—tossed me aside, I could only lay there. I'd come up against Katsuro.

Waking him up would certainly provide a distraction, but would I be able to survive long enough to finish freeing Nimbus in the process? I had to wait to be sure.

I guessed the other vampire wasn't worried about me trying to wake up his rival, and he left me there, gesturing for his minion to get something off a shelf.

Jaz must have entered at some point. She flicked her hand to get my attention. When I met her gaze, I heard her voice in my mind.

Wait. Not long now.

I picked frantically at the threads. I wasn't even halfway through destroying the magic containing Nimbus and if we were close to a confrontation... Well, I needed this thing destroyed.

The minion handed the vampire a container from the shelf. It glinted in the light, maybe crystal or some other sort of fine glass, and had a golden stopper. It was either extremely pretty or ostentatious, and I couldn't decide which.

The vampire turned back to me with that oily grin firmly plastered on his lips.

"As you have destroyed our blood supply, I believe I will see if this can replace the need." He gestured at Nimbus.

I didn't want him to use Nimbus for anything. I picked at the strands of his bindings as quickly as I could, not replying to his taunts.

The vampire tilted his head, studying me.

Shit, could he sense the magic?

Jaz, possibly wondering the same thing, came forward.

"Master," she said with the utmost subservience. "I've been informed there are werewolves at the gate."

She'd certainly waited to tell him. That gave me hope.

The vampire's brow furrowed, and the smile left his lips.

Good.

"Well, deal with it."

She bowed and made like she was going to exit the room.

"Wait!"

Jaz turned.

"This can deal with it for me." He again gestured at Nimbus.

Oh, hell no. I twisted toward Katsuro and yanked the wooden bolt out of his chest before they could stop me.

I definitely heard swearing as strong hands grabbed me and hot fire sank into my neck. I almost lost myself as I orgasmed harder than I'd ever come in my entire life, but the urgency of my purpose let me fight through the haze and destroy the last of the golden threads holding Nimbus captive before I lost consciousness.

He was free, that much I knew. I hoped he would remain that way, though I couldn't do anything else for him. At least not at the moment, possibly ever again. The rest was lost in a chaotic melee of shouts, bellows, and the distant howl of a wolf as my consciousness fled after another mind-blowing orgasm as Katsuro drained my life away. I was content knowing he'd exact some powerful revenge and that I'd done everything I possibly could to rescue my nimbus.

Chapter 27

I stared at the gate. It was an ornate wrought iron thing decorated with apple blossoms, both real and metal. The gate was set in a stone wall that stretched as far as the eye could see on either side of me. It separated me from a vast orchard, apple trees heavy with nearly ripened fruit. Overhead the sky was vibrant blue and cotton puff clouds floated lazily along.

On my side of the fence there was grass at my feet and along the stone wall, but I didn't turn to see what was behind me. Behind me was the past, and I was moving into the future, if I could just get through the gate.

Twister stepped up next to me, and I buried my fingers in his ruff.

We sat and contemplated the gate in silence for a time until an urgent bark got my attention. Nimbus, now on the other side of the gate, rose up on his back legs and put his front paws on the gate. He poked his nose through one of the gaps and whined.

"He is ready for you. Though he's not fully grown, he's been forced into his maturity by the circumstances, as so many of our kind are. You have proven time and again that you are truly worthy of our trust and companionship, and Nimbus will guide you down your future paths."

"What about you?" I kneeled and put my arms around his neck.

He seemed to like this, leaning into the contact.

"I am content."

"Twister, I still want you in my life."

"Truly?" He was clearly pleased by this, ears up, eyes locked on mine.

"Yes, silly." I wiped a tear from my eye, not ready to say goodbye to this magnificent being.

"Then I will return to you in the future. Look for me. It won't be too long." He seemed to wink before placing a paw on my arm and leaning in for one last solid scratching. "Now, go to Nimbus, walk through the gate, and let him guide you to your full potential. Then return to your world and give that evil creature an ass whooping he won't forget."

I giggled. "You said ass whooping."

"I've been in the storm for a while. It was a common phrase when last I bonded a human."

"Okay. Fair." I kissed his broad forehead and stood. "You promise I'll see you again soon?"

Twister glanced at Nimbus, who rooed happily and wagged his fluffy curled tail.

"I promise."

"Okay."

Stepping away from my guide, I put my hand on the wrought-iron gate. It creaked open at my touch, and, with one last deep breath, I stepped through.

Nimbus pressed his head under my hand, and I scratched his ears before taking another step. Pressure built up in my chest, glorious heat and warmth before it exploded out of me.

A wave of golden energy radiated out from the two of us, rustling the leaves in the heavily laden fruit trees. As it passed through the trees, the fruits ripened to a brilliant red.

I sagged as the energy abated, but new knowledge and awareness filled me. Nimbus rooed happily and nudged my hand, so I kneeled on the ground next to him and buried my fingers in his fluff.

"Okay, so what's next?"

He turned to look at me, his soulful brown eyes filled with a golden light.

Now we go home.

***

My eyes snapped open, and I choked on the thick liquid someone was pouring into my mouth.

"She's awake," a familiar voice called.

I couldn't identify it in the confusion of the moment, but I did know it wasn't a bad guy. The voice filled me with comfort and calm. Swallowing reflexively one last time, I gagged on the coppery liquid and almost choked when I saw Jaz pull her arm away from my mouth.

Blood? Ew!

"You were near death," she said. "It was the only way."

"Thanks," I managed to get out before a black and white fluff ball pounced on my stomach, almost making me lose all the blood I'd just drank.

"Nimbus!" I wrapped my arms around him.

He rooed for quite some time, obviously having a lot to say, and it sounded a great deal like scolding.

I just laughed. Then I looked around and sobered. We were still in the study. Katsuro glowered at me from across the room. Jaz still kneeled at my side, and Oliver joined us.

"Oliver!"

He smiled. "Hannah, so glad to see you conscious again."

"Do we still need to escape?" My gaze strayed toward Katsuro. His expression softened, and he inclined his head slightly.

"Yes, sunshine, we still need to escape. And while I appreciate you waking me, please never risk yourself like that again." The same scolding tone that Nimbus had managed colored the vampire's voice.

"No promises." I gently shoved Nimbus off me so I could stand.

He stayed right against my leg, but at least let me get to my feet.

"So, what's the plan?" I was so grateful I wasn't on my own anymore. I went over to Oliver and folded myself into his arms. The shade clutched me tightly.

"They are using guns, which complicates things," Oliver replied. "We can't just blast out of here, despite having the more powerful vampires."

I glanced at Jaz and tilted my head.

"Saving you completely blew my cover, as it were." She shrugged. "I'm not sorry."

"Thank you," I replied, hoping that she was indeed on our side, as everyone kept saying. I just didn't know enough to completely trust her.

"Davin and his wolves, along with Clare and Bridger, are on the perimeter. They are harassing Vito's creatures. Oliver slipped through, but we may have to deal with Drake as well as a few lesser vampires."

"Vito?"

"The vampire who captured us," Katsuro clarified.

"Ahh, he wouldn't tell me his name." I shook my head. Vito, huh?

"Typical," Oliver said. He eased his grip on me, and I stepped away.

"So they know we're here and they're not busting in because they're afraid of Katsuro?" I risked a glance at him. His return look was wary.

"Essentially," the vampire agreed.

"Okay, so I have some powers. Nimbus has some powers. Can we create a shield for the bullets while we run out of here?" I glanced at the cloud puppy.

He wagged his tail. I hoped that was an agreement on his part.

"The main danger is to you and Nimbus," Oliver said. "Bullets are not much of an issue for me, and the vampires can dodge. It is more difficult when we have to protect you."

"What about it, buddy?" I glanced at the fluff ball.

He nodded.

"I think it should be okay, then. Also, Nimbus, can't you just teleport out?"

He wagged his tail again.

"So I'm the weak link and I'll do my best to shield, but above all else, make sure they don't get their hands on Nimbus again." I put my hands on my hips and glared at the others. After a moment, they all nodded.

While Oliver, Jaz, and Katsuro conferred on our route, I attempted to make a shield. The power was there. I could even hold it. I simply had no idea how to make something that would repel bullets.

Finally, Nimbus came to my side and grumbled at me before putting a paw on my leg. Slowly, the energy I held flowed around me into a distinctive bubble shape. It hardened, but not completely, and Nimbus put his paw back on the ground.

"Okay, got it. Thanks."

He rooed.

Once I was ready, the others went to the door. Katsuro listened for a moment before opening it. This required him to destroy the doorknob, which he did with little trouble. The doorframe broke a little, but who cared? Also, damn, that man was strong.

He led, Oliver slipped into the shadows, and Jaz followed. Nimbus stayed right at my side.

At first, we met almost no resistance, and Katsuro was easily able to handle the men they threw at us. Then they seemed to understand we were going to get away, and they dug up some sort of magic user we hadn't expected.

The first blast of energy down the hall would have taken out Katsuro if Nimbus hadn't stepped in with a fierce growl and thrown something back at the man.

Then Nimbus and I moved to the front, and Jaz closed in so we were more tightly protected. Unfortunately, we couldn't get any farther down the hallway. The man we faced was experienced, and Nimbus and I were not.

It was all I could do to deflect the blasts of energy coming at us, and while I'd apparently fully unlocked my powers, I still had a lot to learn.

Oliver finally slipped through the shadows and came out behind the magic user. Mage? Witch? I didn't know the right term and clubbed the man over the head.

He attracted a few rounds of gunfire, but as soon as the magic user was unconscious, Katsuro and Jaz surged forward and handled the rest of the men, while Nimbus and I hurried on behind them.

I was almost shocked when we made it out into the courtyard. It was night, which I hadn't known until then. Floodlights lit the area and people were shooting at anything that moved, keeping the werewolves back.

It didn't take long before the lights zeroed in on us. We couldn't retreat, and the only way to go forward was to brave the open space and all the guns, and I was starting to wear out.

Katsuro took a deep breath, glanced at Jaz, then practically vanished.

Oliver touched my shoulders when my breathing quickened with a touch of panic. My feelings eased until Jaz turned to me with a slight smile on her face.

The predatory look sent my heart racing, and I backed into Oliver.

She'd had us all fooled. We were so screwed.

Dakota Brown

Chapter 28

I screamed when Jaz charged, but she dodged around me and tore into someone I hadn't seen sneaking up behind us.

"I must face Drake," Oliver said. "Nimbus will protect you. As soon as you see an opportunity, run for the forest and the wolves will find you."

In most other circumstances, that statement wouldn't have been comforting, but I certainly wasn't in most circumstances. Well, I'd come to Beechworth because of the rumors that this place was different. I just hadn't realized how different. And yet, how very much the same. At least this time, I wasn't alone.

Oliver shifted into his shadowy shade form, the six-legged wolfish shadow creature that smelled of baked goods. Oliver was the only shade that smelled like cinnamon, and I liked it. Reaching out, I offered a touch, and, after a slight hesitation, he slid his head under my hand like Nimbus would have. I gave him a quick scratch, marveling at the cool smoothness of a living shadow under my hand.

He seemed to wink at me before bounding off and slamming into the other shade—that was just now appearing out of the shadows that clung to the side of the building.

They tore into each other, and tears fogged my vision. I thought about dropping my shield and trying to do

189

something to help, but a stray bullet pinged off the magical bubble just then and changed my mind. That would have hit me. Probably killed me. I needed to protect myself and Nimbus.

Fortunately, the cloud puppy tucked himself between me and the wall to take full advantage of my protection, then stared out at the combatants. After a moment of contemplation, he rooed quietly to himself. I looked out and saw gravel fly through the air, streaming into one of the shades.

I didn't think it would hurt the creature, but it certainly distracted it, giving Oliver enough time to get an advantage and drive the other shade off.

The guns stopped firing one after another and at least one body fell from the rooftops. The lights also began to fail, leaving the courtyard in heavy shadows punctuated by a few bright lights. Katsuro?

And Jaz reappeared, a manic grin made grizzly from a coating of blood on her face. "Let's go."

I followed. Not without misgivings, but I followed.

She led me through the shadows, and straight across the courtyard into the wolves. A pack of wolves that positively mobbed me, rubbing against me and sniffing me as if they couldn't get enough of my scent. They gave Nimbus space until he rooed and touched noses with them, then we were both included in the press.

Before long, Clare and Bridger, along with another large wolf I thought might be Davin, joined us. Some of the wolves had blood on their faces. They were kind enough not to rub it all over me. Davin was positively red up to his shoulders, and he kept his distance though his ears perked when I waved.

Katsuro joined us moments later and not long after, Oliver galloped into our midst, still in shadowy six-legged dog form.

"Let's go," Katsuro said.

We took off into the woods at a run. My vision sharpened with a bit of magic, but it wasn't long before us mere humans struggled to keep up with the others. Bridger was doing the best, but even he lagged.

Nimbus increased his size until I could climb on his back.

"Buddy, be careful, okay? Last time you passed out."

He grumbled but wagged his fluffy tail. I hoped that meant he was better able to control his powers this time. He also bumped into Clare until she climbed up behind me.

Bridger got a second wind, possibly literally. He ran on his own two feet, but I felt gusts of wind and thought maybe Nimbus was propelling him along with us.

Time lost meaning while we ran, though I cast a wary eye to the sky through the canopy of trees. The stars were fading. Dawn had to be soon, and the vampires needed to be under cover before that happened.

The sky had lightened to slate gray from black by the time we broke out into a small clearing. A small hunting lodge with a bunch of surrounding cabins was a welcome sight. Especially when the wolves broke off from the pack and went to different cabins. I guessed this was pack territory.

I averted my eyes as they began to shift. I knew they were comfortable with their forced nudity, but I wasn't part of their pack, and I didn't want to stare.

The group of wolves surrounding us headed for the main lodge. The wolf I was sure was Davin went up the steps first and shifted. Yep, definitely him.

Blushing, I stared down at Nimbus's black and white fluff for a moment until I was sure he was inside. The vampires hurried inside after, and Nimbus stopped by the steps so Clare and I could dismount. She patted my shoulder before climbing off the giant cloud puppy.

I hugged him tightly, before also sliding to the ground. He nudged me gently before shrinking down to his normal size.

We all staggered up the steps, Bridger right there with us, and went inside.

It was warm, well lit, and welcoming, but all I wanted right then was a shower, a bed, and someone to hug me and tell me it was going to be okay. Maybe not in that exact order, but that's what I wanted. Food, I also wanted food.

Davin came over to me, wrapped in a towel.

"Hannah, are you okay?"

"Never better," I stammered, before the tears flooded my eyes.

Nimbus pushed against my side, and Davin wrapped me in a one-armed hug and let me sob onto his shoulder.

"Food!" Davin shouted. "Clean up and get food for everyone!"

I heard people reply in the background, but I was lost to my tears. This was all so much. We were safe, but now the overwhelming fear, well remembered from the last time I'd faced the human side of this operation, combined with my new fears. Fear for me, and for my friends, and for what I'd almost lost. Could I do this again? Did I have a choice?

Nimbus pushed his head under my hand and rooed softly. Davin held me close. Oliver and Bridger hugged me from behind, and I leaned into their support while I cried.

***

Hours later, I was fed, clean, and curled up under a down comforter and on the verge of sleep. Katsuro and Jaz had disappeared quickly, but everyone else had lingered until I was tucked into bed. Nimbus had curled up against my back and snored softly in that adorable way only a dog could manage. He didn't normally snore, but I didn't want to disturb him, either.

I lay there, still on the verge of sleep. There was no question that I was exhausted, but I could not tumble over the edge. Each time I almost made it, I jerked awake.

I heard a soft knock on the door and was relieved to be jerked awake for a different reason.

"Come in."

The door opened, bringing in a hint of cinnamon. Oliver.

"Hey," I said.

"Shouldn't you be asleep, Hannah?"

"Trying," I grumbled.

Nimbus huffed softly and twisted so he could look at me.

"Sorry, buddy."

He gave me a soft nose kiss and went back to sleep. This time without the quiet snores.

I held out my hand to Oliver and when he took it, tugged him down onto the bed so he sat next to where I lay. "I'm glad you're here. Thank you for coming for me."

"Always, Hannah. Mind if I join you for a bit? I'm having trouble sleeping, and it seems like you are, as well."

"Please do." The amount of relief I felt having Oliver there was almost overwhelming. "We won a battle, but we're not anywhere near safe. They're going to come after us again, aren't they?"

"Yes. But we'll be ready. We're going back to Beechworth and preparing the town. They can try to take you and Nimbus, but everyone will fight."

"But, Oliver, that puts so many people in danger. Wouldn't it be better to run somewhere with a lot of sun? Like the equator? Or like a boat that stays in the sunlight all the time? Can a boat even travel that fast?" I was babbling and being ridiculous and we both knew it, but I didn't want an entire town fighting and possibly getting hurt, or killed, just to save me.

He twisted around and pressed his lips to my forehead. "This isn't just about you, Hannah. Yes, we want to save you, obviously, but Vito and his people have been skirting the edges of Beechworth's sanctuary for years now. They've just made a direct attack on something that is ours, and if we don't respond, they'll just keep coming. And now that they've attacked us, we have the excuse we needed to go after them."

"What did they attack that's yours?" I couldn't remember them going after anyone but me or Nimbus. Well, maybe when they'd attacked us at Bridger's house. Or maybe when they'd staked Katsuro?

"You, Hannah. You and Nimbus. You're part of Beechworth and they broke the truce by going after you."

My throat thickened with emotion for a moment before I got control of myself. "But I just moved here. Surely they will say I'm not really part of the truce."

"There's an entire town that would disagree with you, and with them should they argue against it."

"I don't even know what to say. I'm honored."

"And we're glad to have you."

At my invitation, Oliver lay down next to me and wrapped his arms around me so I could snuggle into his chest. Needing to be closer, I tangled my legs with his and pressed against him as tightly as I could.

"I don't want anyone hurt on my account."

"I know, Hannah, but remember, it's not just because of you. This has been coming for a long time, but we weren't going to be the first ones to break the truce."

"Okay."

I inhaled his scent and tilted my head so I could kiss his neck. Oliver's hands tightened on my back and his breath hitched. The energy between us shifted, and he looked down at me, hunger in his eyes.

"Will we disturb anyone?"

Amusement joined the hunger in his expression. "We're in a house full of beings with super senses. Yes."

"Oh." Disappointment tempered my growing lust.

"Hannah, they sent me in here to make sure you were alright."

I perked up. "Did they, now?"

"Yes. Undoubtably, there were multiple willing individuals, but you and I have already been together. I'm sure they won't be surprised if we do more than just cuddle."

My needy desire roared to life, and I licked my lips. "Do you want to do more than cuddle?"

"I would like nothing more at the moment."

I thought I detected a slight tremor in Oliver's hands where he clutched me against him.

Nimbus huffed before jumping off the bed, leaving us alone.

Anticipation chasing away the last vestiges of fatigue, I pressed my lips to Oliver's.

Chapter 29

Oliver's fingers traced across my skin before gently rubbing along the borrowed shirt I was wearing. It was big enough to cover my butt, but not much longer, and I hadn't bothered to put on underwear. Mine was all dirty.

"Davin's shirt looks good on you," Oliver murmured. "Maybe next time I'll dress you up in one of mine." His lips pressed against the bare skin of my shoulder where the shirt didn't cover.

I shivered. "I didn't know it was his."

"I can smell his scent all over it. Mingles nicely with your own." He applied a hint of teeth, and the sensation went right through my center, tingling on its way through me until it settled into a tight, needy ball of lust right in my core.

"I still can't understand how you can be so accepting of me possibly being in a relationship with other men."

"Mmmm, sometimes to get what you want, you have to share." He nipped again.

I gasped, arching my back and pressing into him.

"And what is it you want?"

"Right now? To be buried in you while you cry out my name," he replied, voice thick with lust. "In the future, for you to claim us as your mates. All of us. Our town will be stronger for it, and you will be safer."

My brain short-circuited from Oliver's first words, and I filed the others away for later study.

"Yeah, I think we can do that," I murmured.

He shifted us until I was on my back, and he looked down at me. "You're lovely."

I grinned. "You're a little blurry, but I'm pretty sure I remember you being exceedingly good looking."

He snorted. "Do you want your glasses?"

"No."

Oliver leaned over and nibbled at my neck again, while one hand slid down my side until he found the hem of the shirt.

My needy moan almost embarrassed me, but the hell with it, Oliver clearly liked it. He pulled my shirt up, and I lifted my butt so he could get it higher.

The thrill I felt as his hands caressed my ribs, then cupped my breast, chased away a lot of the fear and stress of the last few days. It would return, but for now, bliss overrode anything else.

I buried my fingers in Oliver's hair and made encouraging noises as he worked his way down my body. I wanted him to take his time, to explore every inch of me. I also wanted him to ravage me completely right now. Since my two raging desires conflicted, I let him pick his own pace.

He scooted down so that he kneeled between my legs and shoved the shirt the rest of the way up. I raised my arms and let him tug it off over my head. Then he lowered his lips to my breast, sucking gently on my nipple and sending tingles of heat and pleasure through me. I cried out as the sensation went straight to my pussy, nearly bringing me to climax. I was soaked, the moisture slicking my legs.

Oliver bent lower, lapping gently and rumbling deep in his throat.

The sound, combined with the pleasure of his tongue against my clit, undid me and I shouted as my orgasm rippled through me.

The shade murmured happily and kept lapping. "You taste delicious, love," he said.

I couldn't answer, not sure what to say, and lost in the sensations he was giving me.

Oliver slid a finger inside me and curled while he sucked at my clit. The pressure of another climax built inside me, and I thrust against his face as he worked my body.

This one took a little longer, but he was patient and kept going until I crashed into another intense orgasm.

While I lay there, recovering, he shed his clothing.

"You still want this?"

"Yes, I really, really do," I replied.

"Roll over."

I did as commanded, and he clasped my hips and pulled them up in the air until I was on my hands and knees.

"Comfortable?"

"Yes."

"Excellent. I may not last long. It has been ages for me."

"Oliver, anything you give me is wonderful."

He dug his fingers into my hips and spread my knees with one of his.

Sweat covered me, and the air felt cool against my skin, contrasting with the heat from his hands and his body.

He took one hand and guided himself to my entrance. I was so wet it only took a little pressure for him to slide inside of me, stretching my walls and filling me completely.

"Oh, fuck me, yes, Oliver, that's amazing," I blurted out, surprised and gratified by how good he felt caged inside me.

"It truly is," he agreed before beginning to move.

I gasped in pleasure as he slid into me again and again. He was just the right size to rub me everywhere inside, and the sensations were overwhelming me into a state of hazy bliss I'd only reached a few other times during sex. I didn't even realize I was calling out his name until another orgasm crashed into me. Oliver went rigid as he followed me with his own orgasm.

We stayed there for a moment or two, both reveling in the sensations. I squeezed down with my inner walls and he grunted softly. "More?"

"If you're up for it."

Oliver laughed. "By the time you've had a few more orgasms, I will be."

"As much as you can manage," I demanded. It had been long enough that I just wanted to be one hot mess of sweat, cum, and exhaustion by the time he was done with me.

I thought Oliver might be on the same damn page by the way he carefully pulled out of me, then replaced his cock with his fingers.

"Let's see how many we can get, shall we?"

***

Hours later, I woke feeling rested and refreshed. Nimbus was back at his spot next to me, and I vaguely remembered Oliver kissing me on the forehead and telling me he was getting up to take care of some things.

I stretched, clinging to the radiant glow of contentment that shielded me from the realities of our enemies and the danger we all still faced. Oliver's words had helped some.

We weren't the cause of this. We were just an additional excuse.

Nimbus rumbled softly and stretched, pressing his back against my side and wiggling around. I took the hint and gave him a scritch before throwing the covers back.

The cool air chilled my naked flesh, and I hurriedly looked around for something to wear. The only piece of clothing was the long t-shirt we'd thrown to the floor last night. It was Davin's, Oliver had said.

Well, it would be better than the still damp towel I'd used to dry off with after showering for the second time last night. I pulled it over my head, freshened up in the bathroom, and left my room to see if someone had my clothing. And food.

Nimbus appeared next to me. Like… appeared.

"Okay, that's going to take some getting used to, buddy."

He rooed happily and wagged his fluffy curled tail.

I could feel the tingles of magic now and almost see a trace of it at the edges of my vision. Maybe that ability would get stronger.

The air in the hallway was cooler than in the closed bedroom, and I shivered, folding my arms under my breasts. This pulled the shirt up enough that I thought my butt might be exposed.

Well, they were freaking werewolves and apparently had no issues with nudity. They'd have to deal. I'd have to deal.

Briefly, I wondered if there was a magical solution, but it would probably be easier just to find out what had happened to my clothing.

I followed Nimbus down to the kitchen. A few members of the pack, a woman and two men, were cooking. I'd have to get their names after I got some clothing and food.

The woman glanced at me and raised her eyebrows.

I shrugged. "I don't know where my clothing ended up."

She grinned, though her expression turned knowing for a moment. "I wouldn't have expected Oliver to be that wild." She laughed.

The blush that colored my cheeks probably went all the way down to my toes. I cleared my throat. "Uh, yeah, my clothes disappeared before that."

The other two werewolves joined in the laugh, and one of them handed me some biscuits and gravy.

I took the plate and a glass of orange juice and sat on the couch, carefully tucking the shirt under my butt. The warm plate felt good on my lap and the food was delicious. I was so focused on the biscuits that I didn't notice that anyone had joined me until I was done.

Davin sat across from me in an armchair, a half-smile on his lips, his eyes glued to me.

"Hi," I forced out, suddenly nervous.

"As much as I like seeing you wander around in my shirt and nothing else, I think we can do better. Your clothing was pretty wrecked. I have Charlotte getting you something more appropriate."

I jabbed my fork at him. "Staring is rude."

He chuckled. "My apologies. You're quite correct." He didn't avert his gaze.

"So, what's next?"

"After we get you clothed?" He licked his lips, then finally managed to look away. "I have ideas, but in reality, we need to discuss the next stage of our plan."

"Davin, the dog just levitated the entire pan of gravy, I swear to god," one of the cooks shouted.

I laughed. "Nimbus!"

He rooed, trotting over with the pan of gravy floating behind him, his tail curled and wagging happily.

"Nimbus, you have to share!"

He set the pan down in front of him and gave it a sniff.

Davin chuckled. "We can make more. I'm sure he's hungry."

"Don't make yourself sick," I ordered, though I was pretty sure a cloud puppy's dietary needs were different than an actual dog's.

Nimbus tested the gravy, decided it had cooled enough, and shoved his face into it, eating hungrily.

I shook my head and turned back to Davin. The look in his eye was hungry and primal. I bit my lip, shivering.

"I'll back off if you don't want the attention," he said quietly.

"No, it's not that. I'm just not used to the situation we are in." I met his gaze.

"Perhaps we should all sit down and have a discussion about how best to proceed. Everything is your choice, and Oliver is a good man and a more than suitable mate. I just think you deserve more." He winked. "As in more mates."

I'd been about to defend Oliver, but with Davin's clarification, I laughed. "Aren't wolves typically monogamous?"

"We're werewolves. Our ways might reflect our wild brothers' and sisters' to some degree, but not completely. I can accept the other men. In some ways, I welcome it. While you can protect yourself, I also want to protect you and Nimbus, and I can't always be with you. If you have more mates, you will have more protection. I trust Oliver and Katsuro to protect you." He took a deep breath. "And even Bridger, if you're interested in him."

"I've barely had time to process all of this," I admitted. "I can't..." I trailed off and waved a hand helplessly, not sure what I was going to say.

"No need to make a decision now," he said. "Let's take one thing at a time. Clothes, because you are very tempting, so scantily clothed, and in my shirt." His eyes shone with lust and a soft moan escaped my lips before I clamped them shut.

I squirmed under his gaze and knew I was getting damp. Especially by the way Davin sucked in his breath, as if tasting my scent.

Someone cleared their throat. I glanced over my shoulder and saw Oliver and Katsuro in the shadows. The vampire's gaze was hungry, and I wasn't completely sure it was lust that motivated that look. He'd recently drank a lot of my blood, and I knew that had to be on his mind. I glanced at Davin.

"Sorry, sorry," Davin said, visibly restraining himself and turning away.

When I looked back toward the hallway, Oliver was alone. I hadn't noticed the bundle of clothing he held before, but he held it up now.

"Care to get dressed?"

"Yeah, probably a good idea." I mock glared at Davin, who held up his hands in surrender, though he had a playful smile on his face.

I got up, leaving Nimbus to his gravy feast and hoping he would clean up his face when he was done, because he was wearing his food like a toddler at the moment. I stopped next to Davin and put my hand on his shoulder, squeezing gently. "I'm very interested in revisiting this topic, but I do think we should all talk first. I need reassurance."

Davin covered my hand with his. "Absolutely."

I went over to Oliver, and he gave me the pile of clothing and a gentle kiss on the forehead.

"Love, get dressed, then go talk to Katsuro."

Frowning, I glanced up at the shade. "What's wrong?"

Oliver sighed. "He's unhappy with how you risked yourself, and he's craving your blood. It's a combination to make any vampire cranky."

I glanced back at Davin, head tilted to invite his advice. I knew he could hear Oliver's quiet words.

Davin nodded and joined us, the heat spilling off his body warming my back, though he didn't invade my space. He was just that warm.

"Oliver is right. Talk to him."

"Hannah," Oliver said quietly. "You do not need my permission for anything but know that I will be okay with any action you feel necessary to take with Katsuro. He needs some reassurance right now, but he's an ancient, powerful vampire. He won't ask for it. He'll just be an ass about it." Oliver smiled. "Feel free to tell him he's being an ass, but, also, feel free to go to him, if you want. It's all right. Once Katsuro has his head on straight again, we'll all talk and work this relationship out, but for now, do what you need to do."

I nodded, clutching the bundle of clothing tight and wondering if I should bother to change into it. Not that I was planning on jumping Katsuro, but maybe being half naked would throw him off some.

Oliver tilted my chin up with a finger and gave me a quick kiss on the lips. I smiled uncertainly and nodded. "I'll do my best."

In the end, I put on the clothing, feeling like I was donning armor. And hey, if it did come down to it, maybe it would be more fun if the vampire had more to take off me. Not that I was planning on getting naked, but, well, a girl never knew when she had several potential mates, now did she.

What on earth was I getting myself into?

Chapter 30

I found Katsuro in the basement. Though to call this luxurious apartment a basement was nearly a disservice. It was entirely possible that Davin, or whoever had built this lodge, had vampires and their comfort in mind when they designed this, and it seemed perfectly suited to someone who had to avoid the sunlight. There was outside access, but the door was heavy, and quite possibly reinforced. I saw no windows, and everything from the plush carpet to the wall hangings and acoustic tiles in the ceiling was designed to muffle sound while still being attractive and comfortable. A fireplace, currently cold, occupied one wall.

The vampire sat in an armchair, long legs stretched out in front of him and a book in his hand. A book I was fairly certain he wasn't actually reading, since he stared off into the distance instead of at the pages.

"Hey," I said.

He jumped slightly and snapped the book closed. His gaze shifted until he focused on me with some of that same hunger from before.

"Hello, Hannah."

I had no idea what to say, so I stood there hoping he would give me an opening.

Unfortunately, Katsuro seemed content to stare back.

Finally, I couldn't take it any longer. "Are you okay?"

Katsuro nodded. "Of course."

"I really appreciate what you did, keeping me safe and then rescuing me after."

The muscles in the vampire's jaw twitched before he nodded sharply. "You're quite welcome. I want to keep you safe." This softened his gaze momentarily before it went distant.

I took a few steps forward, and Katsuro's gaze shifted to my neck before he jerked his head.

"I want you to be safe," he repeated. "You should leave."

"You won't hurt me."

Katsuro licked his lips and rose to his feet, movements so fluid they were inhuman. I didn't back up when he stalked toward me.

"Won't I?"

"No."

"I almost killed you, Hannah," he growled. "If Jaz hadn't been there to revive you, I would have had to turn you to bring you back." He turned abruptly and was across the room before I could blink.

"Don't you think I might have considered that? I don't know a lot about vampires, but I know some of the lore. I don't want to be turned, but I had to get Nimbus free, and you, and Jaz. Yes, I took a chance, but it worked, didn't it?"

His shoulders hunched and he kept his back to me. I went across the room and put my hand on his shoulder.

He moved so fast I didn't even comprehend what was going on until he'd shoved me up against the wall. His breath tickled my neck. He bunched my shirt in his fist and trapped me with his body. There was nowhere for me to go, and a large part of me was extraordinarily happy to be pressed between the wall and Katsuro. I might have been more embarrassed at the thready gasp that escaped my lips and the heat that built between my thighs, but the entire house had likely heard me having sex with Oliver, and it was a little late for modesty at this point.

Katsuro inhaled, likely taking in my scent.

"You can't possibly understand how I felt when I came to my senses with you in my arms, your life fading away, knowing I had caused this. And now, after having had so much of it, your blood calls to me and it's all I can think about. That, and how terrified I am that I will hurt you." His lips brushed my skin as he spoke.

"So, take my blood," I replied, voice a little breathy, heart racing. I wasn't afraid. Well, maybe a tiny bit afraid. But after everything that had happened if it ended like this, at least I would enjoy myself.

"You have no—"

"Stop," I snapped. "Just do it or get over it. I've been running for my life for a couple of years now. I stopped a human trafficking ring by spying on them from the inside. I was terrified for over a year. I had to go on blood pressure meds for six months and anti-anxiety drugs and all sorts of things just to get back to an equilibrium. I saw people killed. I just had to fight for my life again. If you want my blood, take it. If you want to be an angsty ball of mess, I know a good psychiatrist. She's amazing and will help you with all sorts of coping mechanisms. If there's something I desperately need to know, then tell me." They had told me I could tell him he was being an ass.

"Hannah," he murmured. "It's a terrible idea."

"So is wanting my blood so badly it's all you can think about, and then not taking it when its offered. Bite me, Katsuro. Take my blood and take me to bed, or don't but then don't say I didn't offer."

"I don't want to hurt you."

He still held me against the wall, his lips pressed against my skin. I was practically shaking with need, despite being thoroughly ravaged by Oliver earlier.

"So don't."

He still hesitated, so I shifted my weight to one foot and lifted the other, hooking my leg around his and pulling him even more tightly against me. Oh, he was definitely interested. I put my other arm around his waist and dug my fingers into his side.

That did it. I felt him tense before he gently bit my neck, not breaking my skin but letting me know his fangs were fully extended.

I moaned, now thoroughly soaked between my legs again and desperately wanting to be filled and taken by this vampire.

"Spitfire," he murmured. "Are you sure?"

"Yes."

He shifted, bringing his lips to mine, kissing me, requesting entry. I opened for him, our tongues exploring. I ran mine over his teeth, feeling the sharp points of his fangs, enjoying the give and take as our lips melded and he crushed me against him.

Katsuro gripped my ass and lifted me so I could wrap my legs around his waist, one hand sliding up under my borrowed shirt.

I was losing myself in a hazy pool of need when something barked at us.

No, not something. *Someone.*

"Nimbus," I groaned, breaking off our kiss. "Not now."

Katsuro hissed in annoyance.

He barked again. Nimbus almost never actually barked.

"Fuck," I muttered. "What now?"

Katsuro cocked his head to the side, listening.

"You can hear from down here?"

"The soundproofing is good, but it's not that good." He gave me a soft smile, much closer to his old attitude. "We should investigate."

"I'd rather get laid."

That actually got him to laugh.

"Perhaps this will tide you over." He sank his teeth into my neck.

"Oh fuck," I practically shouted as my body reacted to his bite. I was already keyed up and whatever it was that vampires did to a human when they bit them to make it feel good rocketed through me. I came hard, seeing stars. I would have fallen if Katsuro hadn't been supporting me.

Distantly, I felt him take a tiny taste of my blood before he licked my neck and held me while I recovered.

"Tide both of us over?" I murmured through the haze.

"Indeed."

Nimbus huffed, but he didn't sound too annoyed, and when I looked for him, he'd vanished.

"Raincheck then?" I said as Katsuro helped me stand on my own.

"Raincheck. You might want to freshen up, however."

"Yeah." I wrinkled my nose.

Katsuro pointed me toward the bathroom before heading upstairs. When I'd had a moment to collect myself, I did the same, Nimbus joining me when I reached the staircase.

"What is it, buddy?"

He grumbled uneasily.

When I left the basement, I saw why. I froze, not certain the circle of werewolves surrounding an unfortunately familiar face would be enough to hold him.

"Drake," I murmured. The shade that had repeatedly tried to steal Nimbus and kidnap me.

As if he'd heard me, his head turned in my direction, his gaze locking onto mine.

The smile he leveled at me said he was anything but subdued.

I shivered and turned to run. I would not be captured again.

Chapter 31

Oliver stepped out of a shadow at my side and took my arm. "It's okay, we captured him."

"But his powers?"

"Clare has him blocked."

"She can do that?"

Oliver smiled. "She has herbs that we made him drink. He can't escape or use his powers right now."

I turned back toward the living room. "You're sure?"

"I've tested them. They work." The look of distaste on my shade's face was convincing.

"Okay." I let Oliver draw me into the living room.

Drake's gaze flicked between me and Nimbus. The cloud puppy glared at the shade, lips wrinkled as he growled softly.

"I see you managed to convince the creature to stick around," Drake said with a sneer.

"A little kindness goes a long way," I shot back.

Nimbus's growl deepened. A few of the werewolves, though in human form, echoed him.

I hadn't noticed that Drake was bound, his hands in front of him and his feet hobbled. He stood, but there was a chair placed for him.

"So, you've captured me. Well done. What are you going to do now? Torture me? You know I can't betray the bloodline."

"Bad luck for you, your bloodline turned out to be real shits," Oliver said, his normally soothing voice sharp with disgust.

"At least I still have my bloodline."

Oliver stiffened.

What on earth were they talking about? I realized I knew next to nothing about shades. Considering everything that had happened since I'd discovered their existence, I didn't feel too bad not knowing. I probably should find out, though. I was sleeping with one, and I was sure there were plenty of things I needed to figure out about vampires and werewolves that lore got wrong, but before meeting Drake and Oliver I'd never even heard of a shade.

"True. Though I'd rather be aimless than beholden to evil."

"I'd rather not have failed in my entire purpose in life," Drake snarled.

Before Oliver could reply, Davin interrupted. "Perhaps you should reconsider your allegiance."

Drake simply sneered.

"He can't," Oliver said.

"Well, we have some questions." Davin turned his full attention to the shade.

Unfortunately, Drake was unwilling to talk. It wasn't until Katsuro brought his mind control powers to use that we got any answers from the shade, and it took a great deal of work on Katsuro's part.

I almost felt sorry for Drake as the wolves took him away. He was shaking and sweating, and barely able to walk on his own. No one had touched him, but whatever Katsuro had done to get him to talk hadn't been pleasant.

The vampire didn't look a lot better, and he gave me a grateful smile when I sat next to him and took his hand.

Oliver sat on the other side of me, and I pressed my knee against his. He didn't look happy either, though there were many reasons why that could be.

Clare and Bridger had sat off to the side during the questioning.

"Okay, so, mostly we just confirmed our suspicions. Vito was working with that human trafficking group Hannah helped put away." Davin gave me a warm smile. "They were getting their humans from it and making a blood bank of sorts. He got to your DC contact, and we'll need to address that at some point, but it's not our immediate concern. They had hoped to use Nimbus to help their operation after you shut down their main source of blood. I am concerned that Drake thinks they can acquire another nimbus, but that is probably also not our immediate problem."

Nimbus grumbled unhappily. He'd been particularly upset at that revelation.

"What does it mean, though?" I asked. "They're rare, right?"

"Very," Katsuro agreed. "In all my years, I've only seen one other."

I thought back to Twister, and his promise that I would see him again. Perhaps sooner rather than later, Katsuro will have seen three. Though I didn't know my temporary guide well, I certainly missed him already.

"But they come from somewhere, right?"

Katsuro nodded. "It's long been thought they mostly live on another plane of magic and occasionally venture to our world. When they come on their own, they almost always bond with a human, and we suspect they like humans just as much as Earth dogs do."

Nimbus rooed enthusiastically and practically jumped in my lap.

I laughed and wrapped my arms around him. "I like you too, buddy."

"Okay, so we'll take that as a confirmation of that theory," Davin said with a laugh.

"So, if they've figured out how to get to their home plane, that's a problem, right?" I buried my fingers in Nimbus's ruff.

"If I may," Clare said. "I *see* a little in regard to this problem. I think their home plane is still inaccessible to the uninvited. I feel it more likely that they've found a way to trick the cloud puppies, or possibly call them, and with a bit more work, could reliably trap them. It is a problem we should address. They are beings to be cherished, not imprisoned. However, the first thing will be to deal with Vito and his gang. We must return to Beechworth."

"What are we going to do with Drake?"

"Keep him prisoner until all of the beings he's tied to are dead, then see what he wants to do," Oliver suggested.

Davin glanced at Katsuro, and they both nodded in agreement.

I glanced at Oliver, and he read the questions in my eyes.

"I will explain later."

That was good enough for me.

"The hour grows late," Davin said. "We will travel as a group in the evening, once the vampires can go out. Until then, rest. I have teams out patrolling, and hopefully by the time we are ready to leave, we'll have adequate transportation. Then you won't have to ride your nimbus." He smiled at me.

I actually liked giant Nimbus, but it was probably very tiring for him to have to carry me.

Oliver kissed my hand then stood. "I'll explain later. Spend time with Katsuro."

We all still needed to talk, but that could wait.

Davin had already left with a few of his wolves, and Bridger was guiding Clare toward the sleeping rooms. He shot me one last glance I couldn't quite read before he left.

"He does like you," Katsuro said, offering me a hand as he rose to his feet.

I accepted and let him pull me close.

"This is very strange for me. You know that, right? Four men?"

"You deserve all the love you can get," Katsuro said. "Though truthfully, I'm not inclined by nature to share. However, in this case, it makes sense on so many levels that even I think it is a good idea. Bridger may be the hardest to convince." He hesitated. "I still want you to accept my mark, and Davin's. It would be wise if Bridger would also accept them, though I'm not sure if he will."

"Wouldn't that make him subservient to you?"

"Only from an outsider's perspective," Katsuro assured me. "Now, about that raincheck?"

I was instantly and embarrassingly soaked. The needy gasp as my breath caught at the suggestion didn't help.

"I take it you're still interested." His eyes glinted with amusement.

"Yeah." My voice squeaked. What the hell, Hannah. A little decorum?

Katsuro's throaty chuckle just made me wetter.

"I would have thought you'd be satisfied from earlier."

"Damn supernatural hearing," I muttered.

"It didn't take supernatural ears." Katsuro continued to tease me.

"Damn it." I hunched my shoulders.

Katsuro gently led me from the room. Nimbus warbled happily, wagged his plumed tail, and trotted off to the kitchen where I heard more cries of dismay. The werewolves seemed constantly hungry and there was always food out. Nimbus was taking full advantage of his telekinesis.

"Do not fear," the vampire said gently. "No one is judging you. Werewolves especially are very keen on sex, and we're all glad Oliver was able to satisfy you. You're simply adorable when you blush."

That just made me redden more. "I guess I need to make up for lost time. I've been single for several years."

"Then we shall have to do a very good job indeed," Katsuro said sounding quite serious. "It will take all four of us to make up for your deprivation."

I mock glared at him. "Seriously?"

"Yes, sunshine."

By that time, we'd made it back into the basement, and Katsuro showed me into the room he was using.

"If it makes you feel any better, the soundproofing down here is quite good. I intend to put it to the test."

"Fuck," I muttered. "How long has it been for you?" I asked to change the subject, though I almost regretted it after his silence.

"A lifetime," he admitted after a while. "It is difficult to get close to someone when you're in my position. Many are simply looking for advantages. I prefer a more intimate connection."

"And you think you can have that with me?"

He grinned. "I already do."

I didn't press the issue as he took my hand and pulled me close. "No one trying to gain an advantage with me would call me out as you did. And I thank you for it."

Katsuro leaned over and kissed me gently. I returned the pressure, this time urging with my lips and requesting more.

The dance of our tongues and the melding of our lips drew me closer, and I wrapped my arms around Katsuro.

His lean strength reassured me, made me feel safe, as he held me in his strong arms.

"All right if I take your clothes off?" he murmured.

"Generally easier that way." I held up my arms and he lifted the shirt over my head. I hadn't expected a centuries old vampire to have the kind of consideration to ask when we were already clearly heading in the getting naked direction.

Once he had my shirt off, he deftly unhooked my bra and let that fall to the floor.

"Okay, I know they didn't have that kind of closure lifetimes ago," I said, poking him in the chest.

Katsuro laughed. "I do know how they work, sunshine. You are lovely." His fingers traced the sides of my breasts, teasing me as he studied my body.

Since my hand was already on his chest, I fingered the button on his shirt and glanced up for permission.

"Please."

I slowly undid his shirt, tracing my fingers down his front as I did so, feeling the planes of muscle under the soft dress shirt.

He rumbled softly, eyes lidded and thumbs lightly stroking the sides of my breasts as he enjoyed my touch.

Once I had the buttons undone, he quickly undid the cuffs and let the shirt fall to the floor to join my clothing. Then he kneeled in front of me, undid the button on my pants, and tugged them over my hips. He supported me with one hand, while he gently helped me step out of the leg.

Then he looked up at me, tracing his fingers up my thigh. "I'm out of practice, but I don't think I've forgotten everything."

"I'll tell you if you're getting it wrong," I promised with a grin.

"Then let me taste you, sunshine." He eased my legs apart and applied his tongue, gently at first, then more enthusiastically as I encouraged him on.

I buried my fingers in his hair, while he took one hand and palmed my breast. The combination of his mouth and the gentle way he rolled my nipple between his thumb and finger had my legs trembling, and I was grateful for his support, or I might have fallen.

As it was, my body sang from his attention, and shortly, I panted, almost whined, thrilled by the devotion this ancient being was paying me. My body tingled from head to toe, tight and loose at the same time, just about to fall over the precipice. I wanted it so badly. Even this was better than all my previous experiences before Oliver, and now Katsuro.

"So close," I gasped.

He slid a finger inside me and curled it, finding the right spot.

I shouted as I crashed over the edge, legs buckling. Katsuro's vampire reflexes kept me from the floor, and I lay in his arms, languid.

"You're not that out of practice," I slurred.

"Good," he whispered then carried me to the bed.

"Can I?" I gestured toward his cock, which I was anxious to have buried in me, but I certainly wouldn't mind having in my mouth, either.

"Next time. Right now, I want to be inside you."

"Oh, good, me too." I felt a little drunk and sounded like it, but damn that man had talented lips.

"Do you mind if I take a little more of your blood?"

"No."

Katsuro's anticipatory rumble almost put me over the edge again, and the predatory look in his eyes did the rest, triggering a mini orgasm that had me writhing on the bed.

He licked his lips, and kneeled between my legs, stalking me with his expression, making me feel like prey. And a willing prey I was, as the ache between my legs needed to be filled, and I desperately wanted his teeth in my neck.

These men were going to wreck me in all the best ways.

Chapter 32

Katsuro didn't wait long, running his hands down the outsides of my thighs as he kneeled between my legs, devouring me with his eyes. I grabbed his hands and tugged him to me, putting one on my breast and the other on my waist. Amusement combined with the predatory glint in his eye, and he leaned over me, taking his hand from my waist to guide his cock into me while gently kneading my breast with the other.

I was soaking from his earlier attentions, and it took little effort for him to slide in. I breathed out a sigh of pleasure.

"You are perfect," Katsuro said reverently as he moved inside of me.

The expression in his eyes turned from predatory to possessive with a hint of something else I didn't recognize. He watched me intently, shifting his angle at the minutest change in my expression as if he could nearly feel what I was feeling. Maybe he could? Or maybe he could read me that well. Either way, the intensity of his gaze combined with the accuracy of his movements filled me with all sorts of warmth, while sending tingles of pleasure all the way to my fingers and toes.

"Scream for me, Hannah," the vampire commanded me.

I obeyed, shouting as I came hard.

Katsuro rumbled in pleasure, then leaned over me, breath tickling my neck.

"Yes, please."

The sharp prick of pain followed by a flood of pleasure ripping through me, sent me over the edge again as stars exploded behind my eyes. A brief sense of deep connection followed, fading after a moment. But for that second, I felt his ecstasy as if it were my own, and I was sure he felt mine.

We sank down into the bed together, his arms wrapped around me, supporting me, protecting me, and in that embrace, I let myself pretend I was safe from the outside world and that these men would protect me and all I had to do was let them. It was a happy fantasy and I let it chase me into unconsciousness, content just to be held for a while.

***

The trip back to Beechworth was uneventful except that Bridger seemed to be avoiding me.

By the time I'd woken up, everyone was ready to leave, further delaying the discussion I needed to have with the three, or possibly four, men who wanted to be my lovers. We couldn't put it off much longer, but it wasn't like we were trying to avoid it, so much as circumstances were preventing us from having a quiet moment together.

Davin seemed in a fine mood, but Bridger, well, I just couldn't read him. I didn't even know if he truly was interested in me like that. Hell, maybe he was just upset about his house. I hadn't really had a chance to ask him if anything irreparable had happened to it. Or to thank him for his kindness in sheltering me there and everything else he'd done for me.

Why had he helped me? I'd gone from thinking he was a reasonably friendly and helpful nutjob who believed in the supernatural but couldn't actually prove it, to finding out he was right, knew he was right from past experiences, and that he had every right to be a little paranoid. For whatever reason, Beechworth had accepted Bridger as one of their own, just like they'd accepted me. He, at least, hadn't repaid them with a war.

Clare, since she had clearly sided with us, had declared that the bookstore would remain closed for a time so that she could safely stay within Beechworth's boundaries. Even that was my fault. Clare would be missing out on income because I'd come here. And I hadn't even come here for any reason other than that I'd heard rumors the place was different.

The only one who wasn't worse off because of my involvement was Nimbus.

After several days surrounded by others, being alone in my apartment with just Nimbus for company felt strange. Beechworth felt strange. Everything felt strange.

You would think after all the fantastic sex I'd just had, I'd feel amazing. And in many ways, I did. But it also highlighted what I had to lose. And what I'd brought to this community.

Nimbus shifted until he could lay down on my stomach and poke me with his nose.

"What?"

He poked me again.

I buried my fingers in his ruff and gave him a good scratching, but he grumbled and flopped his paw down on my nose.

"Buddy," I sputtered.

A cold draft blew through the room and Nimbus sprang up and pounced at it, much like an artic fox pouncing prey in snow.

"What?" I sat up and stared as fog swirled around the cloud puppy's feet. "What do you have?"

Nimbus growled.

I pulled out my phone and texted Oliver. Moments later, he knocked on my door. I got up and skirted around the fluffy dog while he continued to growl at whatever he had pinned. I let the shade in and dragged him to my bedroom.

"What on earth is he doing?" I pointed at Nimbus.

Oliver tilted his head before raising his eyebrows. "Ahh, he caught the ghost."

"What!" That was almost too much. "Ghost?"

"Yes."

"Why is there a ghost in my apartment?"

"I suppose it likes you?" Oliver went over to Nimbus and ran his hand along the fluffy dog's back. "It's okay, Nimbus, you can let it go."

The cloud dog growled, not moving.

"I don't think Nimbus likes it."

"It won't hurt you," Oliver assured the dog. "Or Hannah."

Nimbus's growl deepened.

"What did it do?" Oliver folded his arms across his chest.

Nimbus sat on the cloud of mist, still holding it down with his front feet, looked Oliver in the eye and rooed, and rumbled, and growled and yodeled for about five minutes. I started timing after the first minute.

Oliver's eyebrows rose.

Nimbus fell silent for a moment then as if saying "and another thing," barked a couple more times.

The shade's gaze went from the cloud dog's to the mist on the ground. Then his hand melted into shadow, he reached down and yanked the cloud mist ghost thing up and stomped out of the room.

I wasn't sure what freaked me out more, the hand shifting thing, the fact that Oliver apparently understood Nimbus enough to get angry at the ghost, or that the ghost had done something to piss off both the dog and the man.

Sitting on the bed, waiting for Oliver to return, I addressed my dog. "What was that all about?"

Nimbus huffed and flopped down on the bed next to me. I buried my fingers in his hair and wondered how I could get more fluent in the cloud dog language. Twister had spoken to me in the transitional place I'd gone to a few times, but Nimbus never had. Was it because he no longer had a body and Nimbus was still alive?

Oliver finally came back. "The ghost will not bother you again."

"Great. Thanks. What did he say?" I gestured toward Nimbus.

"He, rightfully, does not like that the ghost touches you without your permission."

"Oh." That got my eyebrows to rise. "Well, thank you both for protecting me." I had no idea what else to say. "Are you busy, Oliver?"

"No."

"Could you hold me for a while? After being surrounded by people for several days, my apartment feels very empty."

"Of course, Hannah." Oliver's eyes lit up with a smile and he scooted over next to me. After a short, awkward moment, we got ourselves arranged. I lay on the bed spooned between Nimbus and Oliver. The warmth chased away the darkness that had been trying to overwhelm me.

"Hey, you said you'd explain later. If you're still up for it, what was all that with Drake?"

"Ahh." He shifted as if uncomfortable but squeezed me tightly in reassurance. "Yes, I should explain that. You don't know the lore and it is important. Especially if we are to be bonded mates, or even just lovers."

"We are lovers," I protested.

"Well, yes." The press of his lips against my neck soothed me. "And as such, you need to know some of my history, and as the years go on, you'll learn more, but the relevant bits I'll share now. Shades are guardians. I don't know if you would call us a guardian spirit, or a guardian creature, or some sort of fae, but we are tied to a bloodline as guardians. If that bloodline ends, we are set adrift and have no purpose. Drake is tied to Vito's bloodline. Drake has been bound to that creature since before he was a vampire. I don't know if Drake was always evil, but he certainly is now. My bloodline died out. I believe I mentioned that once I had a mate and I lost her. She was tied to the other side of the bloodline. She and they were massacred. I only survived because I wasn't there. I should have been, but we thought one shade was enough and I'd gone off for the evening."

He fell silent, and I gripped his hand, squeezing tightly.

"A mistake that haunts me to this day. I no longer have a bloodline to guard, but this apartment complex is a substitute. It gives me purpose. And now, so do you."

"Oh, so you like me because I give you purpose?" I wasn't sure how I felt about that.

Oliver chuckled. "No, dearest. It's just a side benefit."

"Okay." I brought his hand up to my lips and kissed his knuckles. "So you're a guardian spirit. Nimbus is a super powerful magical dog. Davin is a golden retriever with bite, and Katsuro is… Uh." I lost the thread, unable to come up with something.

"Super powerful," Oliver filled in. "And Bridger. Yes, we'll have to think of descriptors for those two. Super powerful doesn't quite cut it for Katsuro, either."

"I need to find Bridger. I think he's avoiding me."

Oliver nodded. "That would be wise."

Before I could continue, someone knocked on the door, startling a bark out of Nimbus as we all sat up. There was something ominous about that knock, though I wasn't sure how a fist against wood could sound ominous. Angry, yes, or tentative, but foreboding just didn't seem to fit. Still, it did.

We went to the door, and I opened it. Bridger was on the other side, brow furrowed, mouth tight.

"Hey, come in."

His gaze darted to Oliver for a moment before he nodded, and we all went to the small kitchen and sat around the table.

"So, Drake escaped," he blurted out after a short, awkward silence.

And there went all my good feelings from earlier. I knew it wasn't going to be that easy.

"Well, fuck," I said.

Oliver and Bridger nodded in agreement.

Nimbus grumbled in annoyance.

"So, what do we do?"

"What can we do?" Bridger shrugged. "We just have to be ready for an attack."

Oliver held up his phone. "Katsuro has called a town meeting for just after dark. I suspect we'll have a plan of action then. If you'll excuse me, I need to go prepare." The shade left and an awkward silence fell between me and the hunter.

"So…" I said.

"So…" he replied.

More silence.

I buried my hands in my face. "Um, yeah, so we probably need to talk."

"You should let Davin and Katsuro mark you. And Oliver if shades do that kind of thing. It'll keep you safer." Bridger got up and headed for the door.

"Bridger, wait."

"Why?" He turned.

"What about you?"

"What about me? I'm just the crazy hunter."

Before I could protest, he was out the door.

"Damn it. Bridger!" I needed to catch him. We had to sort this out before things got worse. We kept getting interrupted before we could have that all important talk as a group, and Bridger might not even know we were considering him a part of the equation. At least until he said no.

Nimbus rooed and popped out of existence. I ran to the door and threw it open. Moments later, Nimbus returned dragging a reluctant hunter behind him.

"You're not *just* anything," I said as Nimbus dragged him back into the room. "And we really do need to talk."

Chapter 33

Bridger gave Nimbus an annoyed look but allowed me to talk him into staying. I made tea, though I felt like my selection was inadequate compared to what Katsuro and Oliver had gotten me used to drinking. I didn't even try to make coffee. I had instant and that wouldn't cut it. Even the diner had better coffee than that.

Once we had our drinks, I sat across from Bridger.

"Hey, so, let's talk about all of this."

The hunter tilted his head, giving me a quizzical look. "What's to talk about?"

"Well, for one, thank you for saving me. I'm sorry if your house got damaged in anyway and if I can help fix it, I will."

That softened Bridger's expression a little, and his shoulders relaxed some. He took a breath and wrapped his hands around his mug of tea. "It shouldn't be hard to repair. The werewolves already offered, too. And Clare had some ideas on extra protections. I'm just glad we could keep you safe long enough for the ritual to give you your magic."

I couldn't help grinning at that. "Yeah, it's pretty cool. While, uh—" I almost told him about Twister, but then thought I should keep that to myself. If nothing else, it required too much explanation at the moment. "Sorry. Yeah, I think the seed has completely unfolded, but I'm still learning how to use my magic. I think that will take a while."

"A lifetime, likely," Bridger agreed. "But now you have more defenses. You just need to practice. I think that's something we can all help you with."

"Thanks, Bridger. That means a lot that you're still willing to help me."

He averted his gaze, and his cheeks flushed. "Yeah, well, I still want to keep you safe."

"Anything else you want?"

That got a sigh. "What else is there, Hannah?"

"This is all really new for me. I didn't come here looking for anything except a safe place to hide from my past. I feel like I've brought all this crashing down on everyone here." I hadn't meant to go this route. I wanted to talk about our potential relationship.

"So, you weren't looking to get laid by mythical creatures?" Bridger winked.

"Uh, no." I snorted. "I didn't even know they existed. I just came here because the rumors said this place was interesting, and the FBI said it was safe."

"It should be safe," Bridger grumbled. "And before you start blaming yourself again, this conflict has been brewing for a long time. As long as I've been around, anyway. It'll be good to get it over with, honestly. Katsuro can expand his territory into Mayday Hills, and we'll all be better off for it."

"Okay." I clenched my jaw, but a cold nose shoved its way under my hand. I looked down at Nimbus and he perked his ears and wagged his plumed tail.

"See, even Nimbus agrees. Besides, where would he be if you hadn't come here? And we'd all be in a world of hurt if Vito had actually gotten hold of the cloud dog."

"They might be in danger still," I said, remembering what Drake had told us.

"Yeah, all the more reason to get this under control so we can protect the cloud dogs." Bridger reached over and pet Nimbus on the head. He avoided touching me until the cloud dog shifted slightly, making his hand slide into mine.

A tingle of connection rippled through my fingers and down my arm, driving into the well of energy I'd slowly been learning how to use after my unfolding. Bridger pulled his hand back, rubbing at his fingers as if he'd felt it, too.

Bridger arched his eyebrows, eyes widening. "I'm sorry."

"That was all Nimbus." I ruffled his ears again. "But that brings me to my other point. I'm not trying to talk you into anything you don't want, but um, Katsuro, Davin, and Oliver are all considering you part of the 'us' equation, too. Just so you know. You don't have to be, but, well…" I had no idea how to continue with that. It was awkward enough as it was.

"Why though?"

I reached out, palm up, asking for his hand. After a hesitant moment, he slid his into mine. The same tingle of magic joined us again. I caressed the back of his hand with my thumb and watched as his eyes shuttered.

"I didn't come here for anything but escape. I'm finding so much more than I expected. I know you're at least somewhat interested. The guys with the super senses told me, and I was kind of thinking you might be, too. They were just more forward and, well, I haven't really had a chance to talk to you since I accepted that I might actually be interested in more than just a hook up."

"If you're just interested in us because you're going along with what they want—"

I shook my head. "I'd considered that, because truthfully, other than enjoying the eye candy, I hadn't been thinking about anything except upgrading my toys when I had a chance."

That got Bridger's eyes to widen even more. He cleared his throat.

I grinned. "Don't be shy, Bridger. Toys are fun, some are even fun for everyone involved."

He choked a little and his cheeks were flaming. "I'm not experienced with toys, so I'll have to take your word for it."

"My last boyfriend opened my eyes to the possibilities," I admitted. "Unfortunately, we didn't work out in other ways. Well, maybe fortunately." I gestured vaguely to my surroundings. "Or I might not have ended up here."

"So we're back to being glad you came?" This brought a genuine smile to Bridger's face.

"Yeah, I guess. If nothing else, the point about saving Nimbus is very valid."

He grumbled happily in agreement.

"Well, if this conversation accomplishes nothing else, I'm glad I could do that." Bridger squeezed my hand. I hadn't let go yet.

"But to address your point, I am interested. I want this. Oliver is a sweetheart. Scary, but sweet. Davin is cool, though we've only gone on that one date, but he's done a lot to help me, and he clearly likes me. I like him, too. Katsuro is intense, but I like the way he melts for me and the way he trusts me, and I trust him. They're all scary, but they all want me, and I do want them."

Bridger nodded acceptance.

"Okay, so, on to us. I'm not saying we need to jump in the sack right now, but, like, let's consider the possibilities. We can go on some dates, see if we like each other."

Bridger stood, still holding my hand. He tugged me close when I didn't resist, then cupped my cheek. "I'm going to kiss you, if that's okay, Hannah."

"I—"

"I'm only human," he replied to my surprise. "If nothing else, I'm a lot more likely to get my ass killed in the conflict than any of the rest of you. I want to have at least kissed you."

"In that case…" I stepped into him, molding my body to his, and tilting my head up.

He lowered his lips to mine, and I melted into his kiss. Bridger was confident, firm but gentle, at first demanding, then soft and giving. I opened for him, and we explored each other. My heart picked up speed, and I pressed more firmly into his embrace.

The tingle of magic built between us, pulling a needy moan from my lips that Bridger drank with his kiss. He tightened his grip on my back, still cupping my cheek with his other hand.

For a time, the magic simply vibrated between us, but then Bridger shifted somehow and accepted what my magic was trying to offer him. I hadn't even realized I was doing it, but he apparently did.

"I accept," he murmured into our kiss.

My magic slammed into both of us. It was like an erotic ice pick to my core. Not completely pleasant, but certainly not terrible. My vision swam as my body shattered.

"Fuck," I gasped as we broke off our kiss and both went to our knees.

"I'm not sure I knew what I was getting into when I accepted," Bridger gasped.

"I didn't even know I was doing it."

"So, since you've marked me, what does that mean?" Bridger's eyes shone with amusement, and I felt acceptance between the bond we'd just forged.

"Well, I think that means I claimed you somehow kind of like Davin and Katsuro want to claim me."

"You should still let them."

"You might have to accept their marks, too."

Bridger tightened his lips but nodded. "Possibly." Then he grinned. "It'll kill them that we made our bond first."

I smiled. "We are all supposed to have a nice group chat about how we're going to make this work, but we keep getting attacked so we haven't actually been able to do it."

"Maybe we can do that tonight," Bridger replied. "And I am serious. Take their marks. Vito and his gang are no joke and the stronger we are, the better able to face them we will be."

"What if I don't want their marks?" I wasn't completely sold on the idea, after all.

"Then mark them like you did me." He grinned. "Just glad I got there first."

That pulled a laugh from me. "Okay. Hey, you're pretty all right, you know that?"

"Thanks, Hannah."

I leaned in, brushing my lips against his. He responded, deepening the kiss and crushing me against his chest, unbalancing us. We toppled over onto the floor, laughing and kissing until Nimbus woofed, alerting us to someone at the door.

Reluctantly, we pulled apart and headed to the door.

Davin was on the other side, about to knock again. His nostrils flared when I opened the door, and his expression darkened when he saw Bridger behind me.

Shit, we'd all been on board with this, right? Not that I'd made any sort of commitment to Davin yet, but his

236

expression told me he hadn't been as prepared as I'd thought to accept Bridger into our group. Or maybe he could sense the bond somehow.

"Hi, Davin," I said, trying to break his stare.

Bridger came up behind me and put his arms around my waist.

Davin growled.

Dakota Brown

Chapter 34

Nimbus saved me from having to deal with Davin's attitude directly. He trotted over to the werewolf, and by his jaunty walk accented by the wag in his tail, I could tell he was feeling mischievous.

He mimed lifting his leg on Davin. The werewolf growled at Nimbus then went back to glaring at Bridger.

Not about to be ignored, Nimbus, aimed and fired...

Davin yelped as the warm stream coated his leg. "What the fuck, dog!"

Having got the werewolf's attention, Nimbus crouched in front of us and growled, the sound reverberating through my chest as if a much larger animal had made the noise. His hackles were up, practically doubling his size with how long his fluffy coat was, and the number of teeth he showed was impressive.

The werewolf growled back, a sound that didn't normally come out of a human throat. He still managed to make it sound intimidating, but Nimbus didn't back down.

A shift in the shadows caught my attention, and I glanced over to my side. Oliver leaned against one of the walls, arms crossed but not interfering. Taking my cue from the shade, I waited and let Nimbus cow the werewolf. I had no doubt the cloud dog would win this confrontation, though I pulled on my magic in case I was wrong. If Davin even attempted to hurt my dog, he'd learn I had a whole level of crazy he'd never even come close to seeing.

The eye contact went on for a small eternity, and I could feel something going on between the two of them. As if they were pushing on each other with a magic I could barely sense.

Finally, Nimbus took a step forward, snarling.

Davin finally backed down. He didn't exactly submit, but he turned his head and relaxed his shoulders.

Nimbus stopped his growl, smoothed his hackles, and sat, wagging his fluffy tail.

I took a breath, and so did Bridger. When I checked, Oliver was gone.

"I was just coming to check on you. I see you're doing fine."

I raised my eyebrows, deliberately mimicking the eye contact Nimbus had used on Davin.

The werewolf tightened his jaw. "Right. So. You're okay?"

I took that as him backing off even more. "I'm fine, Davin. Do you want to come in? Rinse off your pants?"

Maybe I should have left the last bit off. A flash of anger passed across Davin's features before he schooled them into neutrality.

"I'll swing by my house," he muttered.

"I'm glad you came over to check on me." I stepped away from Bridger and came out into the hallway within touching distance of Davin.

The werewolf took a deep breath. "I apologize for my behavior. As Nimbus has rightly pointed out, it was uncalled for. We have clearly discussed this exact situation and said it was okay. I was simply surprised. The mark was unexpected." His voice was stiff, but not grudging.

"To be fair, Davin, we didn't expect it either. My magic apparently had a mind of its own."

Davin tilted his head and raised his eyebrows. "Both of you are coming to the meeting?" Though he phrased it as a question, it wasn't, and we all knew it.

"Yes, of course."

"Good. The five of us."

Nimbus grumbled.

"Six," Davin amended. "Need to have that conversation that keeps getting interrupted."

"We do. I just hope we don't get attacked tonight so we can actually have it."

That pulled a chuckle from Davin's lips. "Yes. Agreed." He took another deep breath and his energy settled completely. "Again, I apologize." He held out his hand to me, and I took it. Then he offered his hand to Bridger. The hunter took it after a slight hesitation.

"Accepted," Bridger replied.

Davin left. As soon as the werewolf was out of the building, Oliver stepped out of the shadows, laughing his ass off.

"It does a person good to see the werewolf get his tail pulled now and again," Oliver managed to get out between laughs. He wiped at his eye as if brushing away a tear.

Nimbus grumbled at Oliver.

"Of course, Nimbus. It was warranted." He rubbed the dog's fluffy ears.

"How can you understand what he's saying?"

Oliver shrugged. "It's not so much that I understand the words he's using as much as the intent. He apologized for peeing inside. Even if it was on someone who deserved it." He gave Nimbus another scratch. "And I apologize for eavesdropping, though I also believe it was warranted."

"Yeah," I agreed. "No worries."

"How did you mark Bridger? That's quite astounding."

"Um, I don't know. It was something with my magic. It just offered it."

"Excellent. Mark me."

This widened my eyes. "Um."

"Only if you want it. But I do."

I glanced at Bridger. He nodded encouragement.

After a quick look up and down the hallway, I stepped back into my apartment and gestured for Oliver to join us.

The shade followed, and we ended up back in my small dining area staring awkwardly at each other.

Nimbus nudged my leg, and I cleared my throat.

"So, uh, I was kissing Bridger." I blushed, wringing my hands.

Oliver took my hands in his and soothed away the tension. "Yes, that is good. Mates should kiss. Then what?"

"Well, my magic reacted to him." As if summoned by my statement, my magic rose and tingled across my skin where Oliver touched me. "Yeah, kind of like that. And then Bridger just, well, accepted it."

Oliver stepped close, one hand going to my cheek and the other sliding up my arm. My breath came short, and my heart sped as the heat from his body warmed me and the magic tingled through me. He looked deeply into my eyes, and I was caught by the intensity in his gaze and the absolute yearning to be marked.

"I accept," he murmured before pressing his lips to mine.

I returned his kiss, parting my lips and opening my heart. The magic rolled between us, melding us together as our lips danced. Though I was expecting it this time, the snap of connection between us still dropped Oliver and me to our knees.

Trembling, he held me tightly, and this time I saw the shine of tears on his cheeks. After a moment, Bridger kneeled next to us. He put a hand on each of our shoulders. The connection between all of us hummed with energy and sparked when Nimbus pushed his way into the middle, so he was touching everyone.

"See," Bridger whispered. "More powerful."

I shivered as I nodded. "I don't even know what to do with it all."

Nimbus grumbled, and this time I understood that he meant he would help.

"Thanks, buddy." I buried my fingers in his ruff.

"Okay, we should get over to the coffee shop. The sun will be down soon." Bridger stood, breaking the intense connection between the four of us.

Reluctantly, Oliver stood then held out a hand for me.

I let him help me rise, legs a little wobbly after all the emotion and magic.

"Yeah, we should." I rubbed my hands together, again. Nervous at how Katsuro would react to all of this. I knew Nimbus could take a werewolf, but a centuries-old vampire? That might be a different story.

***

The others, including quite a few vampires and werewolves, Mayor Henrietta Clifton—who was one of Davin's wolves, and Clare were already gathered when we made it over to the coffee shop. We'd gone to the back room, though there were guards watching all the exits.

That Katsuro merely gave Oliver, Bridger, and me an appraising look made me think that Davin had to have warned him. That helped my nerves some, and I focused on our current task, which was sorting out what to do about Vito's threat to the town.

We talked for hours without coming up with a real plan. However, I got the impression from my link with Oliver that he expected we'd form a specific plan once everyone left. The people we'd invited into the room were trusted, but then, we'd been betrayed before by someone who had been trusted. There were a lot of good ideas and intel thrown around and everyone agreed it was time to take the fight to Vito. We just had to figure out when, where, and how.

Finally, Katsuro stood. "Thank you all for coming," he began. "We have much to discuss and you have all given us valuable insight. Rest assured, our goal is to safeguard our community, and as it is now clear we must deal with Vito and his gang to do this, they will be dealt with. Not only were humans suffering at his hands, but our people have as well. He has made a direct attack against our own, and now he will pay."

That got a quiet cheer from the crowd.

"Be careful, watch your backs, and travel in groups. If you see anything, even if you believe you can handle it yourself, call for backup. We must know what is going on in our community and we want you to be safe. The time to strike against our enemies will be soon."

This was a clear dismissal, and everyone but my four men, Nimbus, and Clare left.

I moved from the chair I'd occupied in the back of the room to the far more comfortable couch. I could have taken it at any point, but I'd been happy to sit in the back. Bridger came with me, and I sensed the first hint of nervousness from him when he glanced at Katsuro. The vampire still hadn't reacted to my marking the others yet.

"It seems we have several things to discuss," Katsuro said once we'd settled into a smaller group.

Clare spoke up. "I'll leave you here in a moment. I simply wanted to congratulate Hannah on discovering another power. It is wise for you to be joined." She squeezed my shoulder, before casting a look at both Davin and Katsuro. "However you manage it." Then she left.

I expected that she was referring to me marking Oliver and Bridger, as opposed to accepting Davin's and Katsuro's.

The vampire was quiet for a moment before he nodded. "Clare is always wise. How did you do it?"

It was easier to talk about this time since Katsuro didn't seem upset, merely curious. Though I suspected he was not someone to play poker with.

"Bridger and I were talking about all of us and how we should at least consider the possibility of being together. So, like, you know, we were talking about going on a few dates and seeing how it went."

"I wanted to kiss her, at least once, in case I was killed. I am the most likely to end up dead in the fight since I'm only human." Bridger shrugged. "Her magic acted up and I accepted it. We ended up with some sort of bond or mate mark or something. You obviously know a lot more about those sorts of things than I do."

"And after I discovered it," Oliver said. "I wanted this as well. Hannah was kind enough to oblige."

"Very interesting." Katsuro leaned forward, brushing his fingers along my jaw.

The magic tingled faintly, rising at his touch. He pulled his hand away in surprise. "This didn't happen the last time I touched you."

"I have no idea, Katsuro. It just happened."

Nimbus grumbled.

"He believes it is simply time," Oliver supplied.

"I will accept your mark if you accept mine," Katsuro said after a moment.

That shocked the hell out of me. Also, it seemed fair. Was I ready for that? Well, I'd gone there with Bridger and Oliver. It seemed that maybe I should with the vampire, too.

"Okay," I agreed.

"Bridger, I offer you my mark as well. It will give you added protection and lend you some healing properties."

The hunter raised his eyebrows. "Let me think about it."

Katsuro nodded sagely. Then we all looked at Davin.

"I need to reflect," he answered. "The mate bond is common among wolves, but this"—he gestured at the rest of us—"is not, and I must consider my pack."

"Absolutely," I agreed. "So…" I returned my attention to Katsuro. "When?"

The vampire's smile was predatory. "Tonight, sunshine. After we finish making our plan of attack."

A shiver ran down my spine at his expression. He was the ultimate predator, and I was his prey, and he didn't want me to forget it. At the same time, I remembered how considerate he was of me, and how much he cared. Yes, I was his prey, but he was also my mate. He didn't want to consume me. He wanted to complete our bonds and strengthen us for the coming conflict.

And he wanted my blood. So, there was that.

Chapter 35

We had a plan. No one liked the plan, but it was the best we could come up with. Dangle some juicy bait, then pounce. We wanted to hit them hard, but somewhere that wouldn't create a lot of danger to the civilians, and we wanted to pick the battleground.

Now that we had that settled, we were going to have "the talk," and we were all uncomfortable as hell about it.

"So, how exactly is this supposed to work with all of us?" I finally broke the uncomfortable silence. We'd gathered either on or around the couch.

"Communication," Oliver said after a moment with an ironic twist to his lips. "Which, clearly, we are doing quite well with."

"We're here," Bridger pointed out. "That's a start."

"Okay, so we just have to set boundaries. Like, if one of us is having a date night, the others don't interrupt unless invited or there's an emergency." I hoped I was on the right track.

"I think that's an excellent boundary." Oliver shifted on his chair before setting a cup on the coffee table.

Katsuro nodded after a moment's consideration. "Yes. Perhaps we should set up a group calendar so the others know if we have something planned."

It seemed Katsuro, the ancient-ass vampire, was good with technology. I hadn't even thought of that.

"Good idea," Bridger said. "I think I can set up something that will be a little more secure than your average calendar sharing. We'll still have enemies, even after we defeat Vito. Maybe even more because your territory will expand."

"Good thought," Katsuro replied. "With this mark that we will all share, we should know if the other is in trouble."

Davin, who hadn't said anything since we finalized our plan, shifted uncomfortably.

"Yes, we know you still need to talk with your pack elders, Davin. Do not feel pressured into doing something you don't want to do. We can make this work even without."

"I will talk with the pack," Davin replied. "They have accepted Hannah on the assumption that she would take my mark. If she won't, or if my taking hers is a problem for them, I'll have to step away." Davin kept his voice neutral, but somehow, I could sense the hurt that caused him.

Right now, there wasn't anything I could say to make it better. I was accepting Katsuro's mark because he was taking mine. I don't know that I would have agreed otherwise. I had to be on somewhat equal footing with the two powerful men, otherwise I'd feel like a pawn. Of course, where did that put me with Oliver and Bridger? They had no mark to return to me, though Oliver had asked for this and Bridger had accepted before we'd really understood what we were doing.

This was all so damn confusing.

"We need to be open if something is bothering us," I blurted out. "Davin has made a really good start with his concerns, and we need to support that."

He gave me a guarded but grateful look.

"And, at least where our relationships are concerned, we need to treat everyone equally. Politics aside, this is a partnership." I hoped we could figure out how to navigate that.

"Katsuro, Davin, this is your territory. You've been good for the area. I have no issues with following your lead when it comes to politics and securing our peace here," Bridger said.

"And your input, whether you know we're listening or not, has always been valuable," Katsuro said with a smile.

Bridger ran his hand through his hair and tightened his lips before replying. "I guess I knew your people were everywhere. I'm glad you listened."

Oliver tilted his head, indicating assent.

I glanced at Davin, again. He had leaned back and seemed to be distancing himself from us. It hurt, a little. I liked Davin, and I knew he liked me, but if he couldn't handle the dynamic, it would be better to find out now than later. Still, the thought of losing him tore at me. Right now wasn't the time to address it, though. Later, when we would have a chance to talk alone. That would be the best time to talk to the werewolf. My memories of our interrupted date and how kind he'd been and how much he and his pack had done for me. Not to mention how blazing hot he was. Davin would make a good partner if we could work out everything we needed to.

Oliver squeezed my arm and Nimbus laid his head on my knee. I scratched the cloud dog behind his incredibly soft ears and gave my shade a grateful look.

"Well, it seems like we need to leave you and Katsuro to it," Bridger said, slapping his thighs and standing. "Katsuro, I will think about taking your mark."

Katsuro stood as well. "You are physically the weakest amongst us now that Hannah has powers. I'm not discounting your experiences or skills, but it would be best if you could heal more quickly. I will make a blood promise that I will not require subservience from you and will consider anything else you might require of me. I offer this only to strengthen you."

Bridger thought for a moment then took a breath. "Yeah, probably a good idea then. My hesitations are more based on my past, at this point."

"Your past?" Katsuro invited him to continue.

"Yeah, werewolves killed my mother. Tore her apart in front of me." He clenched his jaw before shrugging. "Obviously, it was a long time ago, and, clearly, I don't hate supernatural beings. I just never expected I'd find myself in a position where I'd want to tie myself to one, or several, yet here I am, bound to a witch and connected to a shade and soon a vampire. It's not terrible, just a mental shift."

"Ahh, my sympathies." Katsuro bowed slightly. "Though it was in ancient times, I also suffered many losses to vampires while I was a human. This, perhaps more than anything else, is what drove me to create my own power base and haven, so I could do my part to prevent others from experiencing the same fate."

Bridger and Katsuro shared a quick but meaningful glance that filled me with hope that we'd all be able to make this work despite some of our differences, though that he now considered me a supernatural being was a bit mind blowing. I'd been only human, but now? I guess I hadn't thought too much about it.

Oliver gave me a quick hug then he and Bridger left. We turned our attention to Davin.

"Hannah, we'll talk." He took my hands in his before bringing one up to his lips and kissing my knuckles.

I took that as a good sign, but a pained twinge curled through me as he left.

250

Katsuro offered me his hand. I let him pull me into a comforting embrace.

"He'll come around, Hannah. The pack dynamic requires he consult with his people before he does anything drastic."

"I mean, I have three of you. I shouldn't be greedy, right?"

Katsuro's chuckle rumbled through me, as I was pressed against him. "Nothing wrong with being greedy, sunshine."

"Okay, so how do we do this?"

"The simplest way is a blood exchange," Katsuro said.

I wrinkled my nose.

"It's not that bad."

"You're a vampire!"

"Well, yes." He kissed my hand much like Davin had. "But I promise, it's not that bad. Just a taste. And no matter what else we get up to," his voice dipped into the seductive ranges. "It does require a blood exchange. Even with the werewolves. So, we can just do the ceremony, or we can have sex after."

"Oh, I vote for sex."

He laughed. "No objection. Let's go someplace a bit more private."

"Like, do you have a lair or something?"

The vampire snorted. "No, though we do have an extensive underground complex under the coffee shop where the majority of my vampires live during the day."

"Oh, holy crap, that's so cool. Is it safe though? If the enemy knows where it is, could they attack you there?"

"It's likely that Vito knows where our complex is. It's a standard design in this part of the country. It is also very secure and comes with quite a few built-in protections. We're not helpless during the day, just inconvenienced."

"Okay, good. Just seems like having everyone in one place could be bad if someone had, like, I don't know, napalm or something."

Katsuro took a breath. "Yes, that could be a problem, but I think you will be reassured after a tour."

"I'm surprised you're letting me down there."

"You're to be my bonded mate, of course you can come down. Nimbus, too, of course." He squeezed me gently before shifting us so he could offer me his arm.

I accepted, and he led us out of the coffee shop's back room, the cloud dog on our heels.

Instead of turning toward the main dining area, he led me the other direction until we reached what appeared to be a utility closet. It even had all the necessary cleaning supplies. Another non-descript door led us out the back and into a plain industrial-looking corridor complete with florescent lights and chipped linoleum floors.

"We obviously need a utility closet anyway," Katsuro said. "And it keeps curious innocents from accidentally stumbling on something they shouldn't. There are security cameras and vampires monitor them constantly."

We turned a corner at the end of the hallway and a vampire lounged in a reasonably comfortable looking chair, idly poking at a computer keyboard. She looked up when we approached and stood, bowing.

"M'lord Katsuro."

"Shelby. This is Hannah and her cloud dog, Nimbus. Add them to the authorized list, please."

"Of course. Please, put your hand here." The last, she said to me.

A portion of the desk lit up in the shape of a hand.

"You are high tech here."

My vampire mate shrugged. "Of course."

I did as instructed, and she took a scan.

To my surprise, she repeated the process with Nimbus, her eyes alight with joy at seeing him. He consented to a scratch, then demanded another to her delight.

Then Katsuro placed his hand on the panel, as well, and the door behind her slid open. This was the start of the security that let me believe Katsuro was right in saying they were safe. It would take a literal tank to get through that thick metal door. I followed him through to an elevator.

"There is a stairwell, also, if needed, but the elevator is much faster."

He pushed a button, and we went down.

"Some crazy engineering must have gone into the construction of an underground complex."

"Yes. We've expanded over time, as well. Many of my vampires have modern, advanced degrees."

When we got to the bottom, the elevator opened into a scene out of a Victorian mansion. Except, the more I looked, the more I saw influences from many cultures, including a heavy Asian overtone. Which made sense since Katsuro was Asian.

"Who decorated?"

He smiled. "Everyone, really. It clashes a bit, but we like it."

I followed him through the heavy wood paneled corridors for a way, marveling at the treasures from around the world that everyone had displayed. We went down a wide flight of stairs, took a right and Katsuro led me through another door that opened into a cultivated Japanese garden, complete with robust plant life.

"The grow lights are mildly uncomfortable, and many choose to avoid the gardens, or switch the lights over to something a bit more vampire friendly while they are enjoying them. This is my personal space. A few others enter to care for the gardens, but I and they can tolerate the discomfort easily. I will introduce you to them at some point. They are my oldest companions."

I walked over the wooden footbridge and watched the koi dart underneath. The air smelled faintly floral, and peace pervaded the atmosphere.

"This is amazing."

"I'm glad you like it."

I glanced up at Katsuro. His eyes lit up with joy at my appreciation.

"This way. We will spend more time here and you are welcome any time, day or night."

Nimbus grumbled, dipping a paw in the water and staring intently at the koi.

"No hunting!" I scolded him. I didn't actually know if cloud dogs hunted or not, but I suspected from his interest, that they did.

He huffed, looking abashed.

"This way." Katsuro led us into his home. I didn't know much about Japanese architecture, only what I'd seen in movies, but this seemed to fit with everything I'd observed. He gave me a quick tour of the place. It was beautiful, everything crafted to perfection. His home was smaller than I would have expected from his position, but they did live underground so that might have been part of it.

In the dining area, he seated me at a low table where I sat cross-legged. Nimbus sat next to me and looked expectantly at Katsuro.

Katsuro ruffled the cloud dog's soft ears before leaving the room.

He returned a moment later with a delicate tea service. "A small ceremony before we proceed."

Though I didn't know the meaning behind his actions, it was clear each precise movement had a purpose, and I did my best to follow along with a few of his murmured instructions and match the gravity of his intent. He included Nimbus in the tea service, providing a not quite matching bowl that would accommodate the cloud dog's lack of thumbs. Nimbus was appropriately solemn for the event.

The vampire smiled approvingly at my efforts as we sipped the delicate tea. "If you want to learn, I will teach you some of my culture in the future," he offered.

"Yes, please. I'd like to know more about all of you."

His smile widened. "And, as much as you care to share your past, I'd like to know more about where you came from."

"When this is all settled."

Katsuro inclined his head.

Once we'd finished our tea, he helped me to our feet. "Nimbus, feel free to amuse yourself in the gardens, but please don't eat my fish."

The cloud dog held up his paw as if in promise before trotting toward the closed door and disappearing. I could see his silhouette appear on the other side of the thin walls and he wagged his plumed tail as he trotted back toward the garden.

"Now, shall we?"

I licked my lips partially in nervousness, and partially in anticipation. "Yes."

The vampire smiled, showing more than a hint of fang. He was clearly ready for this, too.

Chapter 36

Katsuro's bedroom was elegantly simple. The bed low to the ground with a deep green comforter that looked extremely soft. He had a low dresser along one wall, a taller wardrobe, all of simple stained oak, and another door that opened off to the side. Presumably a bathroom of some sort.

That gave me a moment of pause. Did vampires have plumbing? I knew he bathed, but was I going to have to get creative to go to the bathroom down here?

The vampire arched an eyebrow at my hesitation.

"Oh, just wondering about bathrooms."

He chuckled. "A fair concern. There are enough humans down here that we installed regular plumbing in all the houses. Take a look." Katsuro slid open the door I'd guessed led to a bathroom, and I looked inside.

"That's not just standard plumbing," I said with a jealous groan. "That's a freaking bathtub with jets that I could practically swim in." Not to mention a really nice walk-in shower big enough for at least two, and a regular toilet and vanity. Somehow the modern appliances didn't clash with the style of the house at all. He even had a wall of plants to help the feeling of being close to the outdoors instead of living under a ton of rock.

"Our water supply is an aquifer near here and we recycle extensively so that the majority of the water we use for frivolous things like a giant bathtub is reused."

"Nice touch." I smiled up at him before stepping back and letting him take me into his arms. I leaned against his chest while he held me. "The humans?"

"Willing," Katsuro replied. "Some are staff. Some are donors. Some are both. Well paid or otherwise compensated. A handful of families that have served some of the vampires for centuries live down here, as well. The only thing they must accept is that if they ever leave our service, they must allow us to alter some of their memories. They will still remember us, but not how to get into our domain or any of the secrets they learn down here. For example, the details about the security system."

"Oh. You didn't ask me?"

Katsuro smiled. "My dear, we're to be bonded mates. This is entirely different. Even if you were to move on at some point in your life, you would still be welcome here and trusted not to divulge our secrets."

"I see. I take it that it would be very rare for a bonded mate to leave?"

"Nearly unheard of."

"You sure you want to be stuck with me?"

Some of the uncertainty I felt must have shown through my voice. Katsuro briefly tightened his grip before turning me to look at him.

"I have never been more certain in my entire life, Hannah. You call to me in a way no one ever has."

The sincerity in his eyes and the solid grip of his hands on my shoulders helped convince me. "We've only just met." I protested one last time.

"Do you have doubts?"

Did I? After a quick moment of thought I shook my head. "No."

"Then why should I?"

"You're like this super powerful being, politically and supernaturally. I'm just me."

Katsuro leaned over and kissed my forehead. "You are more powerful than you know, and your powers will grow as you practice. In time, you may surpass me. I want to watch that discovery and aid you in any way I can. And even if you were simply a human, well, remember, I started pursuing you before you unlocked your powers. I want you, for you, Hannah."

I let myself be convinced. I knew I'd always be able to come up with excuses and reasons why he shouldn't want me no matter what he said. It came down to, this felt right, and I wanted it. I just hoped I knew what I was getting into.

"Okay. Let's do this."

Katsuro's smile was possibly the happiest expression I'd ever seen on his face. He gently cupped my jaw and kissed me.

My magic took that moment to flare up, winding between the two of us as it had with Bridger and Oliver. Instead of pulling away, Katsuro stepped closer, deepening our kiss and letting my magic flow into him.

The bonding took longer, as if my magic had to feel its way through Katsuro's own powers before finding a place to anchor, but I sensed the utmost patience and perhaps even a bit of joy from the vampire through that tenuous thread of connection as he let it penetrate to his very essence.

I kept my feet this time, but only because he was holding onto me. The elastic snap that traveled back through that thread of energy and slammed into me, binding us together was like getting hit with a rubber band. A massive one that pulled his love for me with the band of energy and sent it crashing through me. I had never felt anything quite like it, and it turned my limbs to jelly as the sensation sent tremors of pleasure radiating out from my core.

"Holy crap," I breathed.

Katsuro helped me over to his bed, and I lay down and stared at his ceiling.

He lay next to me, trailing his fingers over my stomach where my shirt had pulled up and exposed skin. His touch sent little tendrils of electric pleasure zinging through me.

"That was quite intense," he agreed. "Ready for round two?"

"Yeah. Should we get naked first?"

"If you would like, then yes, we should."

"You're going to have to help me. I feel like a wet noodle."

Katsuro shifted, planting another kiss on my forehead, before helping me undress. Then he lifted me into his arms, somehow managed to pull back the comforter and his sheets and laid me down.

"Oh my god, I need to get some of these." I was momentarily distracted from everything else by the absolute softness of his sheets.

"That can easily be arranged," Katsuro assured me.

"Cool. You want to get naked, too?"

He pulled his shirt off, shed his pants, and joined me on the bed while I marveled at how comfortable I was.

I sensed his amusement through our connection and poked him gently on the shoulder. "You know, I was reasonably well off before, but not so much that I could indulge in whatever this is." I gestured toward his bed. "These sheets must cost a fortune."

"We shall have to get you spoiled on some of the finer things in life, Hannah." The vampire shifted until he was propped up on one arm, looking down at me.

"I'd like that. So, how do we do this?"

"I will bite my wrist and let you have a taste of my blood." He grinned when I wrinkled my nose. "It won't be as bad as you think. Then, once you've had a moment, I will take a small amount of yours, and then, I assure you, we'll very much be in the mood for sex."

"Great!" I was onboard with that plan. "I'm already in the mood, if that wasn't clear."

He inhaled deeply, as if scenting the air. "Abundantly clear, sunshine."

Before I could delay us any longer, he put his wrist to his mouth and bit down. I winced in sympathy, but I didn't sense any discomfort through our connection. Only joy at finally having someone to join with.

More because of his happiness than anything else, I didn't hesitate when he offered me his arm. I licked the blood from his forearm and fastened my lips over the wound he'd created, drinking the blood he offered. Katsuro shuttered his eyes, a soft groan escaping his lips as I did. This quite obviously was not causing him any discomfort.

The coppery tang of his blood wasn't as unpleasant as I'd imagined, perhaps because his pleasure already filtered through our first connection, and I could feel the power in it as his magic mingled with my own and spread a warmth through me. The power wandered through my body much as mine had with his, not quite taking purchase, but still very noticeable.

I released his arm, and he laid me back on the bed, leaning over me, hunger in his eyes along with a burning desire.

"Still okay?" he asked.

"Yes." I offered him my throat.

His pause as he studied the lines of my neck and the soft hum of appreciation tightened things in my core, and I let out a needy moan.

When he leaned closer, I dug my fingers into his back. The ecstasy of his bite was immediate, and I cried out as he tasted my blood. The bond snapped into place, sending my mind reeling and my body exploding with pleasure. I got the barest sense of the depths of his memories and age before the energy settled between us.

Not sure if I said it aloud, or in my head, I begged him to make love to me. I needed him inside me, needed to feel him as completely as possible.

Katsuro responded, pressing into me, filling me, completing my need to be joined. He rested there once he was fully seated. I let him experience the moment before tugging urgently.

"Yes, my love," he whispered in my ear as he began to move.

Chapter 37

I wasn't sure how long we kept at it, or how many orgasms we had. It turned out that all Katsuro had to do to be ready to go again was take a brief rest and take another sip of my blood. We went for hours, and it was absolutely incredible. When we were finally somewhat sated, he gave me another taste of his own blood, which healed me from the mild blood loss and any other discomforts I might have experienced later from the marathon sex session, and then we both passed out in a post orgasm bliss.

When I woke later, Nimbus was curled up behind my legs and I was cradled in Katsuro's arms. The scent of food tickled my nose and made my stomach rumble.

The vampire stirred and took a breath. "I haven't slept that well in ages," he murmured, kissing my neck. A jolt of need coursed through me at his kiss.

"Shall we get you fed?" He ignored my hungry moan, which was probably just as well. We had things to do today.

"Yes, please."

Breakfast was porridge, some muffins, eggs, and bacon from the coffee shop, along with coffee, of course. After I'd eaten my fill, Katsuro gave me an extended tour.

I felt like I had been transported into an entirely different world as I moved about Katsuro's home. Yesterday, since I'd come down from the surface and still had that experience fresh in my mind, I'd simply marveled at the beauty of it now. Today, waking up down here, was a totally different sensation. The rest of the world felt so far away as we settled into a small sitting area and sipped tea in his small garden. We watched the koi swim lazily or come up for handfuls of food.

"This is so peaceful."

Nimbus rolled onto his back and presented me with his belly. I obliged by giving him a good belly rub.

"So, how exactly are you going to mark Bridger? I don't necessarily get the impression he's into guys."

Katsuro tilted his head, questioningly, before laughing. "I can probably tone the impact down a little bit. Perhaps it would be wise for you to be present and you two can handle the rest?"

"Well, we aren't sleeping together, yet. But I am certainly willing if he is."

Once I finished my tea, Katsuro took my cup and set the service on a tray. "They'll come and take it once we're gone. After this conflict is over, I will introduce you to everyone and give you a full tour of our underground home."

"Thank you." I stood and held out my arms. He wrapped me in a hug and sighed. Through our bond I could feel a great peace, and I let that sensation seep through my limbs as well.

"Though I'd rather stay down here and forget about the rest of the world for a while, as would be reasonable with a new bonding, we have responsibilities." Despite his words, Katsuro kept me tightly enfolded in his arms.

I rested my head against his chest and stood for a time, with Nimbus pressed against the back of my legs. Finally, we released each other and reluctantly headed for the surface.

264

***

Hours later, Bridger found Oliver and I walking with Nimbus. I hadn't had a whole lot of time to enjoy the local parks, and part of our plan was to establish a pattern of going on easy hikes now that we could pretend the initial danger was over. We knew Vito and his people would be coming after us again, but we hoped that they'd think we assumed we were safe now that Nimbus was fully mature as far as his powers were concerned.

I held out my arms and took him in a tight hug. Neither Oliver nor I commented on Bridger breaking our "rules" about being out alone.

"How are you feeling?" He studied me intently for a moment before falling in next to us.

We resumed our walk.

"Rested."

"Good."

He held out his hand, and I took it. Bridger gently squeezed my fingers, and the three of us walked in silence while Nimbus romped around us. The breeze tickled my skin and blew tendrils of hair in my face. I pushed my glasses up the bridge of my nose with my free hand before offering it to Oliver.

The smile on his face and his contentment I felt through our bond was all the peace I currently needed. Though Nimbus's happiness and Bridger's easy walk alongside me added to my good mood.

"Bridger, have you decided if you will accept Katsuro's offer?" Oliver broke the silence after a time.

"It is probably for the best," he answered. "I'm not totally thrilled by the idea, but Hannah has taken his mark and I've taken hers. If I can get extra protection by accepting as well, I should do it."

"Tonight, then?" I glanced at the hunter.

He nodded. "Tonight."

"So, you and I should probably have a talk first." I grinned at him.

"Oh?"

"Yeah, cause, uh, it's intense and, unless you're into guys, you will probably want me along."

Bridger raised his eyebrows.

"Not that you can't, uh, you know, just take care of the extra feelings yourself, if you want, but it's more fun with friends."

That got him and Oliver to laugh.

"Katsuro suggested it, but, you know, whatever makes you happy is fine with me."

"I mean, we've barely been on a date. Have we been on a date?" He wrinkled his brow. "I don't think evading capture counts."

"Right, but we're bonded. Though, if you never want to go that far it's totally fine."

"Why don't you two get ice cream? It's plenty warm and the parlor is quite nice. Then, you'll have been on a date together." Oliver grinned at both of us. "Problem solved?"

Bridger laughed again. "Hannah?"

"I love ice cream."

"Great!" Bridger brought my hand up to his lips and kissed my knuckles.

"I will leave you two alone, then," Oliver replied.

"We have to go past the apartments to get there, right?" I glanced at my shade.

"Yes."

"Leave us there. You're not supposed to be out alone either."

"Very well."

We continued on in companionable silence, and I couldn't help but bite my lower lip. It was either that or walk around with a stupid grin on my face. I was very excited to get my hands on Bridger tonight. Maybe I could even talk him into some time this afternoon after ice cream. That way, our first time together would be just the two of us.

I liked that idea very much.

***

Nimbus buried his face in the vanilla ice cream I'd gotten for him. I had a marvelous lemon-flavored cone and Bridger had gone with rocky road. The trees sheltered us from the afternoon sun while we lounged on a park bench.

Laughing as Bridger told me an outlandish story about some TV ghost-hunter-style humans who'd ended up at the diner and were convinced it was haunted. It wasn't as far as anyone knew.

I briefly thought back to the ghost that Oliver and Nimbus had chased out of my apartment, but my mate was a good storyteller and I soon got wrapped up in the tale.

Once Bridger finished and we had a good laugh, I fiddled with the last bit of my cone, trying to decide if I should bring up my idea about going back to my place. I was just about to say something when Nimbus's head shot up, ears perked, ice-cream-covered nose twitching as he scented the air.

Moments later, a bone-chilling howl rose up from the wolves' territory and abruptly stopped mid-cry. The sound didn't die; it simply stopped as if something had cut it off.

Bridger and I shared a look before we both jumped to our feet, the remains of our ice cream forgotten.

Nimbus grew to giant cloud-dog-sized and ducked his shoulder, grumbling at me to get on.

I climbed up on his back, grabbing fistfuls of his ruff. At Nimbus's encouragement, Bridger got up behind me. Then the dog bounded off toward the forest.

Belatedly, I hoped this wasn't some sort of trap, but if something was wrong with the werewolves, we had to try to help.

And if it was a trap? Well, we'd have to do our best not to get caught in it.

Chapter 38

Someday I was going to do this for fun. Riding on Nimbus's back was a treat I never could have imagined in my wildest dreams. Unfortunately, I'd only ever done this when we'd been in danger or someone else might be in danger, so I couldn't fully enjoy the experience. *Mental note, go for a ride on a giant dog sometime when you're not in mortal peril.*

Nimbus crashed through the trees and skidded to a halt at the edge of a large clearing.

"What the fuck?" I murmured.

"Shiiittt," Bridger said. "What the fuck is right."

The clearing was full of wolves, as if the pack had gathered to have a howl together or something. Except they were frozen. Not like, on ice, but immobile. An irritating current of energy thrummed through the air, and I opened my senses. I couldn't quite pinpoint the origin, but I did know that whatever it was, the energy caused the frozen wolves. Not only that, but as I looked closer, some of the wolves still wore shreds of clothing, and I guessed it had forced them to shift.

"What do we do?" I asked, already knowing the answer. We had to find the culprit and reverse the spell.

Nimbus growled, the sound vibrating through me.

"Yeah, buddy, right there with you," I replied, assuming he was thinking the same thing I was.

"Can you trace the energy?" Bridger asked while Nimbus backed farther into the trees.

We climbed off the cloud dog, and he shrank back down to his normal size.

"It's that way, but I don't know anything more than that."

"Good enough. Can you do anything to keep us from being seen?"

I considered before nodding. "Yeah, I'll do my best." Focusing, I drew my magic around us and concentrated on being invisible. To my vantage point, nothing changed, but I did feel the magic settle onto my skin.

Nimbus gave a full body shake but didn't otherwise complain. Bridger set off in the direction I'd indicated, skirting around the clearing full of frozen wolves. Nimbus and I followed.

It took me a while to notice, but the sky overhead, which had been a bright robin egg blue, was shot through with black. The shadows amongst the trees deepened, making it harder to pick our way and adding an eerie air to the statue wolves in the clearing.

"What the hell is that?" Bridger stared up when he noticed my attention.

"Hell if I know."

Nimbus rumbled, sounding disturbed.

By the time we finished our conversation, all the blue was gone, replaced by a deep black and plunging our world into darkness.

"You know," Bridger said in a deceptively conversational tone. "If I were a super powerful vampire with super powerful magic users at my disposal, I'd have them blot out the sun so I could attack during the day when my enemies were basically sealed underground."

I couldn't even find words to express the horror I felt at that idea.

"Do you think they'll attack the vampires?"

"No, but I do think they'll do their best to keep our vampires contained while they take over the rest of the town. And when they do let them out, it'll be a bottleneck."

"They have to have a backdoor." I wrung my hands together before shoving my glasses up my nose again.

"Well, we can't help them just yet. Let's focus on the wolves because we'll need them to fight the vampires."

"Good point." I took a deep breath and concentrated on freeing the wolves. We could do this.

***

It took a fair bit of time to get around to where I thought the spell originated. When we arrived, we found a large stone plaque flanked by four of Vito's men. One of them was a vampire I'd seen before. The other three I didn't recognize, but I thought they were human by their tanned skin. All four were armed with guns. None reacted to our presence, so my invisibility spell was working.

I took a moment to study the tablet. The three images on it were depicted in exacting detail, one, a human with their face twisted in agony. The middle image depicted a werewolf in "wolfman" form, roaring at the sky. The third showed a wolf collared and chained to the ground.

Even from here, without trying, I could feel the malignant spell radiating off it.

The three of us backed farther into the woods. The slight drain of the invisibility spell was starting to become noticeable. I'd have to drop it soon.

"They're armed and we're not," Bridger whispered. The vampire would hear it if my spell wasn't muffling sound, but I thought it should be or they would have heard us approach.

"Yeah. I'll see if I can make a shield spell. They won't expect us to attack head-on, right?"

Nimbus woofed softly, and I remembered he had powers, too.

"Okay, shield spell, then Nimbus does something. Maybe you can yank their guns out of their hands and toss them away?"

He rooed and wagged his plumed tail. I took that as agreement.

"I'll see if I can use magic on the vampire. What about you, Bridger?"

"Nimbus, can you get me one of the guns?" my human mate asked.

The cloud dog wagged his tail again, keeping it curled over his back in what I assumed was confidence.

Something in Bridger's tone, or maybe the feeling through our bond caught my attention. "Bridger?"

He shook his head. "Don't like killing humans." The hunter tightened his lips. "No help for it, though."

I put my hand on his forearm and squeezed. "I don't see a way around it. Maybe if I knew more about my powers…"

"It's not your fault, Hannah. They chose this life, and Vito chose this conflict, not you."

I took a breath and nodded. "Yeah, okay. I'll try to remember that."

My hunter smiled and winked. "Just remember, fluffball here would be in their hands if you hadn't done everything you did. We're all way better off."

He was right.

I shut my eyes and focused on the strongest shield I could form and put it between us and the bad guys. After a quick glance at Bridger, we jogged toward the bad guys.

I couldn't keep up both spells, though I did my best to hold onto the invisibility as long as I could, but it dropped about the time we reached the vampire and his goons. Fortunately, the vampire hadn't expected anyone to sneak up on him, and we caught them completely off guard.

One of the men got a shot off at us, and the bullet ricocheted off the shield spell. Nimbus rooed loudly as he snatched the guns out of the humans' hands.

The vampire managed to hold onto his but the look on the humans' faces was comical as their guns sailed away before landing at Bridger's feet.

He kneeled and grabbed two of them. I took the third before losing hold of the shield spell. Fortunately, Nimbus had control of the situation. He stirred up a whirlwind right in front of the vampire, deflecting the rapidly fired bullets up and away with his powers. When the vampire's slide clicked open, I fired two shots to distract him while I desperately tried for a sunlight spell.

Sparks flared out in front of me and wrapped themselves onto the vampire, seemingly sticking to him as he screamed in agony and tried to brush them off.

While I focused on the vampire, Bridger took out two of the humans with well-aimed shots. The third human, seeing that things weren't going in his favor, turned and ran.

Nimbus almost seemed to laugh as the human tripped over something and went sprawling into the dirt.

Bridger chased after that human, while I ran over to the vampire.

He thrashed on the ground, but the sunlight spell wasn't killing him, just distracting him. Feeling like an absolute shit, I took careful aim and unloaded my gun into the creature's head.

It worked, and the vampire disintegrated into dust.

"Fuck." I fell to my knees and heaved. While this wasn't the first vampire I'd killed, this felt different. He hadn't been in a position to defend himself, and I'd killed him anyway. Not that I would have been able to keep him contained, but still…

Bridger came back, dragging the third human.

I wiped my mouth and had just enough magic left to fashion some ropes before my powers slipped from my fingers.

My hunter trussed up the human and tossed him to the ground.

Then he and Nimbus came over to me.

"You did the right thing, Hannah," Bridger said, pulling me into a hug. Nimbus pressed against me, and they let me sob for a few moments. Knowing we didn't have a lot of time, I pulled myself together and got to my feet.

"Thanks. I'll finish my breakdown later. We need to rescue the wolves."

Bridger gave me one last hug before we turned to stare at the plaque.

"Well, that's horrific." I reached toward it, fingers spread.

"Don't touch it!" Bridger grabbed my shoulder.

Nimbus growled and tugged on my sleeve with his teeth.

"I wasn't going to touch it, promise." I brushed against the tablet with threads of my magic before recoiling. The magic of the tablet grabbed at my own as if trying to drag me in. "Not that we didn't know this, but that is definitely the source of the spell affecting the werewolves." My intuition told me destroying it would free the werewolves, but how? If I couldn't touch it with my magic, I certainly couldn't touch it with my hand, and I was about out of juice as it was.

Nimbus grumbled before bumping into my legs and pushing me back. Bridger and I allowed ourselves to be herded away by the dog before he turned to face the tablet.

He looked back over his shoulder at us and woofed, his ears disappearing into his floof for a moment as he flattened them to his head before giving us what seemed to be a significant look.

Taking a guess, I covered my ears. Nimbus rooed approval before turning back to the tablet.

Glancing at Bridger, I saw he had his ears covered, too.

Nimbus again increased his size to giant dog and roared at the tablet.

Even with our ears covered the sound was deafening, but not so loud that I didn't hear the crack of the tablet shattering. Or maybe that was an effect of the magic breaking. I wasn't sure, but when I opened my eyes, the magical energy was evaporating, and the stone tablet had fractured into hundreds of tiny pieces. As I watched, those pieces disintegrated into sand before disappearing.

"Good boy, Nimbus." I wrapped my arms around Nimbus's leg, hugging the giant dog.

He rooed happily then shrunk back to his normal size before laying down at my feet, eyes fluttering shut.

"Well, guess that's it for him," Bridger said, kneeling next to the cloud dog and burying his fingers in the dog's ruff just like Nimbus liked it. "Good boy, buddy."

"Yeah, he did a lot for such a young dog. We'll have to carry him." I wasn't looking forward to that, the little guy had grown a lot in the short time I'd known him.

"Let's get him over your shoulders. That'll be the easiest."

Bridger helped me lift the sleeping cloud dog and drape him over my shoulders like a fluffy stole. He wasn't too heavy like that. By the time we got Nimbus sorted, angry growls and yips sounded from the clearing.

A little nervously, I went to look. The wolves were all shifted, and they all turned to look at me almost as one. One of the bigger wolves—I thought it was Davin—trotted over to me, rubbing against my legs before sniffing at Nimbus. Then he spared a glance for both Bridger and the trussed human.

"He broke the spell after we found you. Somehow, they're blotting out the sun. I think the vampires are attacking town. I guess I didn't have to play bait after all." So much for our plan to draw the enemy out and pick the ground for our fight.

Davin grunted before barking, literally, commands at his wolves. Two fell in with us, two more flanked the captured human, while the rest faded silently into the woods, heading toward town.

"Okay, so now what do we do about the darkness? If they've committed all their vampires to this attack, we're going to need something to fight them. Werewolves are good, but until we can get our vampires above ground, they're going to be seriously outnumbered."

Bridger nodded. "Is there someplace safe we can take Nimbus?" He addressed the wolves.

The lighter blond one nodded and trotted off into the woods. We followed.

Chapter 39

The werewolves led us to a small cabin. As this was their territory, I suspected it was less a hunting cabin and more a place for them to crash after a particularly tiring day running as wolves or gorging on deer.

After a quick note that the cabin was adorable and well-constructed, I followed the wolves inside. I'd gawk later. We had lives to save first. The door latches were levers, and the wolves easily worked the mechanism with their noses.

One wall of the cabin had several large bunks with comfortable looking beds. I lay Nimbus on the bottom one. He woke up long enough to make a nest with the comforter and the pillows before he was snoring softly in that adorable way only a dog can manage.

"So, what do we do?" I turned to Bridger.

The werewolves both gave full body shakes before shifting back to human form. I averted my gaze to give them a bit of privacy. My assumption that this cabin belonged to the wolves was further strengthened when the man grabbed some sweats out of a cabinet and handed them to the woman before dressing himself. I hadn't had time to meet all of Davin's wolves with everything else that was going on, but these two looked familiar. I couldn't place their names, though.

"Now, we figure out how to bring the sun back," Bridger answered.

"Yes, that has to be our main priority. Davin will be hunting the magic caster, but without vampire backup, we may be outnumbered," the male werewolf confirmed.

The pressure of their gazes as they studied me was almost too much. I turned away and hunched my shoulders, trying to think. With a little rest, I could likely create more sunlight spells, but that was a very small thing with as big as this fight was.

As I racked my brain for ideas, the feeling that I needed to meditate tickled at the back of my thoughts.

"I need a minute." I sank to my knees and focused on my breathing until I could turn my thoughts inward and chase them down into the transitional place where I'd unlocked my magic and met Twister.

I found myself walking down a path between a forest of apple trees, branches heavily laden with fruit. I picked one and took a bite. Crisp, sweet flesh crunched between my teeth, and flavor exploded in my mouth. By the time I'd finished the apple, I reached the end of the pathway. A round door I'd never seen before stood in my path. It was golden with coppery highlights flickering along the surface as if sunlight played over the surface.

Approaching, I clasped my hands together in front of me. "We need help. The vampires are attacking my friends, and they're hurting countless people and beings besides those of us in Beechworth. I'm not practiced enough to do this alone. Please?"

I bent over and put my hand on the round brass knob, feeling its smoothness under my fingers and the warmth that radiated out from it, and the door. I didn't fear anything in this realm, but I hesitated to open the door. With no idea where it led, I just hoped the answers I needed were on the other side.

Taking a deep breath, I slowly twisted the handle.

The door opened inward under its own power, and I released the handle. I got the impression I wasn't supposed to go through the door, but to wait. It wasn't a human-sized door—unless that human were a child. The light through the door flared blindingly bright, and I averted my eyes until it faded.

When I blinked the sparkles from my eyes, the door had vanished. In its place sat a dog. This dog had a boxy face with a long snout, floppy ears, and short, burnished golden brown fur. She wagged her tail, thumping it on the ground.

I held out my hand, and she came forward and pressed her head under it for pets. She radiated warmth much like the door had. If this obviously magical dog had anything to do with sunlight, I wouldn't be surprised.

"Are you going to come help us?"

The dog nodded.

"Thank you." I scrubbed her ears again then took a step backward, intending to retrace my steps to my body and consciousness.

Instead, I was jerked back. I snapped my eyes open to see Bridger shaking me.

"Sorry, Hannah. We just got word from Beechworth and it's bad. We need to go. If nothing else, we might still need to use you as bait."

"Great," I muttered.

"I will stay with Nimbus," the man said. "I will guard him with my life."

"Thank you." I didn't want to leave him, but he'd likely be safer here than with me.

After a moment, I remembered what I'd seen in the transitional place and looked around, but I didn't see the dog anywhere. Pushing away the feeling of disappointment, I went outside and immediately felt like an ass. The dog waited for me at the door, tail wagging.

"Hello." I ruffled her ears, and she dropped her jaw in a doggy grin.

"Who's this?" Bridger asked.

"She answered my call for help. Otherwise, I don't know."

"Good to meet you." Bridger also gave her a scratch behind the ears then we fell in behind the female werewolf and headed toward town.

***

"Fuck," the werewolf cursed.

It didn't look good. The darkness had allowed Vito's vampires to come out and play. All the streetlights had come on with the unnatural darkness, illuminating a line of heavily tinted cargo vans waiting in the streets of downtown. I guessed that was how the vampires traveled. Now they were loading captured townsfolk into them. Many were people I recognized from the various shops around town. They were not combatants. The screams and shouts of battle sounded from the direction of the coffee shop.

"We have to stop the vans." I pointed at them urgently.

Before I could say more, the new dog burst into motion. She sprinted out of the underbrush we crouched in and sped toward the nearest vampire. The dog was astonishingly fast, and she skidded to a halt in front of the vampire.

He turned and glanced at her before baring his fangs. Instead of being intimidated the dog opened her mouth but instead of a massive bark, blindingly bright light poured from her open jaws.

The vampire didn't stand a chance. He went up in flames, screaming out his death as others looked his way. At first his companions didn't seem to understand what was going on, but after the dog unleashed her weapon on the next vampire, they clued in. 'Panic ensued' was a mild way of putting how the vampires amongst the enemy reacted to a dog wielding literal deadly sunlight. The less-impacted members of the party managed to switch their focus to attacking the dog, but the vampires scattered.

For a moment, I was worried about the dog's safety, but she skillfully evaded each attack. As the vampires scattered, wolves came out of hiding and attacked. Others shifted to human form to help rescue the captives.

"Okay, so, let's head toward the coffee shop." I glanced at Bridger, and he nodded, so we hurried in that direction. "Wait, do they get cell reception when they're underground?"

"I don't know. I haven't spent that much time texting Katsuro."

I dug out my phone and called Katsuro.

The call went to voicemail. "Damn. Either they don't, or Vito had one of his goons take out their connection."

"Probably the latter. Katsuro strikes me as the type to want internet access for his people. If nothing else."

"Yeah." I sent him a quick text letting him know what was going on, just in case, before turning my attention back to our surroundings.

Though it was darker in this part of town, we got to Oliver's apartments with little trouble. The main fighting surrounded the coffee shop, and we could see what was going on while remaining crouched in the shadows.

I guessed that quite a few of the enemy were inside the coffee shop trying to get through to the sanctuary. Or, at least, they were keeping the entrance blocked while the rest of Vito's people took over the town.

While we watched, Vito himself, with several vampires and Drake, his shade, came out of the coffee shop.

It seemed as if Davin and a few of the others had been waiting for this opportunity. They charged out from wherever they'd been hiding, a few in human form, most in wolf. Oliver slipped from the shadows and launched himself at Drake.

My heart was in my throat as I watched them struggle. With their shadowy natures and the unnatural darkness, it was more that I caught flickers of them as they blocked out the light.

Davin and the other wolves went for Vito and the other vampires. I thought they were going to succeed, but then Vito pulled out a gun, and he was vampire-fast and deadly accurate.

Two of the wolves fell without a sound, reverting to their human forms. Davin took a hit and fell back, shouting in anger and pain.

"I really wish I had my rifle," Bridger muttered.

I wished he did, too.

Vito leveled the gun at Davin. The other wolves backed off. Oliver had Drake in an arm-lock. He let the shade go when Vito pointed at them.

As though I were glimpsing the future, I could see what events would unfold if nothing changed. Vito would kill Davin with the silver in his gun, then Drake would get the upper hand with Oliver. They would find Bridger and me and kill us. Nimbus would be in danger again, and my vampires would fall. All of that would happen if I didn't do something in the next few moments.

But what? What could I do against an ancient, powerful vampire?

I had no time to think, so I did the only thing I could. I played bait, or at least a distraction.

"Hey!" I shouted as I raced toward them.

I wasn't in bad shape by any stretch of the imagination, but it had been a long day, and I wasn't a runner. Still, I made good time and had everyone's attention. Davin held his hand to his side and stared at me as if he couldn't quite figure out what I was doing.

Bridger shouted something, and Oliver, well, I could feel his terror through our bond. Drake grabbed him before he could come to me.

I just hoped that the dog with the sunlight powers would catch up before this latest idiocy got me killed.

Gasping, I stumbled to a halt between Davin and Vito, his gun now pointed directly at me instead of the werewolf.

Davin growled unhappily, but there wasn't anything anyone could do.

"I'm pretty sure you want me more than you want some werewolves. Looks like you've won. There's nothing we can do against your magic and your vampires. Why don't you let Davin go?"

"My dear, you're in no position to bargain," Vito began.

Just then I felt a soft brush of fur under my hand on my left, and a vibrant warmth on my right. The dogs had arrived.

"I think I am," I shot back. "Let Davin go, and I'll tell Nimbus to back off. You can get your revenge on me."

"You make no mention of the vampires?"

"I think I'm more valuable to you than the werewolves, but I doubt you want me more than you want Katsuro."

Vito chuckled. "You are surprisingly clever and wise for a human. Maybe I'll turn you and make use of you that way."

I didn't bother to hide my shudder. Vito studied me, his oily gaze coating me in an imagined filth as he surveyed what he thought would be his next prize.

Nimbus rooed softly, and I sensed him gathering his energy. The new dog huffed, and before Vito could agree or disagree with my terms, they attacked.

Nimbus yanked Vito's gun skyward with his powers. The new dog dashed forward, blasting the vampires with the sunlight pouring from her mouth.

Davin grabbed me and dragged me away from the fight. "You're crazy, Hannah," he snapped, now sheltering me with his body.

"It worked."

"Where the hell did you get a sunlight-puking dog?" Davin shoved me around the corner of the coffee shop.

I snorted but otherwise didn't answer. There would be time enough for questions later. Especially since I wasn't exactly sure myself.

"Stay here. They still need me." Davin glanced at me, and I nodded. The werewolf dove back into the fight. I peered around the corner, watching and grabbing for my magic. If I was recovered enough, I might be able to help.

Bridger had used my distraction to join the fight. He and Oliver were guarding each other while they fought the vampires. The new dog's sunlight weapon was devastatingly effective, and the coffee shop had emptied as Vito called more vampires to shield him. He sported burns but was too powerful to simply kill that way. Too bad.

"Nimbus!" I called my cloud dog to me.

He popped into existence next to me.

"We need to see if we can free our vampires."

He rooed in agreement.

Hoping the guys and the sunlight dog had the battle in hand, I crept back and headed for the service entrance.

Nimbus trotted along ahead of me, his tail curled over his back.

When we got to the service entrance it was predictably locked. I pushed on the door a few times just to make sure and pulled once. Nothing.

Nimbus huffed before vanishing. Moments later, he pushed open the door, front paws on the crash bar. His teleporting abilities were handy.

I slipped inside and we let the door close behind us. Emergency lighting gave just enough illumination that I could see. Nimbus knew where we were going, too, so he led the way as we crept through the hallways. We would likely run into at least one vampire, and I prepared myself as best I could to fight them.

The hallways were empty, but the storage closet that led to the entrance wasn't. They knew I was coming, so I charged in and blasted outward with my own version of the sunlight spell. Vampires screamed as the motes stuck to them and burned.

Nimbus kicked up with his wind powers, clearing a path, and I ran through while they were distracted.

In the entry room where the control pad was, I saw two more vampires. I blasted them with the sunlight spell and, hoping I wasn't making a mistake, slammed my hand down on the pad.

Nimbus stood at my side, pelting the vampires with torrential wind to keep them back.

A speaker crackled.

"It's me! Hannah!" I shouted. "We have them distracted."

The doors glided open, and an entire horde of very angry vampires boiled through.

They moved quicker than I could follow, but flickers of color and form blurred past me. Nimbus dropped his wind attack and sank to the ground. I kneeled next to him, burying my fingers in his ruff.

"Very good boy." I hugged my cloud dog close.

Jaz appeared next to me, practically out of thin air. "Go below. We will handle the rest."

Before I could agree or disagree, she was gone and the wind of the enraged vampires passing faded. The door slid shut, but I suspected it would open for me if I put my hand on the reader. I didn't want to simply hide, but I knew I was out of power. Really, what else could I do but get in the way. Though one thought did occur.

"Nimbus, that new dog, she needs to know that some of the vampires are friends."

He huffed, ears perked, tail flagging over his back in alarm before he ran off and vanished. The cloud dog would warn her. As soon as he came back, we'd retreat below to rest and wait.

All in all, a solid plan. Until Drake swirled out of the shadows next to me.

"Shit!" I grabbed for any thread of magic I had left, but it was gone.

The shade's hands closed on my arms in an iron grip I had no hope of breaking. Still, I tried, using all the techniques the FBI had taught me. They would have worked against a human, but Drake was nearly as strong as a vampire, or so he seemed at that moment.

He twisted one of my arms up behind me and wrapped his arm around my throat, cutting off my air. Either would have been enough to subdue me. I went still.

"Let's go end this, shall we?" he hissed.

With no choice in the matter, I let him drag me out through the coffee shop. I thought about one last attempt at freedom, but Drake nearly dislocated my arm, and I gave up. This time, someone was going to have to save me.

Chapter 40

Feeling worthless as the enemy shade dragged me out through the front doors of the coffee shop, I was at least glad to see all my men still alive. They had the upper hand, until they saw me.

The sky was lighter now, but dark enough for the vampires. It had gotten late while we'd fought, and they must have dropped the magic blotting out the sun. And this day had started so good, and now I felt completely hopeless.

Katsuro had Vito on his knees, Davin held a gun on someone else who might have been the mage from the aura of energy circling her, and many of the others were on their knees with their hands behind their heads. Oliver and Bridger weren't in my line of sight, but I could sense them, so they weren't dead, at least. Not yet, anyway.

I didn't see the dogs.

A faint thread of hope that they could save us one more time was the only thing that kept me from weeping in despair. Logically, the guys shouldn't trade their victory for me, but I, and Drake, knew they would.

Everyone froze when Drake pulled me out into the twilight gloom and cleared his throat loud enough for the supernatural beings to hear.

Then Vito laughed. He started to get up, but Katsuro shoved him back down.

Drake twisted my arm harder, and it took everything I had not to shout in pain. I did end up on my toes, trying to keep him from dislocating my shoulder. Katsuro must have sensed it through our bond, however, and he stepped away from the other vampire.

"And still, you lost," Vito said as he finally got to his feet. "All that effort, all those lives lost. If you had simply cooperated…" The vampire's head evaporated in a red mist, and the rest of him crumpled to dust moments later.

It took a moment to process what had just happened, and then chaos broke out once again. I jerked away from a suddenly unresponsive Drake and sprinted toward Katsuro, since he no longer had his hands full with the other vampire. Davin still had the magic user pinned, and with the loss of Vito, it didn't take long for the others to fall into line.

The vampire tucked me against his side with an iron grip that let me know he had no intention of releasing me any time soon.

Oliver and Bridger joined us after a bit. Bridger had a rifle slung over his shoulder.

"Oliver was kind enough to get my rifle," he said. "It seems he can slip through the shadows with objects though it takes a little longer. I thought about taking out Drake instead of Vito, but I was loaded for vampire, and based on what Oliver had told us, I thought taking Vito out would also incapacitate Drake."

He was right. The shade lay on the ground moaning softly, not responding when a pair of werewolves went over to drag him over to the rest of the captives.

Nimbus and the new dog trotted into view, looking pleased with themselves, tails wagging.

Katsuro and several of his other vampires gave the brown dog wary looks, but she seemed content to return to my side. Sitting opposite Katsuro, who still held me.

When Nimbus saw the ring of captives, he got a look in his eye I could only describe as mischievous. He rooed, then grumbled happily, before expanding to his giant dog size. He had to be exhausted after everything he'd already done. What could possibly be worth expending more effort?

Wagging his now giant plumed tail that he had tightly curled over his back, he trotted toward the captives, turned sideways to them, and lifted his leg.

I didn't even try to stop him, though I did wrinkle my nose at the pungent smell of a large quantity of male dog pee.

The cries of dismay from the captives got me laughing.

Bridger chuckled. "He's got a good point."

Oliver kneeled and held out his hand to the new dog. "Hannah, where did you find a sun dog? They're even rarer than cloud dogs."

She trotted forward and shoved her head under his hand for scratches.

"She's lovely." Oliver sounded positively enchanted as the sun dog pressed against his chest with her body. She'd remained reserved, if friendly, with me, but she did seem to like Oliver quite a bit. Ironic, considering he was a creature of shadow.

Katsuro cleared his throat. "Yes, her assistance was key in overthrowing Vito."

She turned her attention to Katsuro, and he flinched before bowing formally. "My thanks."

The sun dog huffed and wagged her tail before again burying her face in Oliver's chest.

"I think she likes him," Bridger said.

Nimbus, bladder empty, shrank back to his normal size and trotted over to us before laying down at my feet.

I managed to dislodge Katsuro enough to kneel and hug my dog. He'd done so well, and I murmured into his thick mane just how proud I was of him while tears leaked from my eyes.

"I suppose I should be glad he didn't get huge before he pissed all over my leg," Davin said coming up to us.

That broke through my tears, and I laughed.

"Hannah, you have done so much this night to save all of us. You, Bridger, Nimbus, and our new friend. We still have a great deal of cleanup to accomplish, but I would rest better knowing you were truly safe. Would you please take Nimbus below and get rest?" Katsuro took my hand and pressed his lips to my knuckles.

"I was going to, when Drake showed up and ruined that plan," I admitted. "Jaz told me to go below."

"There is no blame or fault. You did the best you could, and truthfully, none of us would be here if not for you. Go. Rest. Once all these creatures are dealt with, we can go back to more pleasant pursuits."

I knew what he had in mind, and I grinned, but truthfully, I was completely exhausted and falling into his extremely comfortable bed sounded amazing.

Nimbus rose and went with me when I headed back to the coffee shop. Bridger and Oliver flanked me, and the sun dog stayed right at Oliver's side.

***

After several days of whirlwind activity, Davin and Katsuro had finally deemed it safe for me to return to my apartment. I was curled up with Nimbus on the balcony overlooking the coffee shop and hoping I'd finally get a chance to relax and settle into my new home. With all the turmoil, I didn't really feel like I lived in the apartment. Of course, after Katsuro's super soft sheets and insanely comfortable bed, my sheets felt scratchy, and my bed felt a little uncomfortable. Maybe I would have to upgrade.

I shifted and scratched Nimbus gently behind the ears, and he rested his head on my chest while we lay on a bed of blankets together. Of course, we could have been laying on a bed of rocks and everything would have been just perfect since I had Nimbus with me. The only thing that would make it better is if I had one, or more, of my men with me.

He perked up, glancing at the door moments before I heard a knock.

It wasn't one of the guys I was bonded to, or I would have felt their presence. Also, I'd told them just to enter unless the door was locked, which, right now, it wasn't. Especially now that I was bonded to Katsuro, and Oliver was one of my mates, none of the residents would dare mess with my stuff. I could have left a fortune of money out in the hallway and as long as they knew it was mine, it would stay put. Honestly, I probably would have been safe beforehand, too. I still really didn't know any of the other residents because they all preferred to keep to themselves, but according to Oliver they were decent sorts.

Grumbling, I got up after Nimbus did.

When I opened the door, two of Davin's werewolves stood there. I recognized them from forever ago when I'd first been introduced to some of the wolves. The woman was Rachel, and the man, Jamie.

"Hi," I said not sure how to interpret their visit.

Everyone had been so busy in the last few days since the fight that I'd hardly interacted with anyone but Katsuro, Nimbus, and Oliver. Even during the day while Katsuro was supposed to be resting, he'd been busy, though we had managed a few minutes together here and there since I was staying at his place. Oliver had smothered me with attention when I'd first returned to my apartment, but then duties had called him away. I wasn't upset that I didn't have anything to contribute at the moment. I just missed seeing my friends.

"Hannah, would you and Nimbus join us? We have pack business we must discuss."

I licked my lips nervously before nodding and slipping on my shoes. I shoved my glasses up my nose and glanced at my cloud dog. He wagged his tail happily, so I guessed whatever it was couldn't be too bad. The dog usually had a good sense of what was going on.

The werewolves led us down to the parking lot and the customary old truck. I knew some of the werewolves drove newer vehicles, but it seemed like most of them preferred the old trucks.

Jamie drove and Rachel sat in the middle of the bench seat. Nimbus hopped up and sat between my feet after I got in. At least they hadn't sandwiched me between them. That made me feel a little less like I was a prisoner and more like I was a guest. Hopefully, that feeling continued.

Jamie turned off the main road onto one of the dirt two-tracks that I knew led out to pack land. We bounced along through the forest in silence for a few minutes until we came to a small group of other old trucks. Jamie parked and we all slid out. The scent of food grilling wafted in on the air.

Nimbus rooed happily and bounded off into the woods. I relaxed further, knowing he wouldn't leave me if he thought there was actual danger. Really, I was only nervous because of recent events. I trusted the wolves. I just had leftover fear. My stomach growled though, and I hoped whatever the wolves were up to, it involved food.

"This way." Rachel gestured toward one of several paths that led from the parking area into the woods.

The path was short and led to a clearing where several of the werewolves cooked over charcoal grills. The clearing was set up as a permanent gathering area with picnic tables, the grills, a currently cold firepit, and small shed probably for storage of the cooking supplies.

They had laid out the fixings for burgers, hotdogs, and sides.

"Grab something to eat," Jamie said just as a cry went up from the wolves around the table. The plate of cooked hamburgers lifted up and floated away.

"Nimbus!" I shouted.

The cloud dog appeared very briefly out of the underbrush before turning and vanishing, stolen plate of meat zipping off after him. My last impression of the cloud dog as he disappeared into the forest to enjoy his meal was the jaunty flag of his fluffy tail.

Several of the werewolves laughed. A few sighed, and they went back to making more hamburgers. Fortunately, the ones on the grill had survived Nimbus's thievery and I was able to get a hamburger.

Though I still didn't know why I'd been invited, everyone chatted amicably, and the atmosphere was relaxed. I felt the tension ease out of my shoulders as I grabbed a seat at a table and ate my lunch while I watched the others.

A ripple went through the crowd at some point, and everyone turned, signaling Davin's arrival. It didn't surprise me that everyone noticed, or that everyone stopped what they were doing until he waved—a gesture that seemed to acknowledge the entire group—then went over to get food. My core tightened, and desire did funny things to my stomach as I met his eyes.

The chatter started again, and Davin came over to join me. His gaze lingered before he seemed to realize he was staring at me and turned his attention to his food.

"I didn't know you were going to be here," he said, genuine surprise in his voice.

"I didn't either." I chuckled. "Jamie and Rachel came to get me. I don't know why."

"You're certainly welcome." He offered a guarded smile before concentrating on his food. "Where is Nimbus?"

"Took off with a plate of burgers."

Davin laughed and shook his head. "Well, after everything he did to save Beechworth, he's more than entitled to them."

"Don't let Nimbus hear you. Your food will never be safe again."

Davin winked. "Seems like it's already not safe."

"True enough. So, is this like a weekly cookout or something?"

"We're having a gathering to honor those we lost in the fight and handle some pack business. Fortunately, though the fighting was fierce and there were casualties, we didn't lose too many lives." His shoulders sagged.

"Ahh. You and Katsuro have kept me out of most of the cleanup. How many did we lose?" Sorrow welled liquid in my eyes.

Davin cast his gaze downward before answering. "Five of my wolves and ten of Katsuro's vampires. Other casualties were limited to injuries, fortunately. The enemy lost many more."

"Yeah." I thought back to the vampire I'd killed and shuddered.

Davin put his hand on my forearm. "We all did what we had to. If we hadn't defended ourselves, so many more would be dead, or worse."

I nodded. I knew that. It didn't help a whole lot right then, but I knew in the coming weeks I'd remember, and it would help me heal.

We sat in silence for a while. At some signal I missed, Davin stood and headed for the area around the fire pit.

Nimbus emerged from the underbrush and dashed for the food table. This time the werewolf cooking just put a plate down for him to get to.

Nimbus huffed as if disappointed he didn't have to steal it but dug in anyway.

"Before we honor our fallen, we have a few things we need to discuss. Who wants to start?" Davin addressed his people.

"We do," Rachel said. She, Jamie, and several others stood.

I saw Davin's eyebrows go up in surprise, but most of the others nodded in agreement.

"Hannah," Rachel began. "We know you and Davin are interested in becoming mates. We know Davin hesitates because of the bonds. However, we, as a pack, find you more than worthy. You saved us from the magic that held us painfully in our shifted forms. You selflessly threw yourself between Davin and Vito to protect him and provide a distraction so he could be defeated, and there are so many other things you've done recently to prove to us that your heart is kind, and strong, and more than worthy to be an alpha of our pack. We feel Davin should accept your bond as you should accept his."

"Besides," someone else shouted. "He's fucking miserable without you, and we're tired of him moping."

Davin sputtered a protest at that, but he didn't deny it.

"Davin?" I glanced at him, the flutter starting up in my stomach again.

He stared at the ground and ran a hand through his hair, as if embarrassed. "I am miserable without you, and I will accept all you offer. I just hadn't thought my pack would support it."

"Well, we do!" a few of them called in unison.

"So, get on with it! We will need a mating celebration after we lay our fallen to rest," Jamie continued.

"Right now?" Davin arched an eyebrow.

"I doubt Hannah is quite up to that," Rachel replied dryly. "But tonight would be nice. Then we can have a celebration tomorrow."

Davin turned his attention to me, hope lighting in his eyes. "What do you think?"

"Pick me up for dinner tonight, and we'll decide then?" The pressure of nearly the entire pack staring at me was a little too much to make a decision right then, anyway. Though little thrills of anticipation jolted through me at the thought that I might have my werewolf tonight.

"Sounds perfect." Davin bowed formally in my direction much as Katsuro might have, then turned back to the sad business of honoring the fallen pack members.

Chapter 41

Jamie gave me a ride home after the pack ceremony. Davin promised to be by in a couple of hours, which I needed after crying for nearly an hour along with the wolves.

Oliver met me and Nimbus at the door of the apartment complex. His sun dog, who he called Aurora, was at his side. She'd made it very clear she had accepted him as her person and Oliver was happy to have her. Nimbus and Aurora sniffed. She gave him a reserved look and he planted his paw on her snout.

"My dearest, are you okay?" Oliver pulled me into a hug.

"Yeah. The pack had me out to remember their fallen."

"Ah." He tightened his grip on me.

"They also decided Davin should accept my bond, and I should accept his. So, Davin is taking me out for dinner tonight."

Oliver kissed my forehead. "Excellent. I'll tell the others. Do you need anything?"

"No. Just a little recovery time."

"Do you want company, or to be alone?"

That was a good question. "Company, for now at least."

Aurora grumbled at Nimbus, who simply flopped over onto his belly and swatted her in the face again.

"Nimbus, be polite."

He grumbled happily, ignoring me.

Oliver released me from the tight hug and walked with me up the stairs and to my apartment.

"We need to find you a house," Oliver said as we went inside.

"A house?"

"Yes. There is not room for all of us to gather here, and Bridger's home is too far away to be convenient."

"I can't afford a house." Suddenly I realized I had missed at least one rent payment and perhaps my other bills as well. *Shit.*

"I would not worry overly much about money," Oliver replied. "All of us together have plenty. Perhaps once things settle, you will finally get a chance to work on that book you mentioned ages ago, and then you will have some income from that, as well. There is no need for you to stress."

"I think I missed some bills." I sighed.

"All of the utilities are owned locally. No one is worried, Hannah. Let us take care of you, as you have taken care of us in this conflict. We'll work out a balance as time goes."

I took a breath and nodded. "Okay. I won't worry about it right now. We can all talk about a house together if we want. Having some place where we can all gather probably is a good idea."

"Let me make you tea." Oliver went to my kitchen where he had apparently upgraded my tea selection.

I let him take care of me while I went to my closet and tried to figure out what to wear. I settled on an outfit that I hadn't had a chance to wear yet. Nothing fancy, because I hadn't yet gotten around to buying anything fancy, but comfortable enough and it looked nice. I laid it out on the bed, then went back to the kitchen to drink tea with Oliver.

Nimbus and Aurora occupied themselves, wrestling in the living room.

***

Davin texted to let me know he was on his way up, which I appreciated. Oliver had stayed with me until about a half an hour ago, and I'd appreciated the company. By the time Davin knocked softly on my door, I'd regained most of my equilibrium and shaken off the sorrow of the ceremony we'd had for the fallen earlier.

"Hey. I hope this is okay." I gestured at my clothing. "I don't have anything nice, yet."

"You're perfect," he replied. Davin had dressed slightly nicer than me, but not so much that I felt underdressed. "I have two thoughts for dinner. I could take you out again, or, it turns out,"—he winked—"I'm a pretty decent cook. I have a couple of steaks that are just right for this occasion. Totally your call."

I hadn't actually been to Davin's house yet. "Let's go to your place." In theory we were going to end up there anyway. Unless we had to do this under the full moon in the middle of the forest or something. In which case, hopefully we'd have a cabin nearby.

Seeing Davin smiling nervously at me, hope shining in his eyes, drove home that this was really happening. Butterflies of anticipation emerged from their slumber in my stomach and fluttered around.

I returned his nervous smile with my own and held out my hand. Davin pulled me against his chest and wrapped me in a hug.

"I'm grateful for everything you've done for us, Hannah." His breath tickled my ear. "I'm grateful for Katsuro, Oliver, and Bridger that they have helped you find a home here and have kept you safe. And I'm grateful

299

for Nimbus that he was willing to put me in my place, and for everything else he's done. If nothing else, I'm glad you are in our lives. I very much hope you still want to share bonds."

"I do," I tightened my arms around him.

After a long hug, Davin loosened his arms. "So, about that steak?"

Nimbus rooed.

"Yes, I have one for you, too." Davin ruffled the cloud dog's ears, then offered me his arm. I let him take it and we headed for his place.

***

"He didn't!" I laughed and took a sip of red wine. Dinner, a perfectly cooked steak and a delicious salad, was only a memory of dirty plates we'd already put in the dishwasher. I sat, perched on the couch so I could look at Davin, who sat next to me, also drinking wine and telling stories.

"I swear. Oliver wore the hat for a month straight, holes and all. Little Jimmy was so proud he made one for me, too. I still have it. Eventually he got interested in other things and stopped knitting for a few years, but recently he took it up again." Davin shrugged. "He got some flak for it from a few of the less flexible pack members, but as long as he holds up his duties, what do I care? Besides, knitting is a valuable skill. I had a word with a few of them and they quit bugging him about it."

I finished the last of my wine. The bottle was empty, so I set it on the coffee table. Nimbus had passed out after his steak dinner and was flopped over on his back, legs in the air.

Silence settled around us, full of anticipation, but also uncertainty.

Davin shifted before carefully setting his glass down next to mine. "You don't have to do this, you know. You should be safe now, and everyone knows you belong to Beechworth. Katsuro's mark is more than enough to protect you."

"Davin, I know I don't have to do this. Neither do you. You don't have to accept my mark. You don't have to tie yourself to someone who already has three mates. If you want a partner who will be focused only on you, that's okay with me."

He took my hand. "I do want you, Hannah. I'm drawn to you. My wolf adores you. I'm miserable without you. I do have some thoughts on our living situations, but we will have plenty of time to work on that in the future."

I glanced around Davin's living room. He had a very nice, but modest for what I had expected of a pack leader, two-level home on the edge of town. It backed up to the forest and had a huge porch and a walk-out basement. The back yard was simple but well maintained and had several vibrant flowerbeds. Davin admitted that a few of his pack members took care of the yard for him. He didn't have a green thumb. The house itself was well furnished but a touch impersonal. As if he didn't spend much time here.

"What were your thoughts?"

"We get you set up with a nice house with a vampire-safe basement on the edge of town but close enough that none of us have to travel far to reach it. It should have enough rooms so that we all have our own space if we're staying over but be small enough that we're never too far apart."

"Did you have one in mind?" I smiled at him, thinking he must.

"I have a lot in mind. We'll have to build the house."

I raised my eyebrows. That thought was daunting. "Like, us build it ourselves? Or hire someone?"

Davin laughed. "We have a talented construction crew."

"Okay. I was going to say, I have aspirations to write a book, not build a house." I shoved my glasses up my nose and took a breath. "I'm certainly okay with that if we can figure out finances. I technically have a job, but I haven't talked to Clare since the fight and she pays well, but not enough for me to buy anything."

"I'm not dismissing your concerns, but you have no need to worry about money ever again. Katsuro and I will set you up with a healthy bank account that will be yours no matter what happens to the rest of us. It will be your money to do with as you please. We will all chip in for the house, and you will make it our home."

"Are you sure? I am not taking you all as mates just so I have access to your money." Truthfully, until Oliver had brought it up the other day, I hadn't even considered it.

"We know. And we're sure."

Some of the stress I hadn't realized I'd been carrying eased from my shoulders. I hadn't exactly been worried about money. I had enough for a year or so still, but I hadn't considered being able to get a house or any of that. The government would have paid for all of that, except I hadn't felt right taking the money.

Davin smiled when I turned my attention back to him. "You smell more relaxed."

"I guess there's just so much still to sort out. I haven't really had a chance to settle in, and so much has happened."

"Well, take all the time you need, Hannah. Even for this."

I leaned forward, putting my hand on his thigh and gently working my way into his space. "I've taken all the time I needed, Davin."

He accepted my invitation, shifting until he could cup my jaw with his hand. "How do we do this?"

"We kiss, and you accept the energy that will surge between us." I could already feel it building in my center, along with a different sort of needy energy building in my core as my arousal grew in anticipation. "What do we do for yours?"

"Sex," he said. "And biting. Which I think you're already okay with. Some blood exchange. More sex."

I laughed. "That sounds excellent."

Davin ran his thumb along my cheek. "I'm going to kiss you now."

The butterflies that had started up earlier at my apartment had settled with food, but they exploded into a flutter of anticipation in my stomach, and the feeling went straight south and centered between my legs. The needy moan that escaped from my lips wasn't even embarrassing. Davin touched his lips to mine. I scooted forward so that I could straddle his legs and deepen our kiss.

I parted my lips, and Davin responded, rumbling in pleasure and letting me lead the kiss as my energy rose. Our lips danced as my magic pressed against Davin's. He allowed it to meld with his and as our kiss intensified, the bond snapped into place.

Lust surged through me. Davin groaned, his fingers digging into my back as he pulled me tightly against him.

"Perhaps we should have started this in the bedroom," he said when he came up for air.

"It's not that far."

"Fair point." Davin scooped me up in his arms, stood, and carried me into his bedroom. The casual display of his werewolf strength was impressive and made me feel delicate. Not something I was used to.

"Isn't being a werewolf contagious?" I murmured, remembering that we were about to share blood.

Davin snorted. "No. Hereditary. At least for natural werewolves. Some magically afflicted wolves have historically been known to spread their curse, but for us, it is simply how we are born."

"I have so much to learn."

"And a lifetime to do it in, Hannah."

Davin set me gently on his bed. I'd taken my shoes off hours ago, and he gently massaged my feet. "Okay if I undress you?"

Grinning in anticipation, I nodded. "Yes, please."

He gently removed my socks, first, before digging strong fingers into the soles of my feet.

I flopped back on the bed and stared at the ceiling. "Bliss," I murmured. "I could die happy, now."

"Mental note, foot rubs," Davin replied with a laugh before working his way up my calves until my pant legs stopped the progression.

The bed dipped as he settled next to me and touched my stomach. In response, I sat back up and lifted my arms so he could remove my shirt.

"Some time we will do this differently," he said. "But right now, I want you naked."

"I want me naked. And you, too." I attempted to make my voice seductive. It must have worked because his pupils dilated, and he jerked my shirt off over my head. Not quite gentle, but not rough enough to be displeasing.

I helped him get my pants off, though he did take a moment to appreciate the lacy black bra and panties I'd worn for the occasion. Those landed in the clothing pile quickly, and I pulled down the comforter while Davin stripped.

Watching as his muscles rippled while he moved, I couldn't help but drool a little. Werewolf physique was stellar, and I couldn't wait to explore him with my hands. Davin was used to being naked around others, and he dropped his pants as quickly as he had removed mine. He didn't wear underwear, and while I'd seen him naked briefly before, this time I let myself look. He wasn't huge, but decently sized and nice and wide. I couldn't wait for him to fill me, and I scooted back on the bed and ran my hand up my ribs, gently brushing along my breast while I waited.

Davin inhaled deeply. "You smell amazing. So ready. So perfect for me, as if you were made for me. I've never smelled anyone better."

Understanding that it was a werewolf thing, I took it as a compliment, even though it sounded a little weird to my non-werewolf ears. I didn't have a good response, so I held out my hand.

He crawled onto the bed and took my hand, pressing my fingers to his lips.

"I'm going to make you so wet. I'm going to take you from behind, and just when you're on the verge of coming, I'm going to sink my teeth into your shoulder."

His voice was low and gravelly and tightened the muscles in my stomach. I was already dripping, I was sure. He wasn't going to have to work too hard to get me soaking.

"Take me however you want me." I arched up, wanting him to hurry.

Davin rolled me and got me up on my knees. "Soon we will have a discussion about your likes and dislikes," he said. "Unless there's anything I need to know right now."

"No. This is all fine."

"Good."

His fingers feathered along my hips and ass, caressing my skin. Davin scooted me over and slid me back toward the edge of the bed before sliding my knees apart. The soft touch of his fingers along my inner thighs sent shivers of anticipation through me, and when he softly stroked my folds, I sucked in a breath.

"Mmm, looking forward to dessert," he rumbled.

When Davin's tongue parted my folds, I sighed happily as heat and pleasure curled through me. When Davin's lips found my clit, I pushed greedily against him, and he obliged by sucking harder and sliding a finger inside me.

I cried out as he found my G-spot and stroked it expertly while sucking my clit. Squirming, I shoved back into him, gasping and shouting for more.

When I finally shattered all over his face, my legs and arms gave out, and I crumpled to the bed.

"I'm not done with you yet." Davin crawled up on the bed with me, holding me while I trembled from my orgasm.

"Good."

He held me for a while, fingers playing gently over my sweat soaked skin. Once I was ready, he helped me to my knees.

"Ready?"

"Yeah."

He fitted his cock to my opening and pushed inside me, slowly at first, then more quickly. He was right, I was wet enough that he was able to enter me with no resistance other than my body adjusting to his girth.

Once Davin was fully seated, he paused. I squirmed, wanting more, wanting him moving inside me, wanting to complete our bond.

The werewolf obliged, giving a few experimental strokes before slamming into me.

I cried out his name, clutching the pillow in my fists and letting the sensations ride through my entire body. I could feel his pleasure as if it were my own through the bond I'd created with him. It would just get more intense when we completed his mating bond.

My core tightened, and Davin leaned over me. Just as I felt my orgasm cresting, that delicious tightening before release, the werewolf sank sharp teeth into my shoulder.

I shouted as the bond snapped into place, and my body shattered around him. I felt his orgasm as if it were my own. The sensations flooded through me. Stars flickered through my vision as my head swam with pleasure.

Davin pulled out of me before I was ready. I cried in dismay, not wanting to be separated from him, even by that much.

"You have to bite me back for it to take hold," Davin ordered, turning me so I faced him.

I didn't have vampire fangs or even partially shifted werewolf teeth, but I gave it my best as I sank my teeth into Davin's shoulder. He shuddered against me, and another wave of pleasure curled through my body. The bond tightened as I tasted blood, and another orgasm rocked my core.

We collapsed into each other's arms and lay there, reveling in the endorphins of our bonding. I intended to keep him up for hours before we got real rest. By the time we were done, we were going to be exhausted, and I was totally here for it.

Chapter 42

A few days later, at the earliest point of twilight that Katsuro could comfortably be outside, I gathered with him and the other guys, Aurora, and Nimbus and looked at a property. It was thirty acres that backed up against the forest. A creek meandered across the lower part of the property, and we stood on higher ground outside of the flood plain.

"This is where the house would go." Davin gestured toward the ground at our feet, a very golden retriever feeling coming from him as he excitedly showed us the property.

"It's not too far from the coffee shop." That was important to me. If nothing else, I wanted to easily be able to hang out there. That was also Katsuro's home, and Oliver lived very close. Bridger was the only one who lived out of town, but we couldn't do too much about that. Though I hoped to convince him to spend the majority of his time at my new place. We'd see.

"It looks perfect," Katsuro replied as he stared out over the expanse of land, a gentle breeze playing with his dark hair.

Bridger wrapped his arms around me from behind and pulled me against his chest. I leaned back and let him hold me.

"I have no objections," the hunter said.

Oliver glanced at Aurora before adding, "It is quite acceptable."

Nimbus grumbled happily and bounded down the incline, tail waving jauntily over his back.

"Perfect. Katsuro and I will sort out the property purchase and get in touch with the local builders. We'll have your home built in no time, Hannah." Davin grinned like a puppy who'd just been given a bone. I had no problem letting him handle all of that. Especially as excited as he was about it. Ever since we'd bonded, he'd had a ridiculous grin on his face, and it made me happy every time I saw it.

"If you'll excuse us?" Katsuro bowed toward me ever so slightly before lightly touching Davin's arm and leading him away toward the vampire's SUV. He did, occasionally, drive.

Oliver gave my arm a gentle squeeze then headed off toward the forest with Aurora. Nimbus gave me a quick glance before bouncing off after them. He pounced on the sun dog, before dashing off. She took off after him fast as a sunbeam, and it wasn't long before he was chasing after her instead.

I laughed and turned in Bridger's arms until I faced him.

"It occurs to me that you and I got interrupted the other day." I kissed him lightly on the lips. "I think it's occurred to everyone else, too."

The hunter smiled. "I had noticed, believe it or not. However, I felt your priorities were straight and didn't feel I should complain."

He said it so deadpan that it took me a moment to burst out laughing. He chuckled and pulled me tightly against him.

"Survival is kind of a pressing need." I grinned at the hunter.

"So, barring another attack, your place or mine?" He brushed a bit of hair out of my face.

"Your place," I said. "If nothing else, it'd be nice to have a little more space."

"Sounds good. Do you want to follow me out, or drop a vehicle off somewhere?"

"I'll follow you. That way, you don't have to drive me back."

"I never mind driving you around, Hannah, but that's fine."

Hand in hand, we headed for the parked cars. I'd finally gotten mine back from the werewolves. After it had been tampered with so that the handles would drug me, they'd wanted to go over it with every type of cleaning ability they had, and the thing smelled like a new car. I'd still felt a little hesitant the first couple of times I'd driven it, but the wolves hadn't found any other traps, and I'd gradually relaxed back into enjoying the vehicle.

Nimbus appeared in the passenger seat as I pulled away from the curb.

I ruffled his ears. "You could have stayed with Aurora."

He carried on for a few minutes, and I nodded along.

"Well, I'm glad you're here."

Nimbus woofed in agreement.

It didn't take overly long to get to Bridger's place. It wasn't as quick as getting to some of the spots in town, but the drive wasn't awful, either. I hadn't been out here since it had been repaired, but they'd done a good job, and I wasn't actually sure what had been damaged.

When we got out, Bridger opened the door for me, and we went inside his bunker-style home.

"What would you like to drink?"

"Water for now, thanks." I followed him to the kitchen and leaned against the counter while he got me and Nimbus both something to drink.

The water here was so fresh. I knew he was on a spring well and it tasted better than any city water. Nimbus lapped his up before trotting into the kitchen. The refrigerator door opened, and something floated out of it.

I glanced at Bridger, but he only smiled and kicked the door shut after the cloud dog had taken his prize.

The low feeling of anticipation and arousal centered in my groin was building to a needy roar. I needed Bridger, and I didn't want to wait long to have him. We were already bonded, and I had to have that physical connection too.

"Do you think you will still take Katsuro's and Davin's bonds now that the danger has passed?"

Bridger shrugged. "Maybe. I'm not in a hurry." His sense didn't change to discomfort through our bond, so I suspected he was okay with the idea, just not in a rush as he said. "So, how's being an alpha of a werewolf pack?"

"More meetings than I expected." I laughed. "Though they don't expect me to be a real werewolf or anything. I'm more of a figurehead, I guess."

"That will change as you learn more, I suspect." Bridger came around the counter and held out his hand.

I took it and he pulled me to him. His lips met mine. A feeling of completion fell over me. Bridger backed me into the wall by the counter and cupped the back of my head with his hand, his other going to the small of my back. I dug my fingers into his ass, pulling him closer. Being pressed between him and the wall filled me with all sorts of ideas, and I ran my leg up his.

"So, want to show me your bedroom?"

"Yeah, I really do."

He led me down the hall, pausing to push me up against the wall and make out with me, or tear off a piece of clothing, leaving a trail behind us from the kitchen to his room. By the time we made it into the bedroom, all I had left were my panties, and Bridger just had a pair of boxers on. The back of my legs bumped into his bed, and Bridger went to his knees, taking my panties with him, then his hands went to my hips and his mouth went to my pussy.

Groaning, I spread my feet, giving him more access. He worshiped my clit for a while, sending tremors down my legs. I used his shoulders for balance until I was barely able to stand. Then we adjusted so I was laying back on the bed, legs spread wide while Bridger worked me with his lips and fingers.

"Oh, fuck," I gasped out. "Yes, just like that." I shattered, and Bridger made a happy sound before he stood and slipped out of his boxers.

"You have birth control, right? Do you want me to use a condom?"

"Yes, and it's up to you. Last test I took was clean, and I've only been with the others since."

"Yeah, I'm clean, and it's completely up to you, Hannah. I'm okay either way."

"Then no, I don't want you to use one."

"Got a position you prefer?" He helped me get all the way onto the bed and lay next to me, fondling my breasts while we spoke.

"I am fond of quite a few and always willing to try others." Mostly, I just wanted him inside me.

He grabbed my hips and rolled me until I was straddling his legs. "How about this?"

I hadn't expected him to want me on top for the first time, but I wasn't going to complain. I ran my fingers down his velvety length and enjoyed the way it twitched under my fingers. He sucked in his breath in pleasure. I

313

teased him, and myself, until he was even harder, and precum dripped from his head.

"Ready?"

"Yeah," he breathed. He helped position himself at my entrance, and I slid down on his length.

His eyes shuttered as he groaned. "Feels so good," he murmured before grabbing my hips and thrusting into me.

It took a moment for us to find our rhythm, but once we did, the combination of the feeling of him moving inside of me, and the pleasure through our shared bond had me floating with ecstasy.

"I'm close, Bridger."

"Yeah, me, too," he replied, voice thick with lust.

We came together. Now that I'd had all four of my men, I felt complete. Soon we'd have a place we could all share, and I'd really make Beechworth my home.

***

The next day after a long night of sex and cuddling and a delicious breakfast that was almost lunch, I'd left Bridger's house. He'd promised to swing by tomorrow, so it wouldn't be long before I saw him again, but I still wanted him closer. I wanted all my men closer. The house idea was feeling even more right for our situation than it had when Davin had brought it up.

Raindrops pattered on the windshield, giving moments of warning before the skies opened up. A sharp flash of lightning crackled across the sky, followed seconds later by booming thunder.

"Okay, it was cloudy this morning, but I hadn't expected a storm like this."

Nimbus perked up, glancing around, head tilted as he stared into the storm. The wind kicked up, and a branch fell across the road. I slammed on my brakes. Nimbus rooed, tail wagging like crazy.

"Buddy, what is it?"

He vanished and reappeared outside. When I didn't follow, he turned and barked at me then reappearing in the passenger seat. The cloud dog gripped my sleeve and tugged before vanishing again.

Grumbling, I turned the car off, pulled out an umbrella from the door pocket where someone had thoughtfully stashed it for me and got out. The wind tugged at my umbrella and my hair, and fog misted my glasses as I followed Nimbus into the storm. He wouldn't have pulled me out here if he didn't have a really good reason.

We threaded our way through the trees for a few minutes before he sat down next to a tree and wagged his tail so hard I thought he was in danger of spraining it.

"What is it?" I kneeled and saw a tiny puppy. "What the…?" This pup was just barely old enough to be away from its mother. Eight weeks old maybe? "Little one, what are you doing out here all alone in this storm?"

I grabbed the puppy and tucked him into my shirt. He was soaked, hair thick and fluffy like Nimbus's but more of a grayish color. It hit me… "Twister?"

The little dog gave a soft roo, and this time I couldn't see because my eyes were full of tears.

"Oh, buddy, you said I'd see you again and here you are. Let's get you inside and warm. I'm so happy you're here."

The little guy squirmed around until he could lick my nose.

I gave Nimbus a quick hug, and then we trudged back to the car. Even with the umbrella I was soaked, but home would be warm. I couldn't wait to text the guys and tell them all about Twister. I wondered if he'd have the same powers as Nimbus or different ones.

Still, while I'd felt complete before, it was as if the last puzzle piece had fallen into place, and I could truly call Beechworth home.

Epilogue

Mayday Hills had folded like a house of cards once Katsuro moved into the territory. They hadn't let me come along, which I wasn't upset about, but what little fighting there had been was brief, and Oliver was treating Aurora to as many steak dinners as she pleased for her efforts in the takeover. Some of the vampires and other supernaturals had pledged to Katsuro and Davin. Some had moved on. Some continued to live their lives the same as they always had, semi-unaware of the politics of the region.

Now that everything was secure, Katsuro had brought me into Vito's stronghold in the city and we were going through his papers. With my background in accounting—how I'd discovered the trafficking ring in the first place—I had a good head for numbers and patterns.

I was shuffling through Vito's files when something caught my eye.

"Guys?" Hands shaking, I held out the file, almost dropping it before Katsuro could take it from me. The file detailed the sale and distribution of cloud puppies, and I had no doubt that these dogs weren't being sold into loving homes.

Oliver and Bridger crowded around. Davin sensed my alarm from the other room and joined us, Jaz following on his heels.

Katsuro handed the file off, and everyone looked through it before they all glanced at Nimbus then focused on me.

"We have to do something."

Stay tuned for more in the Companions of the Convergence world.

Author's Note

Thank you so much for reading my reverse harem tale! More is coming soon! Reviews are so very important and are greatly appreciated! Even a line or two will do!

About the Author

Dakota has two passions in life: writing and cinnamon tea. Tea so strong she ought to be able to see her future when she drinks it, and the writing? Well, she hopes it makes you see stars when you read it. She creates reverse harem romance novels filled with things that go bump in the night. That handsome werewolf walking down the street? The suave vampire you're just dying to get a taste of? You'll find them enraptured by charming, smart ladies ready to make those bad boys work for their affection. When not writing, Dakota can be found on the back of a horse out on the trail or tending the animals on her farm.

Other Works

Mountain Magic Trilogy (complete)

Becoming
Demon's Touch
Reckoning

Ocean Enchantment Trilogy

Siren's Catch
Siren's Song
Siren's Storm (forthcoming)

Pizza Shop Exorcist (complete)

The Price of Possession
The Price of Exorcism
The Price of Magic
The Price of Souls
The Price of Rebellion

Horsemen Against the Apocalypse Duet

Seeking War
Apocalypse Interrupted (forthcoming)

Dreambound Trilogy (Complete)

Nightmare's Dance
Nightmare's Fall
Nightmare's Flight

Pizza Shop Monster Hunter
Monster's Price (stands alone)

Companions of the Convergence
Only Human in Strangeville (stands alone)